clap

J. W. Diaz | clap

review

Copyright © 2000 J. W. Diaz

The right of J. W. Diaz to be identified as the Author of
the Work has been asserted by him in accordance with the
Copyright, Designs and Patents Act 1988.

First published in 2000
by REVIEW

An imprint of Headline Book Publishing

10 9 8 7 6 5 4 3 2 1

All characters in this publication are fictitious
and any resemblance to real persons, living or dead,
is purely coincidental.

ISBN 0 7472 6832 0

Typeset by Palimpsest Book Production Limited,
Polmont, Stirlingshire
Printed and bound in Great Britain by
Clays Ltd, St Ives plc.

Headline Book Publishing
A division of the Hodder Headline Group
338 Euston Road
London NW1 3BH

www.reviewbooks.co.uk
www.hodderheadline.com

'Life is an incurable disease.'
      — attr. Dr Scarborough

'A prick has no conscience.'
                    — Anon.

chapter one

(Capricorn, October 7–8: Health matters take priority. Renew old friendships, but don't believe everything you hear.)

'Drop your pants, Mr . . .'

'Farr. Ricardo Farr.'

Farr hesitated. Then he told himself not to be foolish; he had come to the hospital to be examined, after all. What did he expect?

He hurried to undo his belt, freed the button fastening the waistband, unzipped the fly and let the trousers fall around his ankles. He would have preferred to have taken them off properly and folded them over the back of a chair. They were linen – perfect for the climate – and while of Italian design and expensive, they were easily creased. He wore them to impress; what else were good clothes for? Farr had the feeling the doctor would have resented the additional time this would have taken, and would almost certainly have regarded him as excessively fastidious.

'And the shorts.'

Did he think he would get away with just talking about it? Can't stop now, Farr thought.

Too late to back out, to run for the door.

It helped that Dr Garcia was patient, his face blank. He

wasn't amused or disapproving. He didn't try to catch Farr's eye. Dr Garcia didn't seem in the least interested in who he was. If his face expressed anything at all, it was that this was routine, it was work, it was carried out if not a thousand times a day then at least several dozen, and there were many, many patients still waiting out there today: so, his face said, let's get on with it, shall we?

Slightly reassured by these thoughts, Farr had to bend his knees and push the boxer shorts down over his hips with both hands. Not all the way, just to his thighs. Then he straightened up. The boxer shorts were shot silk, striped in two shades of blue.

Farr felt his dick was all shrivelled from embarrassment. He couldn't tell Garcia that. In fact, Farr didn't dare look down at himself because if he thought he saw just how small it was right now, and how ridiculous he must look to anyone watching, he would feel a great deal worse.

'You'll have to hitch your shirt up for me.'

'Oh. Sorry.'

Farr pulled up the bright blue and yellow shirt. Blue sky, yellow jungle, tigers romping in the long grass; a Cuban Rousseau run amok on the Caribbean island. Farr had chosen the design and bright colours to match the fake gold Rolex on his left wrist and the fake Raybans in the breast pocket.

Garcia didn't touch. He was wearing latex gloves, but he made no move to handle Farr's testicles.

'It hurts?'

'It stings, doctor.' Farr tried to smile.

'When?'

'When I pee.'

'Have you noticed a discharge? Thick, yellowish?'

'Well . . .' Then the smallest hesitation. 'I think so.'

'And the reddened skin there on the inside of the thigh?'

Garcia pointed with his forefinger.

'It's sensitive.'

'It feels irritated by your clothing?'

'Yes. B-bit like sunburn.'

'I see.'

Did he? It wasn't a place the sun reached very often.

There was a pause. Farr waited. Dr Garcia looked. Intently. The way he looked didn't make Farr feel too bad. The process seemed too clinical, too impersonal to take offence. So far the reality was far better than the imagining. When Farr had woken that morning, his first thought was that a stranger, someone he didn't know, would sit staring at his pecker (no doubt making some comparative judgement about its general size and length in his own mind). The notion had appalled him, brought the blood rushing into his cheeks. He very nearly turned away from the hospital at the last minute. He had clenched his jaw, grinding his teeth and squeezing his hands into fists so the nails dug into the palms – just to steel himself to enter the premises, to walk up the steps and report at reception. It was much worse than any visit to the dentist.

Dr Garcia was no stranger, in fact.

Farr didn't know him so much as know of him. If he had been a praying man, Farr thought, he would offer up a prayer right then that Garcia had absolutely no idea who he was, either.

Farr wanted the doctor to say something, but he didn't. He could hear the wall clock ticking the seconds away, like the drip of a faulty tap. At last Garcia pushed himself backwards, using his feet as levers, rolling away from Farr and still seated in his chair. The chair legs ended in castors so he could propel himself back to his desk, swivelling round and turning his back to his patient.

Garcia was looking at Farr's medical card. Farr assumed that was what he was doing. Farr could no longer see his face, just the back of his shiny hair, Garcia's right hand fiddling with a cheap biro, rolling it between his fingers. He felt Garcia did this deliberately so he wouldn't watch him button up. He noticed Garcia still had the gloves on. Looking down at him from behind, Farr thought Garcia a neat man, the way only people with fine, straight black hair and nut-brown skin with chiselled features are neat. Economical with his movements, someone self-contained. A true professional, Farr thought, who could never be messy or careless. Almost feline, and not an ounce of spare fat on his compact frame. Well, that was the Blockade. Almost every Cuban was on a compulsory diet, thanks to the Americans. Why did Garcia irritate him so? Farr experienced an irrational and almost violent urge to tease him, to bring the seed of doubt about his wife's appetites almost to the surface, to needle him with it. Why? Why did he want to hurt him? Farr told himself it was because Garcia seemed to represent all the virtues of ordinariness, an ordinariness Farr longed for, yet whose qualities he knew he could never possess – the qualities of reasonableness, patience and loyalty, a certain modesty of spirit.

'Not yet.'

Farr had pulled up his shorts and was reaching for his trousers. Garcia must have heard him move.

Farr froze, then pushed the shorts down again.

'I need to give you a serological test.'

'What does that mean?'

Farr felt emboldened now his private parts were no longer being scrutinised.

If Garcia answered the question, Farr didn't hear it.

'This will hurt a little.'

It happened so quickly, almost in a single movement. There was no time to protest or retreat. Garcia had turned round, rolled back to him and was now holding his penis firmly with one hand while with the other he held what looked like a cotton bud – the sort of thing women used to clean their ears and put on eyeshadow.

The intention was clear, but Farr had no time to react.

He could smell the latex.

Garcia was pushing the cotton bud into his prick.

Straight in.

Farr's response was involuntary. 'Ah . . . Jesus!'

Farr thought that was it, but no; no it wasn't. Garcia was pushing it in deeper. A half-inch. More. Bastard! Now he was withdrawing it steadily, and the sting became a sharp, deep pain that struck deep into Farr's abdomen, his stomach, like a blade shoved right up his rectum; his balls felt as if they would shrink right back up into his scrotum and he expected the broad-bladed stabbing spear of the Zulus to come out of his throat. Impaled. That's how bad it felt.

He wanted to be sick.

Sweat broke out on Farr's forehead.

Shit.

He couldn't look.

He wanted to scream: stop!

'You can get dressed.' The chair spun round. Garcia had turned away from him again; something flat like a small plastic dish, no bigger than the top of a jam-jar lid with what looked like wax in it appeared in Garcia's hands. He was scraping the surface with the tip of the cotton bud.

'Well, doctor?'

Farr was doing up his buttons and zip, hurrying and feeling relieved. Smiling, even. Feeling friendly towards Garcia now the worst was over (and let's face it, Farr thought, it was every bit as bad as he had feared, but he told himself it was some consolation at least that no women had been present, no nurses, to witness his humiliation and laugh at him behind his back). Dr Garcia clearly didn't know him. Dr Garcia wouldn't make a scene. That, at least, was something. Farr could go. The sun was shining out there. Farr told himself the world knew nothing of what had just happened, and even if it did, it couldn't have cared less.

'Sit, please.'

Garcia had discarded the gloves. The cotton bud and the dish were gone. He was writing something. Writing neatly in a small, crabbed hand. Neat fingers, nails even and clean, small black hairs on the backs of the hands; doing it slowly and carefully, yet knowing exactly what he wanted to write because he didn't pause or look out of the window the way Farr did when he was compelled to write anything. Like a letter, for instance. Farr hated writing letters. He hated writing anything. It gave him cramp in his right hand and he could never read whatever it was five minutes after he had written it. If he could recognise every third or fourth word he might guess the rest – that was the best he had ever been able to do. Farr turned his attention to the voices and the sound of feet in the corridor outside. He waited, hating to be made to wait, worried now, bothered by the test and the writing and above all Garcia's silence. He glanced up at the clock, anxious to take his mind off all this, and noticed the picture of the President himself, a portrait taken at least twenty-five years earlier: vigorous, intense, a forefinger raised in admonition – Farr thought history had not yet marked the young guerrilla in combat fatigues with the limits of success.

'When did you last have full intercourse?'

The question took Farr by surprise.

'Last night . . . er, this morning.'

He's playing with me, Farr thought. He knows me. He's pretending not to, seeming to treat me like anyone else, but he's working it out, setting it all up.

Garcia seemed to freeze. The way he held his head, chin stuck out, was a question mark. His posture seemed to say: well, make up your mind – which was it?

'Last night and this morning. This morning was the last time.'

Garcia nodded in acknowledgement.

6

'Come back in a week. I'll have the result then.'

'A week?' Farr sounded stupid even to himself, grappling with the disagreeable notion of having to return to the hospital at all. Did he have to go through something like this all over again, only worse? The thought of that packed, foetid waiting room – all those people staring at him – was bad enough. He thought one of the girls out there had recognised him already.

'Can't you tell me now?'

'I'd rather we knew for sure.'

'Off the record, doctor.'

Farr thought of offering him money.

'Off the record?' Garcia said it as if the phrase had no meaning, sounding strange on his tongue. Foreign. Off the record? What's that? Instead he handed Farr an appointment slip, and their eyes met as Garcia stretched out across the desk to hand him the paper. It was as if the doctor was seeing Farr for the first time. Reaching out from behind his white coat and desk, and looking at Farr not simply as a suppurating and diseased sex organ, but as a person.

Farr, who had put his hand in his pocket and crumpled up a ten-dollar bill in his palm, immediately gave up the idea of a *douceur* to speed things up.

'This is your current address here in Santiago – eight, Santa Rica?'

Farr nodded. 'Yes.'

'You haven't put down your occupation.'

Farr laughed uneasily, and Garcia stared at him.

It was a hard look that demanded an answer.

'I'm in the service sector.'

'Yes?'

'You know how it is, doctor. A little of this, a little of that. Getting by as best I can. Like everyone else.'

Farr shrugged, opening his hands, palms up.

7

He smiled broadly but felt uncommonly awkward.

'*La Lucha.*' Garcia said it straight-faced. A statement, not a question. Not judgemental.

'That's it, doctor! Thanks to the Blockade, we're all on the hustle nowadays.' Farr beamed. He was going to add 'even doctors', but decided against it. Considering how it felt to have a cotton bud shoved up his penis, he certainly didn't want to offend the man. Next week it might be a blowtorch. If Garcia knew what Farr and Mrs Garcia got up to on Tuesday and Friday afternoons, he would have ample reason.

Be nice, Farr told himself.

Garcia was studying the forms on his desk.

Giving nothing away, Farr thought. Cautious. Meticulous. Garcia looked like a husband and father, someone who kept going on a state salary, rode to and from work on one of the three million Chinese bicycles imported to beat the petrol shortage, relied on ration cards, kept to the rules. Someone who ate rice and beans like any *campesino*, and tried to find a justification for his family's poverty and having no way out of it.

That's what being respectable meant, Farr thought; the type who'd throw a fit if he thought he was being offered a bribe.

'Tell me what you think it is, doctor.'

It was said confidingly. You can tell me. I trust you.

But Garcia had made up his mind. It was as if he knew Farr would find it hard to return, to face up to it, and it would be even harder if he told him all there was to tell now. Dr Garcia had to give Farr some incentive to make him come back, and the only incentive was fear of the unknown.

'Farr,' said Garcia. 'Farr. I know that name. You write the horoscope. My wife insists on buying the *Diario* for that reason alone. She reads hers – and mine – out loud every day.'

'What sign are you, doctor?'

'Taurus.'

'Ah. The sign of common sense.'

'Thank you, Mr—'

Garcia looked down at the file in front of him to find the name.

'Farr.'

'Thank you, Mr Farr, but I have to say — no offence meant — that I don't believe in it. Astrology, I mean.' Garcia nodded towards the wall clock.

Eleven-thirty a.m.

'This time next week, Señor Farr. Don't be late.'

Farr got as far as the curtain at the entrance of the doctor's cubicle.

'Mr Farr?'

Farr turned.

'Do you practise safe sex?'

Farr's hesitation prompted another question, or rather an expanded version of its predecessor in case Farr had not grasped what he meant. 'Do you use condoms?'

'Who can afford condoms in Cuba, doctor? Even supposing one could get hold of them?'

There was nothing safe about Farr, sexually or in any other respect. He had dropped a hint there, just the vaguest of suggestions — but Garcia showed no sign of picking up on it.

'In that case try to keep yourself to yourself until next week, all right? No unprotected sex. Please.'

It sounded as if Garcia said it all the time and knew it was futile. Farr thought, what man — or woman — with Cuban blood and living under a Cuban sky could keep himself to himself, or herself to herself? And who could possibly obtain condoms in Santiago or anywhere else on the island? Unless his name was Farr and he played *La Lucha* for every lousy American dime he could get. Then he might have a fighting chance.

chapter two

(Capricorn, October 8–9. Expect strangers bearing gifts. Follow your instinct, but remember, financial matters loom large in your sign.)

The hospital entrance was crowded with patients, their friends and families. They sat on the steps and talked to one another, shared food and drink, waved hats and copies of the Revolution's newspaper, *Granma*, to cool themselves in the heavy, motionless heat, gossiped and laughed. A well-behaved, patient crowd doing what Cubans had learned best: to wait in line, cheerfully, without complaint. They might not have fridges and Volkswagens and Coca-Cola to turn their island into a consumer heaven, but they had one another. Farr suddenly felt absurdly, tearfully sentimental. He had an irrational urge to hug the nearest of them, to put his arms round their necks and kiss them on the cheek. If this wasn't Cuba one might almost say God-fearing, Farr thought, not that God had anything to do with it. He stepped carefully between them, watching where he put his feet as he made his way to the lot where he had left his car.

No matter how preoccupied he was, Farr prided himself on never failing to notice what he called a New Business Opportunity. He identified one almost at once, a teenage boy with his right foot and leg in plaster being carried down the steps on a stretcher by two perspiring orderlies, a woman in saffron yellow Farr took to be the boy's mother waddling behind. It was all very well, the woman was saying loudly to no one in particular and everyone in general, they had given her son a painkiller in there – in the hospital – while they set his leg and put on the plaster cast, but told her none could be spared to take home. Nothing for a boy with a multiple fracture, and it wasn't even his fault! The bones were smashed in several places and sticking out of his skin when he was brought in! What was she supposed to do when the drug they had given him wore off? She rolled her eyes dramatically and threw her hands heavenward, her bright red mouth and heavily rouged cheeks working furiously. How was he supposed to manage? She had asked just for aspirin, but the doctor said there wasn't enough even of that. Only for emergencies. Mother of God! Wasn't her boy an emergency? Hadn't they fixed him up in the accident and emergency section? The youth, Farr noted, was pale, sweat beading his upper lip and plastering his hair to his forehead. He was muttering something, evidently trying to turn round to tell his mother to shut up, but the orderlies, struggling to keep him on the stretcher, told him roughly to keep still. The mother was still waving her hands about, oblivious both to her son's embarrassment and to what amounted to her own potentially disastrous criticism of the medical authorities and, by implication, the leadership itself.

Didn't the stupid cow know what she was in for if she spoke out like that, in front of everybody?

The kid knew. His face said it all. Farr reached the bottom of the steps and stopped listening to the shrill voice.

Why hadn't he thought of it earlier?

Our children are our teachers.

Painkillers. The cheapest available. Powder might be best.

That way Farr could make up the doses himself, perhaps diluted with a little dried milk. Why not?

He made a mental note to add painkillers and condoms to his wish list, along with sanitary towels and batteries.

Farr started to figure out the costs and likely margin of profit. Assuming, of course, that his mule did as he was asked and didn't get stage fright and fluff his lines in customs.

Then Farr would be up shit creek and no mistake.

The Lada chugged steadily past the monument of jagged stakes and beckoning arm of independence hero Antonio Maceo, for ever mounted on his rearing bronze charger. Farr had the windows down, his elbow resting on the sill, fingers lightly touching the hot steering wheel. There was no traffic to speak of – few people could afford the petrol or spare parts to keep their jalopies going. He manoeuvred around two *camellos*, local buses crammed with an improbable number of people, through a group of cyclists and passed a crowd at a bus stop, neat in their T-shirts and slacks. Waiting. Passive in the noonday heat, careful to keep to the shade of the big mango trees, to move as little as possible, their eyes following the faded sky-blue Lada's sluggish progress. Behind them, a wall was covered with posters of the Pope superimposed on earlier revolutionary tracts, the old Pole's image already torn and fading.

Only a communist or a criminal – criminal in the widest possible sense of the term – had his own wheels nowadays.

Funny how these things worked out, Farr thought. Months went by and nothing happened; and then, all at once, everything seemed to converge.

Garcia was an example. Of all the people who had to examine him that morning, it had to be the head of the section. As if it wasn't enough to be humiliated – it had to be, quite literally, at the hands of the cuckold himself.

God alone knew what would have happened if Garcia had suspected him as the instrument of his wife's infidelity.

What would he have done?

Farr had a sudden image of a gleaming steel scalpel held in one of Garcia's latex-covered hands.

As if on cue Farr felt another twinge between his legs, a brief spasm of pain he tried to ease by shifting in his seat.

He wanted to pee again.

Was this Amelia's doing?

Farr knew he wasn't the first. How many other lovers did Amelia have during the siesta? How many other videos did she get to watch in the afternoons in the shaded rooms of her men friends? Video was her special code word. When she called him she used the word 'video' to arrange something else entirely.

Farr didn't really believe in God at all. Not the kind of God who responded to prayers for rain, a cure for cancer or an American visa. God as life's Lucky Dip simply didn't wash with Farr. But he thought it felt uncomfortably as if Providence was punishing him for his many sins and doing so precisely where it hurt most – and putting his cure in the hands of a man Farr had dishonoured. In Cuba, men died violently for a lot less.

Just the wrong kind of look at a married woman was enough.

He pushed the thought away. Only one thing was worse than Amelia's being the source of his mystery affliction – and that was that he might have unwittingly made her a present of it. Amelia wasn't just anyone. He didn't make love to the slender, petite doctor's wife because she was somebody else's wife and therefore could make no claims on him (though it was true that the illicit nature of their affair excited him considerably). It wasn't because she was the one who took charge of their couplings, calling him up to say she wanted to watch a video (that too added piquancy to his desire). There was much more to it. Farr thought of Amelia as a strategic asset, not in direct commercial terms, but as a long-term prospect of far greater importance. Someone to be brought into play when all else had failed and an appeal of last resort had to be made to people with power, real power.

Such as Amelia's brother, Captain Gomez of State Security.

Now it could all go horribly wrong.

What if an infected and maddened Amelia, out of a desire for revenge, told both husband and brother about the afternoon trysts in the room he kept at Las Americas?

No. No, she couldn't. He muttered to himself, lips moving: don't even think it.

This time next week he would know the very worst.

That evening Farr guided Maria up the steps to a vacant table. He knew the hotel veranda as a zone of neutrality, its status agreed by combatants on all sides. Calm prevailed here, a kind of temporary peace where both the foreigners and their new-found partners, hired for the single trick or by the day, had what they wanted. But just beyond it, Cespedes Park was a free-fire zone, cruised by girls and boys offering their services as guides, translators, fixers, drivers and much, much more. No local – male or female – could enter the Casaverde's premises without a guest's invitation, and the only guests who could afford the pricey rooms were foreigners. As for Farr, he looked foreign to most Cubans, and Cuban to most foreigners. The best, or worst, of both worlds, he told himself.

An outsider everywhere, he thought.

At home nowhere.

He made a show of playing the gentleman, gallantly pulling out a chair for his best girl, helping her to get comfortable before he went around the table and sat down opposite her.

Without thinking he spoke in English, playing his role as foreigner, the part-Englishman of impeccable manners.

'What will you have?'

'Mojito, darling.'

Farr knew the 'darling' was said to lay claim to him, to stake her possession of him, if only for this half-hour.

Maria's dark eyes were appraising, reading things in his face Farr tried to keep from other people.

He would have to tell her.

Warn her – if she didn't already know.

'Señor?' A waiter Farr recognised stood at his elbow.

'Mojito for the lady, please, Tomas. I'll have a beer. Make it a Cristal.'

When he'd gone Maria put out a hand and touched Farr's arm.

'What's bothering you, Ricardo?'

'Later.'

'Is it important?'

'Later. Not now.' Said with finality.

'When does your friend arrive?'

'Wednesday. He's not my friend. He's a colleague.'

Maria shrugged. It made no difference to her.

'He has dollars,' she said quietly, as if speaking to herself. 'That's all that matters, isn't it?'

Farr said, 'We'll have a drink here. At nine. That's your cue. I'll introduce you as my cousin . . .'

Maria was the only girl he brought to the Casaverde. She didn't have to solicit outside on the street. She was his best worker. She operated by appointment only. She was dark chocolate, almost six foot two, and in her midnight-blue lurex she stood out like the Statue of Liberty on July 4. The term statuesque just didn't do her justice, and the foreigners couldn't get enough of her. To them she must seem the very epitome of Cuban love. *El secreto del amor.*

Farr's other girls in the downtown area, Inez and Lydia, weren't in her league. Not yet. With time and a little more coaching they might be good enough.

'You think he'll believe that?'

'He can believe what he wants. People always believe what they want.'

'You think the worst of everyone, Ricardo.'

'And you, Maria? What do you think?'

She shrugged, looked away at the other tables.

Inspecting the competition. Not that she should have any worries on that score, Farr thought. The other *jineteras* were no patch on her. Oddly, women worried about the envy of other members of their own gender, even whores, while men fretted about their status. Even pimps. Especially pimps.

Farr prided himself on his ability to assess another man's wealth in a glance. The shoes were the key. Good quality leather meant the other fellow had access to dollars. There were two kinds of people, finally, those with dollars and those without – and Farr was only interested in the former.

Tomas was back with their drinks. Farr poured the beer foaming into his frosted glass and raised it in mock salute. Maria lifted her rum, mint and ice and they touched glasses.

'My beautiful Catholic,' he said, smiling at her.

'Don't.'

Instinctively she put a hand to the little gold crucifix at her throat.

'Don't what?'

'Don't make fun of me. Or my religion. You hurt me with your teasing. You're cruel. You don't love me.'

Love? He didn't know the meaning of the word, any more than he understood the term faith. But he didn't tell Maria that.

'This morning it was love, my sweet. This is business.'

Farr didn't believe a word of what he'd just said, but he hoped she did.

'And what do I tell him?'

'Whatever you want, sweetie.'

'I'm a dance student.'

'That's good.'

They're all dance students, Farr thought.

'You think he believes me?'

'It doesn't matter.'

'And then?'

'You'll take him to the Tropicana. He wants to see it. I've arranged it. The best seats.'

'Really?' Her eyes shone at the thought.

'Yeah – fifty bucks each.'

Now he had her attention.

'Then?'

'He'll bring you back here.'

'We fuck is what we do.' Her voice had an edge to it.

'If that's what he wants. If he's capable after all that overpriced rot-gut rum they serve there.'

'What about me?'

'If he likes you – and I'm sure he will, Maria – he is going to pay you twenty dollars a day for your services as guide and escort, and another dollar for your travel expenses.'

Maria was pleased at the price but didn't want to show it, Farr noted. She was pleased because twenty dollars was twice the going rate. He knew she was pleased because she didn't argue, or ask him how much his share would be.

Pity the poor Cuban family without a pretty daughter.

'For how long?'

'For the duration of his visit.'

'Which is?'

'Five days, maybe more.'

'Five days' fucking and I'm worth two front seats at the Tropicana.'

'No one's forcing you, honey. You can walk away right this minute. It's supply and demand. The market sets the price, not me. And you're better off than most.'

A lot, lot better than three dollars a trick, Farr said to himself.

Maria tried a new tack.

'You know this man, Ricardo?'

'Not really.'

'He's American?'

'Yes.'

'What's his name?'

'James.'

'James.' She said it as if tasting the word.

'That's right.'

'Maybe James young and handsome. Maybe he take me to Miami.'

The dream of every Cuban female jockey.

If pigs flew.

She was watching him, looking for a reaction.

'Maybe he will at that, Maria.'

'Ricardo, you know what my horoscope said?'

'No.' Farr knew he was supposed to be interested because he wrote them. But after doing it for five years he was fed up with the whole exercise, especially as the *Diario* paid so pitifully and he had such difficulty getting the words down.

'It said I would meet someone who would become a good friend and that if I lived up to the challenge new vistas would open up to me. Ricardo, what's a vista?'

Farr wasn't listening. He needed to urinate again.

Shit, his dick was on fire.

He had to tell her.

Farr noted with regret that his beer was finished.

'You don't really care. You never care. You're a bastard.'

'You're right there, Maria. I am a bastard, quite literally. Let's take that walk. I have something to tell you.'

chapter three

(Capricorn, October 9–10. Congratulations. Relief
is at hand and the day is yours – but you have some
way to go before the war is won.)

Farr stepped forward, placing himself squarely in front of the
foreigner. He stuck out his hand and smiled broadly.

'Mr Plush? Ricardo Farr.'

'Hey, buddy!' The visitor dropped his bags and Farr felt a
wet palm clasp his fingers.

'Good to meet ya, Ricky. How'd you know it was me?'

Farr was careful to wipe his hand surreptitiously on the seat
of his pants when Plush wasn't looking. He picked up one of
the bags, the bigger of the two. He was pleased to note it
weighed a ton. He didn't mind the effect the weight had on
his arm and shoulder. On the contrary. Farr thought it was
beautiful. Oh, blissful pain! The mule had arrived! Oh, glory!
Life had suddenly taken on a far rosier hue than of late. Never
mind it felt like his shoulder was going to be wrenched out of
its socket.

He didn't answer his visitor's question and anyway Plush was
talking again. Something about an Irish grandmother. How did
Farr recognise him? It was obvious, but Farr didn't say so. Farr
didn't say he had hung well back from the barrier. He didn't
carry a sign or push forward with the other tourist touts and

pimps as the arrivals came through. He didn't want to make a spectacle of himself in front of Gomez's men. He wanted to keep it all low-key so he could slip away unnoticed in case there was any trouble. (Farr, on his way to the airport, had pictured in his mind's eye the terrible image of Plush being dragged away in handcuffs, each of the American's protests rewarded with a blow from a policeman's rubber truncheon, while triumphant customs officers scuttled along behind clutching the precious contraband.) In any case, he had been looking for an American and he was pretty sure he would know him when he saw him. The second of the twice-daily flights from Havana connected with the Cubana flight from Mexico City; there weren't going to be too many WASP arrivals.

Even so, he didn't expect anything quite so obvious.

'This way, Mr Plush.'

Maria would be disappointed.

Farr made a mock-deferential bow and a simultaneous sweeping movement with his free hand towards the exit.

'It's James, Ricky. We're already colleagues, but I have this strong feelin' we'll be real good friends by the time this here trade show is over. You okay with that case?'

Farr winced inwardly at the contraction of his first name, but he wasn't going to complain. Plush seemed friendly enough. Farr was anxious to know for sure what was in the suitcase. He couldn't wait to get it back home and sorted out. Right now he wanted confirmation that there had been no hassle from customs. Next, he wanted to set his plan in motion, get Plush fixed up with Maria. He had the Tropicana tickets ready in his breast pocket. It was all a matter of maintaining cash flow. Warren Buffett was a great believer in a healthy cash flow, and Farr was an ardent admirer of the Warren Buffett approach to investment. Find something people want over and over again and buy into it. Buy when the price is right and watch it grow. Warren Buffett had found

Coca-Cola. Farr had found sex. Everyone wanted both, again and again.

'Jeez, it's night and it's still hotter 'n hell.'

Plush took a large white handkerchief out of his trouser pocket and wiped his face with it.

Farr didn't have the heart to tell him it was the dry season and as cool as it got. Instead he busied himself heaving the suitcases into the back of the Lada. He put the heavy one in first, then the smaller one on top. Just in case they were stopped and the cops decided to make a rudimentary search. Better they found the American's pyjamas and washbag than several kilos of aspirin. You couldn't be too careful these days. Farr was wondering how James T. Plush Jr was going to fit into the front passenger seat. The Lada was small and boxy, and the seats were designed for Russian dwarves with legs cut off at the knees. Plush was a very tall man. He had a narrow chest and enormous hips and backside. He gave new meaning to the term pear-shaped. Farr thought English girls were pear-shaped, but they were nothing like this. Plush wore fancy cowboy boots with three-inch heels and a big white stetson. In that get-up he must be over seven foot, Farr thought. Like a colossal toadstool, he tapered up to the huge hat. Not that Plush seemed bothered in the slightest at the prospect of sitting doubled up, his knees on either side of his large ears. He was just standing there, waiting, hands at his sides, sweating profusely and not doing anything to help while Farr loaded up the Lada, which now had a decided tilt towards the rear end as if it were sitting up begging. Except talk. Come to think of it, Plush had been talking constantly since he emerged from the customs hall. Not to Farr specifically. Just anyone.

Plush was saying something about Texas. That it was southern, but not Old South. Texas was special. Texas was big. Everything in Texas was big. Then Plush was talking about his Irish

23

roots again. He was speaking quietly in a gentle monotone, without a break, without any pretence at punctuation. It was sleep-inducing stuff. Farr had switched off, thinking about Maria and Amelia and the occasional sharp pain in his pants, but something made him try to lock into the monologue again.

He interrupted his passenger's flow.

'James, I don't understand. You didn't need an Irish passport to come to Cuba. All accredited journalists, even US nationals, can get visas nowadays. Especially if you're covering the trade show.'

'Yeah. I know. But I thought it was kinda safer. I wouldn't attract so much attention as an Irishman,' Plush said. He had taken off the stetson and balanced it on his knees. It blocked his view out of the windscreen.

Farr shrugged. Inconspicuous was not an adjective Farr would have applied to the giant in fancy dress beside him.

'Well,' Plush said with an embarrassed laugh. 'That's not the whole truth, amigo.'

'No?'

'Truth is, I played up the Irish grandparent angle to convince the foreign desk I was eligible for the trade show and could get in without any hassle. It showed initiative, y'see.'

'I see.'

Farr didn't.

Why was he so keen to come to Cuba for a trade exhibition?

'You got a ration card, Ricky?'

'Sure.' Farr wasn't going to admit to it being a forgery.

'What do you get with it?'

'A piece of bread a day. Three eggs a week. A portion of chicken or fish once a month.'

'I thought Cubans ate pork.'

'Most people can't even remember the taste of pork.'

'You don't say!'

'A family of four gets a small bottle of cooking oil four times a year, and milk is only available to children under eight.'

'Man, that's some revolution.'

'It's not the revolution, James. It's the American blockade. If you go to hospital you got to take your own bedsheets. If you're a schoolkid you have to share textbooks and your exercise book gets reused over and over. They just rub everything out and start again. If you're a doctor, you get a single bar of soap a month to wash your hands.'

'Now that's crap, Ricky.' Plush had gone red in the face. He was angry. 'It's your Soviet friends who went down the tube in ninety-one. That's what really happened here. Your Red friends screwed up and you're payin' for it.'

My friends?

Farr thought, thanks for putting me right on that score.

'In Cuba it's called The Special Period in Time of Peace,' Farr said. There was an awkward moment's silence, relieved by the sight of the hotel up ahead.

'Ever thought of becoming one of those rafters, Ricky? Whaddya call 'em?'

'*Los Balseros*.'

'Yeah.'

'It's two hundred and fifty miles to Miami and I'm scared of sharks, James.'

'But you'd have a better life in Miami. Money, a car, a house. A real job. These rafters get a hero's welcome, you know. They get taken care of until they're settled.'

'Can I offer you some advice, James? In the spirit of friendship?'

'Sure thing, Rick. I'd welcome it.'

'Two pieces of advice, actually.'

'Shoot.'

'First. Don't talk politics. It's not that you'll get yourself

into trouble, but it puts at risk whoever you're talking to. Make
sure first you know who you're dealing with.'

Plush turned his round, sweaty face towards Farr.

His mouth was pursed. He didn't like the advice.

'And the second?'

Farr wasn't sure if Plush was taking in what he said or
not. There was something in his voice that said that he, the
renowned foreign correspondent, knew better.

'If you go with a girl—' Farr hesitated. For a macho Cuban
the whole idea of using a condom in the first place was
repugnant and God knows, Farr didn't want to put Plush
off the idea of sex, rather the reverse – 'use a condom. Even
a nice girl. Any girl.'

Even dance student and third cousin Maria.

Well, he's been warned, Farr thought.

'Thanks, buddy. It's appreciated. I knew I was in good hands
here. Is this the place?' Plush's tone was at odds with his words,
suggesting he was ready to write Farr off as a political deviant
and a damn nuisance. Now he was peering out of the side
window at the illuminated façade of the Casaverde.

'This is it, Jim.'

You call me Ricky. I'll call you Jim. See how you like it.

But Plush was off again, this time rattling on about his job
as chief of the newspaper's Austin bureau and what awesome
fun it was to run his own outfit.

It was very late when Farr got home. Perversely, he was feeling
nervous because everything had gone so well. Plush had given
him the big suitcase to take home, and he managed to lug it
up the stairs of the old damp-stained *edificio* a step at a time,
relieved for once that there was a power cut because he didn't
want the neighbours to see. Once in his living room – the
entire place consisted of one quite large room with a cupboard
of a bathroom and a tiny kitchenette in the corner – Farr sat

on the case to rest a moment and counted out the five days' daily allowance Plush had advanced him. At thirty bucks per diem that was a hundred and fifty US straight off. A twenty-dollar bill for petrol. A small fortune to most people. Plus a hundred dollars for the Tropicana tour's best seats when Farr had only paid ninety.

That was a ten per cent profit right there.

It got better. Plush had taken at once to Maria. His eyes looked moist and he stammered, repeatedly licking his lips and fidgeting when Farr made the introductions. The bit about Maria being a distant cousin and dance student went down easily, too. Farr offered to pay for the contents of the suitcase, but Plush wouldn't have it. No, he said, unable to take his eyes off Maria's considerable physical assets. The newspaper understood Farr was working in difficult circumstances and was more than happy to try to make things a little easier for him and his family. It was the least they could do. Hell, he didn't even get a retainer and that was something they might look at again later. Plush, his face flushed either from the *cuba libres* he was knocking back, or whatever it was Maria was doing to him with her foot under the table, explained that he bought the stuff in Mexico, so technically he wasn't breaking the US trade embargo. He went on at enormous length about it. Farr could scarcely keep the disbelief off his face. He still wasn't a hundred per cent sure Plush meant what he said.

He asked Plush twice. It was all for free?

He started to unpack now, fingers trembling with excitement.

He made separate piles of each commodity.

Batteries. Six to a pack. Thirty packs. Condoms, eighteen to a box. Thirty boxes. Farr sniggered to himself – that was five hundred and forty shags. Ten packs of sanitary towels, six to a pack. Fifteen bottles of aspirin, a hundred and fifty aspirin to a bottle.

What was this?

Two hundred and fifty prescription sleeping pills.

Four hundred painkillers.

Toothpaste, twenty tubes.

Toilet paper, two dozen rolls.

Farr started tapping out the figures on his little pocket calculator. He checked and rechecked.

It couldn't be.

Farr told himself he could live for two years on what he could get for this on the black market.

Uh!

That burning sensation again.

Farr started stacking the goodies away in the usual hiding place, under the floorboards. Lovingly. He made little piles of the boxes and bottles, cellophane packets and tubes. Almost caressing them into order.

My babies.

An hour later he was stretched out on his bed, on his back, shirtless, pants undone and staring into the darkness, listening to the whine of mosquitoes and thinking about the money and feeling the waves of sleep start to lap at his brain when the telephone rang.

His telephone hardly ever rang.

It went on ringing until Farr managed to stumble over to it in the hallway.

'Yes?' Breathless, sweat on his back.

'Mr Farr?'

An unfamiliar voice.

'Felipe Gomez. Captain Felipe Gomez. I think we met once. Through my sister. Amelia. Forgive the late hour. I tried to reach you earlier. I have a favour to ask of you.'

Farr said nothing. All he could hear was the terrible pounding of his own blood in his ears, as loud as the surf during the hurricane season.

'Are you there, Mr Farr?'

Farr's response was a strangled 'yes'.

'You know my office? Can you come round in the morning? Say between ten and eleven? I assure you it's a small matter to you, but of some importance to me. Can you do that?'

Farr thought, do I have any choice?

'You know where it is?'

'I think so.'

Who doesn't know it?

Only the whole world and his uncle, that's who.

Shit, Farr thought, Amelia's spilled the beans.

Gomez sounded so damn calm and reasonable.

Friendly, even.

Everyone knew what these security police interviews were like. It was a conveyor belt. Once you got on, you never got off again.

chapter four

(Capricorn, October 10–11. It's hard to appreciate,
but other people do have feelings. Try not to take
things too personally.)

By nine the next morning Farr was back at the Casaverde. Plush
had left a note for him at reception, saying he was waiting at
the poolside. He quickly spotted the American reclining on a
folding beach chair, facing away from him towards the stretch of
clear blue water. All Farr could see was the stetson protruding
above the high back of the plastic chair like the funnel of a ship,
and what appeared to be a long cold drink with a miniature
umbrella sticking out of the bits of fruit, along with a purple
cocktail stick shaped like a devil's trident. Plush was holding
up the glass and sucking meditatively at a multicoloured straw,
the plastic kind that has a bend in it.

Farr approached quietly. In between noisy sucks Plush
was speaking, nodding away and laughing. Farr expected
to see Maria crouched down beside the chair, massaging
Plush's spindly white legs or working sun cream into his
squishy gut, patiently pretending to listen to his mumbo-
jumbo.

All part of the service, Farr said to himself.

He was surprised to find there was no one else there.

'Morning, Jim.'

Sweat plastered curls of light brown hair to a pink and fleshy chest and paunch.

'Ricky! How you doin', son?'

Plush didn't turn. Instead he raised his glass in salute.

'Just fine, Jim. How did it go last night?'

There was a certain lubricious ambiguity in the phrasing of the question, but it seemed to be lost on Plush.

'It was a great evening. We had a real swell time. Man, are those dancers somethin'! Struttin' around on high heels with candelabra on their heads. Incredible! Thanks to you, Ricky. All thanks to you. Wouldn't have missed that for all the world. A once-in-a-lifetime show. Have you had breakfast? They got everything here. Eggs any way you want 'em, hash browns, pancakes and maple syrup. Freshly squeezed orange juice. Great coffee, too. I'm impressed. C'mon, let me order something for you. Be my pleasure . . .'

'Thanks. But I've already eaten.'

Candelabra weren't what impressed most male visitors to the Tropicana show, Farr thought.

'Take a seat, Rick.' Plush flapped a free hand towards an empty beach chair. 'Maria will be along in a minute. She's a great gal. Did you know her daddy was a revolutionary in those hills back there, along with Che and Fidel?'

'The Sierra Maestra — yes, I heard something of the kind.'

Farr thought, bitch is stealing my war stories.

'She's a great kid. Terrific body. Sweet temperament. Lovely sweet smile. I'm mighty grateful to you for introducing us. I never met anyone like her before.'

I'm sure you haven't, Farr thought.

'That's okay, Jim.'

There was surely one part of the anatomy that made all Cuban women different. Special.

'Why don't you have one of these rum punches?'

'Too early for me.'

'Aw, this is my third and I'm gearing up for a fourth.'

Then he was in for a surprise when he tried to stand up, Farr thought.

'Have you told your office you're here?'

'Oh, sure. C'mon, loosen up and have a drink, Ricky.'

'No, I'm fine, thanks.'

'Suit yourself.' Plush sucked noisily at the straw, then tried unsuccessfully to hook out a large chunk of pineapple.

'What's your plan today, Jim?'

'Well, Maria suggested showing me the sights. I wanna see that garrison where the revolution began . . .'

'Antiguo Cuartel Moncada.'

'Moncada garrison. That's it. I unnerstan' they got Che's boots and Fidel's uniform and the bullet holes are still right there in the walls. I want to pick up a little local colour for our stories. Later there won't be time for moochin' around town.'

Our stories? What did he mean?

'Fine by me, Jim.'

'How about we three meet up for dinner?'

'Sounds good.'

Farr groaned involuntarily as another stab of pain hit him in the testicles.

'You okay?'

'Sure.'

'You look kinda pale.'

'I'm okay, Jim.'

'Shall we say nine o'clock – here at the hotel?'

'That's good.'

As he walked away, threading his way between the poolside tables and chairs, Farr could still hear the drone of Plush's voice behind him. He seemed to be reading aloud from a guidebook. Maybe he'd run out of things to say himself.

'Founded by the Spaniards in 1514, Santiago was Cuba's

capital from 1524 until 1549. Today it is Cuba's official "Hero City" for its role as a stronghold of nationalism and birthplace of revolution . . .'

Farr bumped into Maria in the lobby as she swept out of the lift like an exotic bird. She was wearing a long blue wraparound beach dress that billowed behind her.

New, by the look of it, Farr thought; most likely it was bought from one of those overpriced boutiques in the foreign currency mall on the mezzanine.

'What the hell are you doing?'

'Shhh! Don't speak to me like that! I was taking a shower in our room. You got a problem with that?'

Our room, Farr repeated to himself. Our room?

'No . . .' Farr was caught on the wrong foot. 'I just didn't expect to see you wandering around the hotel on your own.' He made no effort to keep the irritation out of his voice.

It intruded on Farr's territory, and Maria knew it. He — not Plush — was the one who provided his girls with access to foreigners in their hotel rooms. What else were pimps for?

'I'm not wandering around. What do you take me for?'

A whore, that's what, Farr said to himself.

'Anyhow, James he say it okay. He tell reception I can come and go as I please. Okay?' Maria's tone was haughty, defiant.

'How was it?'

'How was what?'

Farr noticed foreign guests spilling out of the pair of gilded elevators were turning their heads to stare at her, the dowdy foreign women with hostility in their eyes, the men with barely concealed lust. Maria knew perfectly well what Farr meant, but her face wore a stubborn look. She felt offended, and she showed it by sticking out her jaw, setting her mouth in that obstinate way of hers when she felt aggrieved.

'Last night,' he said.

'Perfect,' she snapped, raising her chin.

Farr thought, slut's hiding something.

'Yes?'

'He was the perfect gentleman.'

'He didn't do it is what you mean.'

Maria looked away.

'Couldn't get it up, or what?'

Why did he say these things?

She looked at Farr now, eyes blazing.

'He say he want to get to know me better.'

There was a careless destructiveness in Farr's heart. He liked to see Maria angry. It pleased him. It would never have occurred to him that he might feel anything for the girl. Envy was as alien and abstract an emotion as the term love. Farr could envy a neighbour his wealth or his power, his car or his clothes – even his horse – but never his woman. Now he was interested to see if Maria would make a scene right there and spoil it for them both. Whether her female vanity would outweigh her appreciation for the power of the few dollars she earned. He told himself he was feeling this way because he was afraid of his meeting with Captain Gomez, infuriated by the needle pain in his groin and generally exasperated by the breezy savoir faire of that ugly American sitting out there in the sun getting drunk.

They were walking across a deep-pile carpet towards automatic glass doors that led out onto the patio where the potted palms and the pool were.

'Maybe he's a *maracon*, Maria. Maybe he likes strong, good-looking boys with big dicks. You thought of that? Maybe you should have offered him a blow-job, huh?'

Why did he do it? He didn't know. He knew it was a vicious and mean thing to say. Farr's feelings seemed to range from the brutish and callous to extreme sentimentality, and he didn't know why it was that way.

35

They had reached the double doors.

'No, Ricardo. I think maybe he a little crazy, but he not *maracon*. He talk all night. Never stop. He hold my hand. I sleep and I wake up, he still talking. I go to toilet and he talk all the time. I take a bath and he talk. I think James very lonely man. Unhappy.'

Farr shrugged. Who cared as long as he paid up?

'I got to go. We're meeting here tonight. Nine. All three of us.'

Maria gave him a half-smile, uncertain.

'You remember what I said, Maria. He wants to do it, you use a condom. Promise me. You promise me, Maria?'

She looked at him keenly, narrowing her eyes as if she was a little surprised, trying to figure him out, read his expression.

The glass doors sighed open and a gust of warm, sticky air hit them. Farr was turning away when she called out to him.

'Ricardo?'

'Yes?' He stopped, looked back at her.

'You not jealous, are you, Ricardo?'

She looked pleased at the notion that he might be, watching him closely now to see if her words had found their mark.

She would like nothing better than to get her hooks into me, he told himself. But it'll never happen.

Farr smiled back at Maria, masking his next thought: sorry to disappoint you, my sweet. No *puta* will get the better of Ricardo Farr. Never.

Farr knew where the security police headquarters were. He had passed the place before, looking carefully the other way. It never did to look at it or its employees openly, or point the way the tourists did, sticking their forefingers rudely out of the window, shoving their cameras carelessly at whatever took their fancy. If they knew what really went on in there behind the crumbling yellow walls they wouldn't do it. He had heard the stories too, just like everyone else, but this was the first time he'd driven right up to it deliberately, parked in the oil-streaked lot out front and, knees quaking, climbed the steps to the reception desk.

Palms and feet leaking perspiration, his eyes avoiding the hard, indifferent faces of the armed guards.

Trying to look pleasant without being unduly obsequious.

Farr had applied both deodorant and aftershave after a strip-wash that morning, but already he could smell the rank, almondy bitterness of fear emanating from his own armpits.

The place was dilapidated like every state building, stained black with damp on the outside. Inside, the dim corridors were noisy with slamming doors, footsteps, shouts and orders, raucous outbursts of laughter. Farr was asked to write his name down and was given a numbered slip of paper.

They didn't even look at him.

There was no body search.

His hands were shaking and he put them in his pockets.

The lifts weren't working, so he tramped up the stairs.

Behind a brown door bearing the number 9, Farr found an open-plan office, four desks in it, all occupied. Gomez rose to meet him, coming forward with a smile on his round face.

'I'm Felipe Gomez. You must be Mr Farr.'

Farr did not know what to say or do. His shirt stuck to his back. His legs ran with sweat from climbing the stairs to the third floor – and from nervousness stoked by a vivid imagination.

They shook hands.

Farr felt dull with fright.

'Shall we get some air?'

There were fans on each desk, but they weren't working.

Farr followed Gomez dutifully. He had time to inspect the secret policeman. He wasn't what he expected. He put Gomez at about twenty-eight to thirty, slightly plump, with a straggly beard and moustache, his thick tousled hair brushed back from his forehead. By Farr's standards Gomez was shabbily dressed. Without his secret policeman's pass or swagger of self-assurance, he would never get a foot in the Casaverde's doors before being chased off by the doorman and porters. He wore a T-shirt with horizontal grey, red and yellow stripes that only accentuated his spreading gut. His tan trousers were clean and pressed but very worn, and the navy-blue shoes on his feet looked as if they had been re-soled many times. He wasn't wearing socks and he wasn't packing a gun.

He looked like any other middle-rank civil servant.

Dirt poor, but unlike most people he was almost chubby.

He did not look like someone on the take.

An honest security cop was a dangerous animal.

'We'll take my car.'

It was a huge Chevvy, at least forty years old. Not that Farr knew much about cars. It had a white top and red body. The chrome and paintwork had been lovingly cleaned and polished, although Farr noticed the tyres were mismatched. The big leather seat in the back could easily have seated six people.

Farr was tempted to say it would make a fine taxi, but he bit down on his tongue just in time. This was not the time to discuss New Business Opportunities. He made a mental note of it nevertheless. Gomez looked like a man who might like a decent pair of shoes, and maybe the honesty might wear a little thin at Christmas or New Year.

'Where are we going?'

Gomez didn't answer the question directly.

'You're my excuse to get out of that damn office.'

Gomez smiled shyly, like someone enjoying breaking the rules. Nothing more was said until they drew up at a headland south of the city and parked in the shade of a banana tree.

'See? We're alone. It's both very public and private at the same time,' Gomez said. His tone was calm, friendly.

'And beautiful,' Farr said, starting to relax.

There had been a point at which he thought he was being driven to his place of execution. It would be easy enough for Gomez to avenge his sister's honour, if that was his intention.

'It's one of my favourite places. I don't get enough petrol to get out into the country, but on the other hand if I don't use up my petrol coupons they'll take them away from me. So now you know – this is how I do it. I bring my family out here at weekends sometimes.'

Gomez led the way. Farr listened to the sound of the breeze in the palms as the two men moved in and out of the luminous shadows. They sat at a rustic wooden bench and table near the edge of the cliff with a fine view of the sea. Out in the bay the air seemed iridescent, glowing above the grey-green waves.

'My sister said you were someone with his ear to the ground. Someone with a feel for what's going on in this town of ours. You've met her, of course. Amelia.'

It was a statement, not a question.

Had she told him – everything?

Farr felt he was slipping into quicksand.

The wrong word, he thought, and he was a goner.

'I'm flattered, Captain, of course. But I'm not sure I would know any more than someone in your position . . .'

'You know Amelia's husband, Dr Garcia?'

'I've met him. Very recently, in fact.'

'He's well respected. He heads a department at the hospital. He's a specialist on diseases of the urinary tract, I believe. Sexually transmitted diseases, or STDs.'

Gomez paused. He pulled a Havana cigar out of his shirt pocket and offered it to Farr.

'No thanks. I don't smoke.'

'The damn things will be the death of me, but I can't resist them.' Gomez removed the band, bit off the end, turned his head and spat out the tobacco leaf and cupped his hands to light it. The first match was a dud, the second missed. He managed it with the third, turning the cigar carefully to get an even burn.

He broke each of the used matches in two. Farr assumed it was a way of making sure they were out so they didn't start fires. An old army habit, perhaps.

Captain Gomez puffed hard to get the Havana going.

He was taking his time. His leisurely manner was making Farr's heart beat furiously. Was he doing it deliberately? Was it part of his technique? Did he do this while someone else turned the handle of the electric generator and the electrodes fried a suspect's balls? Farr could feel the sweat gathering on his temples despite the sea breeze, but he resisted the temptation to wipe it away. He didn't want to appear scared.

'Last year Dr Garcia formed his own medical association. I mean by that an independent association.' Gomez let his eyes flicker towards Farr's face, watching for a reaction.

'That upset some people. It made things awkward for Amelia. Because I'm her brother, you see. It's family.'

Farr waited.

Upset some people.

I bet, Farr thought.

'Next week there's a trade show. You know about it. You'll be helping the foreign journalists with their story, no doubt.' Gomez looked down at his feet. He paused a moment, drew on the cigar, and when Farr failed to confirm or deny this, he continued. 'There are sixteen countries sending delegations. Forty-three firms. Five main themes. Tourism. Aviation. Telecommunications. Banking. Construction. As a journalist yourself you know this, of course. It may be in your report where I read of these matters.'

Gomez took a long draw on his cigar and let the smoke swirl out of his nostrils. He looked up at Farr.

'There are four hundred thousand people in this city, Mr Farr. There will be maybe four to five hundred business visitors. Maybe as many foreign journalists. Many, many will be US nationals. Not all of them will be here for legitimate purposes. Security is going to be a big priority for us. We want things to go smoothly, without incident. We don't want anything to happen to these people while they are our guests here in Cuba. You follow?'

'Sure.' Farr nodded.

'Good.' Captain Gomez inspected the end of his cigar.

'What I'm saying to you isn't official, Ricardo. It's between us. Between friends. A confidential matter between friends, okay?'

'Fine.'

'See, the Leadership has been planning this trade show for a long, long time. The timing is chosen with great care, and I'm not talking about the weather. It's a national security issue. You might call it our Cuban Trojan Horse. To break through the Blockade. You see? Not all at once, but bit by bit, brick by brick, we make a hole in this wall the imperialists have built around us. Little by little.'

Gomez made a jabbing motion with his cigar as if trying to knock a hole all by himself in the trade embargo.

'And where do I come into all this?'

Gomez dropped the wet stub of his cigar to the ground. He stamped on it and then jabbed the stogie with the toe of his shoe as if it was a cockroach he was trying to exterminate. When he had tired of it he stood up straight and smiled at Farr. He looked almost boyish and not at all sinister.

'Ah. That's it, Ricardo. Amelia said you were a smart guy, and she's right. She reads those horoscopes you write in *Diario*. They're not my kind of thing, I have to tell you. But she said you would understand, and now I know it too. That's exactly why I wanted to talk to you. Why I need your help.'

chapter five

(Capricorn, October 11–12. Don't imagine people
are conspiring against you. Give it time, and at all
costs avoid self-pity.)

Cespedes Park was transformed by the Monday morning when
Farr set out once again for the hospital. A special enclosure
had been put up for the trade stands, and the clatter of
hammers and power saws rang out among the trees where
the hospitality chalets were going up in rows, like tents at a
medieval joust. Banners overhead welcomed Cuba's American
Brothers (not comrades this time, Farr noted). Nearby, in an
open space, several hundred youths and girls in identical blue
workshirts and carrying red banners practised marching and
countermarching to the sound of a bass drum, tramping back
and forth until their feet kicked up clouds of dust and their
shirts turned black with sweat. The familiar chanting, growing
to a roar: 'With Fidel, our whole life!' Workers were cleaning
the fountain (Farr couldn't remember when he had last seen
it working properly). Red bunting fluttered across approach
roads and the national flags of the participating nations hung
from lamp-posts in clusters like bunches of brightly coloured
flowers. Whitewash had been liberally splashed on walls and
the bollards of trees. Farr noticed that hoardings listing the
foreign firms taking part included South and Central American

subsidiaries and franchises of some major household names in the States. Computer and telecommunications firms. Tobacco giants. Auto manufacturers. Chemical corporations. The big fruit traders. Washington would not be pleased.

The dollar was like water, Farr thought. It found its own level, rising like a subterranean spring to the surface and seeping through every crack and fissure in the edifice of sanctions. Greed was unstoppable. A force of nature like gravity. Unavoidable. Irresistible. Pitiless.

What did Cuba really have to fear most?

Gomez had meant it as a rhetorical question.

Sanctions or the greenback?

Revolutionary Police were more in evidence, Farr saw, the officers patrolling two by two on foot in peaked caps and denim fatigues, pistols on their belts.

There were fixed checkpoints at major intersections where there had been none before, wooden boxes set up on platforms to give the police a three-hundred-and-sixty-degree view and a clear field of fire.

What did they expect, he wondered, a second Bay of Pigs?

Farr's mind was focused on the sting. He was twisting in the driver's seat, trying to relieve the feeling of having had his prick tweaked with red-hot pincers. It was only a few minutes to go.

Father, I have sinned . . .

Now was his moment of truth.

It would almost be a relief to know.

He was kept waiting. Other patients were called and they vanished into booths. New patients took their place, leaning or squatting wherever they could. There weren't enough seats. The place was packed. By the time Farr had lost any sense of embarrassment at sitting there, a white-coated woman doctor had called his name out and come up to him with a message that Dr Garcia was unavoidably delayed. He had had to attend an important meeting at the last minute.

When Garcia finally appeared, he said nothing but nodded to Farr and held the plastic curtain aside to let his patient go ahead of him into the cubicle. Garcia sat down behind his desk. He had a pile of buff-coloured files — his morning's backlog of patients — and quickly found the one he was looking for.

'I apologise for keeping you waiting.'

Farr said nothing.

'I have your results.' Garcia's eyes briefly met Farr's.

Farr could see his own name at the top of the sheet.

He smiled but thought: well, get on with it!

That pain again.

Farr winced, contracting his stomach muscles.

'Do you want the good news or the bad news first, Señor Farr?'

At the very moment Garcia pulled the file closer to himself, looking down at the papers and tapping his pen, Farr had a flashback to his meeting with Captain Gomez. Gomez had driven him back in his Chevvy to where the Lada was parked. All the way back Gomez had talked about history. It was apparently one of his favourite topics.

Farr hadn't interrupted. Not a word. Not until they drew up outside Santiago's secret police headquarters.

Gomez was in full flood. He seemed to have relaxed in Farr's company, and now he kept one hand on the steering wheel and waved the other around for emphasis.

'Look. Look at this city of ours. You see the slogans on the walls? Socialism or Death. In every barrio, *Revolucion*! But what does it all mean? Our own children here in Cuba don't even really know. Why? In my opinion it's because they're not being taught properly. Maybe the teachers are too young. They don't remember. They have no personal experience of the struggle. They're just words in a book, scrawled on a wall . . .'

Gomez turned, taking his eyes off the road. He had the disconcerting habit of maintaining eye contact with Farr while he talked and letting go of the wheel to punch the seat between them for emphasis. He was getting himself quite worked up.

'You think you're some kind of big-time player, Ricardo. To that crowd in Miami you're nothing. You have to understand that if those people get their hands on this country, there will be no place for a man like you. I'm talking about crime with a capital C. Organised. The Mob. Extortion rackets, drugs, prostitution, big-time. A little guy like you gets a choice; work for them and they squeeze every lousy US cent out of you, or you're shark meat. You think I'm kidding?'

Gomez didn't wait for a response.

'They got plans for Cuba, my friend. Big plans. Casinos, hotels . . . the money's waiting in the banks, so are the architects' plans and the construction companies. Even the Spanish-language edition of the *Chronicle* has got an entire fucking printing works all packed up in containers waiting to be flown in and set up in Havana. Do you understand any of what I'm saying?'

Gomez thumped the seat harder with his fist.

'They're just waiting for us to go belly up. Sure, the President's cautious, stubborn. Wouldn't you be? Is it any wonder when the Mafia is waiting to move in here and turn the clock back to Batista's days? They want to turn this island into a damn Disney park, Ricardo, and we'll be the clowns. Sure we will. Suckers in fancy dress. We'll be the underclass, fucked every day by rich Americans. A man won't be able to call his life his own. Not you. Not me. You want professional football and baseball, Ricardo? Sure you do, because you tell yourself it's big money. But it's also corrupt, my friend, and behind the corruption is a whole lot of violence to keep ordinary folk like us in our place, backed up by the US Marines and all in the name of freedom. Not our freedom, though. Oh, no, not ours.'

The Chevvy nearly hit the pavement. Gomez grabbed the wheel just in time.

'And those bastards in Washington lecture us about human rights! What do they know about human dignity, huh?'

At last, to Farr's relief, they stopped. Gomez kept the Chevvy running and waited while Farr found the door handle and clambered out.

'Ricardo?'

Gomez had calmed down somewhat.

'Yes, Felipe?' Farr ducked down and looked at him through the side window. Trying out the first name. Farr thought that if he could call a secret police captain by his first name it must mean he had some degree of immunity from the conveyor of oblivion in that down-at-heel place.

'You'll remember what we talked about, won't you?'

'Of course, Felipe.'

'Just between us, right?'

Farr nodded emphatically.

He didn't say it, but he could think it and it was this: maybe the Blockade was more useful to the *Comandante en Jefe de la Revolucion* than it was to the island's blue-eyed enemies in Washington. Maybe Fidelistas like Gomez knew they were finished without the embargo. Maybe it was their last defence.

'Dr Garcia will listen to you, Ricardo. You're a man of the world. A man without ideology. Without religion. You survive by your wits. Amelia said you were a survivor. He'll respect that in a way he won't respect one of us. Try to explain to him. Try to explain that there is a lot more to Cuban independence than sugar and soap. There's a moral price. And we all have to pay our share. Will you do that for me, Ricardo?'

Farr thought his secret thoughts.

Cuba could never accept defeat even when it stared the population in the face and made the kids cry from hunger.

Era cuestion de dignidad.

Farr opened his mouth to reply, but Gomez spoke again.

'For Amelia, too.'

Farr couldn't meet his gaze.

'Yes, of course. I'll try, Felipe.'

'Do you promise?'

What a question, Farr thought.

It was nothing short of blackmail.

'I promise I'll try.'

'The good news,' Garcia was saying, 'is that what you have is curable. Almost instantly. With the right drugs the symptoms would disappear – within a week. Even less.'

What does he mean – the right drugs?

Farr moved his weight from one cheek of his buttocks to the other.

'And the bad news?'

'I don't have the right medicine. I'm sorry.'

Sorry?

Garcia looked up at Farr. He had a strange expression on his face, one Farr had not seen before. The doctor looked ashamed, certainly. And, yes, it was anger. The doctor was angry. The vein lying against his smooth olive-toned skin stretched tight across his forehead was beating away rapidly, twitching like a viper. Garcia was clenching his jaw rhythmically almost in time to the pulse above his eyebrow.

He was twisting the pen furiously with his well-scrubbed fingers.

'What – can you repeat that?'

Farr's mind grappled hopelessly with what the doctor was saying. Had his ears deceived him? Was he dreaming?

Garcia's words echoed in his mind: couldn't be cured?
Couldn't?

'The hospital does not have the antibiotics to deal with your problem, Mr Farr. I'm sorry, but there it is.'

He flung the pen down on the desk.

'What the hell am I supposed to do? Wait till my pecker falls off?'

Farr checked himself. He felt the colour rushing into his face, his voice rising hysterically.

Couldn't be cured?

Farr took a deep breath. Keep calm, he told himself.

'Did you have sex since we last met?'

'What did you say?' Farr was gripped by wild panic. It took him a moment to backtrack, to focus on the question. 'Oh, no. No, I haven't. No, I didn't.'

'I need the names of your sexual partner or partners.'

'Fuck cares about that? You can't do anything for them, anyway. And I'm your patient. I'm sitting here. Not them. I'm the one you should be concerned about. Not . . .'

What was he going to say? Dr Garcia was looking at him strangely.

Amelia – the name shot into Farr's mind.

'Yes?'

'What have I got? Tell me, for Chrissakes!'

'Mr Farr—'

'Don't tell me I'm—' An appalled look stole across Farr's face. Not that. Not HIV!

'It's gonorrhoea, Mr Farr.'

Farr expelled his breath sharply.

'For a moment . . . I thought . . .'

'There are seven hundred and fifty thousand new cases reported every year in the United States alone. Normally this would not be too much of a problem. It's caused by a bacterium, gonococcus. I'm anxious to trace your sexual partners, Mr Farr, because very often people who are infected, especially women, show no sign of symptoms . . .'

Farr lost all patience. He spoke roughly. 'It's a simple case of the clap, doctor. Just give me the damn pills or injections!'

'I can't. I'm sorry.'

'Can't or won't?'

'Can't.'

Farr thought: was this Garcia's revenge?

'If you'd just listen and try to stay calm, Mr Farr.'

Garcia looked suddenly tired and drawn. He leaned back in his chair and breathed deeply. He put his neat hands across the front of his white coat and laced the fingers together.

'Normally I would prescribe ampicillin or amoxillin. These are pencillin-based and usually very effective.'

'So?'

Farr grimaced as the needles stabbed him again. The pains were becoming more frequent. Every time they hit him they made him hold his breath and he felt quite dizzy.

'Right now, here in Santiago, we have a particularly virulent strain. It's resistant to pencillin. I know because I have many cases. Twelve diagnosed in the last week. Twenty today. Pencillin-based antibiotics have been administered and they have not been effective. Totally ineffective, in fact.'

'Well, you've got to get the right stuff, haven't you?'

Farr glared at Garcia. His look said, are you thick as shit or what?

'Easier said than done.'

'Doctor—' Farr smiled '—Cuba has the best health-care system in the entire Americas. The best anywhere in the developing world, or so we're constantly told, and now you're telling me . . .'

'Used to be the best. Was the best.'

'Used to be?' Farr sounded stupid even to himself.

What subversive talk was this?

'Maybe my gonorrhoea is different . . .'

'No. No different.'

Garcia leaned forward. His eyes flickered towards the curtained entrance to his cubicle. His voice dropped. 'Listen to me, Farr. Just for once, shut up and listen. We have an epidemic on our hands. That means the incidence of infection – the rate at which the disease spreads – is out of control . . .'

Dr Garcia was still talking quietly, trying to explain; something about an appeal to the authorities, a delay in the start of the trade show, an attempt to contact the Havana representative of the International Committee of the Red Cross. The added difficulty of diagnosis because the disease was often masked by something called clamydia, and sometimes there were no symptoms at all to alert the sufferer. Despite Garcia's appeal to pay attention, Farr was only half listening. In a brilliant microsecond, a terrible fraction of a moment's understanding, Farr grasped the substance of what Captain Gomez had been talking about and what he'd promised in return. What Dr Garcia was saying – the chalets going up in Cespedes Park, the Party youth workers rehearsing, Amelia naked except for her stockings on the floor of the hotel room, Maria in her lurex and fuck-me shoes, and even Plush and his absurd hat – all had in common.

Farr bent forward slowly and rested his forehead on the edge of Garcia's desk and let out a long moan of anguish.

chapter six

(Capricorn, October 12–13. You give wise counsel,
but ask yourself whether you're as good at listening
to others as you are in telling them what to do.)

'If gonorrhoea isn't treated,' Garcia was saying, 'then the
bacteria invade the bloodstream. When that happens they attack
the joints, heart valves – even the brain.' Garcia took Farr by
the arm, guiding him down the crowded corridor, steamy with
humanity. Old women and children, hospital orderlies, pretty
nurses as virginal as nuns in their starched white uniforms, old
drunks, expectant mothers and the lame parted before them.
Farr noticed the doctor's white coat acted like magic, as an
instantly recognisable symbol that people deferred to, made
room for. Garcia might be poor, but he had respect, Farr
thought. His coat was like a badge of office. It was a lot more
than Farr could claim for himself.

'But the most frequent consequence.' Garcia was saying,
speaking loudly over his shoulder, 'is something called PID.'

Garcia stopped and turned. They were standing outside
a door that appeared to Farr to lead to a women's ward.
His heart sank. He hated the sight of sick people, especially
women.

The smell alone of all that chemical or whatever it was was
bad enough.

'PID affects one million women in the United States every

year. It scars the lining of the Fallopian tubes. Or it can prevent the passage of the fertilised egg into the uterus.'

Garcia pushed open the swing door, holding it open and waiting for a hesitant Farr to follow.

'Right here we have examples of what I'm talking about.' Garcia smiled at a woman patient lying flat on her back in bed. 'This lady here had her egg implanted in the tube itself; it's called an ectopic pregnancy, and had we not intervened in time she would have died. We're going to see a lot more of it, too.'

'Hello, doctor.' She could barely lift her head.

'How are you today, Ana?'

'Better, doctor.'

Garcia moved on, pulling Farr by the elbow. He spoke in a low, hushed voice so the bedridden patients wouldn't hear.

'She's still very weak . . . lost a lot of blood. Now an infected woman who is pregnant may give the infection to her infant as the baby passes down the birth canal during delivery.'

Farr shivered despite the heat.

Do I have to hear this?

'All these people in here are suffering the long-term effects of infection. They were never diagnosed until the secondary or tertiary symptoms appeared. Needless to say, we don't have enough beds, enough sheets, enough blankets—'

'What happens to a man if he isn't treated?'

'In the long run? Sterility. Cardiovascular disease. Aneurism.'

'Aneurism?'

'Blockage of blood vessels to the brain. Leading to strokes, paralysis – eventually death.'

Garcia glanced back at Farr.

'Seen enough?'

'Er, yes. Thanks.'

'I'll walk you to the entrance. We're getting so many cases now we're having difficulty coping. It's the so-called sex industry that's doing it. We're all working flat out. I don't get home until ten or eleven at night. Sometimes later. I try to catch up on paperwork on Sundays. My wife says the kids don't remember what their father looks like!' Garcia smiled wearily, watching Farr for his reaction.

'You're not married, Mr Farr?'

'No.'

'Forgive me asking, but you're not a Party member, are you?'

'Do I look like one?'

'I didn't think so, no. Not with that Rolex.'

'It's a fake, doctor. Made in Hong Kong.'

Farr surprised himself with his unexpected honesty.

'Still . . .'

They walked in silence until they reached the steps.

'What can I do to help?'

He's been waiting for me to ask that, damn him.

Garcia thought for a moment, pursing his lips.

'Well, for a start, give me the names of your sex partners. If that embarrasses you, persuade them to come in and be tested independently. But it must be done. And quickly.'

'What's the point if you can't help them?'

Garcia sighed.

'We desperately need the antibiotics.'

'If I'd known a week ago . . .'

If he'd known earlier he wouldn't have made promises he couldn't keep to Captain Gomez. But then Gomez hadn't been entirely frank with him, either.

Garcia shrugged. 'That's too bad.'

'I'll try. But I can't promise anything.'

'I appreciate it. Maybe one of the newspaper people . . .'

'Can you write down the names of those antibiotics for me? I was never one for spelling . . .'

'Sure.'

Garcia pulled a pen from his coat, Farr found a scrap of paper in his trouser pocket. It was a receipt for ninety dollars from the Tropicana tour group. He turned it over and hoped Garcia wouldn't notice.

Garcia went all the way with Farr and waited for him to get into the Lada. He was explaining his interest in STDs. How it was, in the fifteenth century, that syphilis had caused terrible pustules all over the bodies of its victims, how the flesh peeled off the sufferer's face with death following within weeks. Yet this same disease had evolved or 'learned' to hide its symptoms, and prolonged its sufferers' lives to help it spread . . . when Garcia started talking enthusiastically about the lesions caused by STDs and how helpful they were in spreading infection, Farr shuddered inwardly. He tried not to hear more.

'You're Cuban?'

'Of course.'

'Forgive my saying so, but you don't look entirely Cuban.'

'No?'

'It's the pale eyes,' Garcia said.

'My mother,' Farr said, not wanting to be drawn.

'I don't wish to pry.'

'That's okay.' It wasn't, but what else could he say?

'Your mother is American?'

'She's dead. She was British. English. From a place called Croydon, not far from London.'

'Your father was Cuban.'

'Uh-huh.'

'They met here? In Santiago?'

Garcia didn't give up easily.

'Havana. They met in Havana.'

Garcia wanted more. Farr remembered what Gomez had said to him and decided to humour the doctor.

'Okay. My father was head porter at the Riviera. Built by

the guy who bankrolled Batista. They called him the Jewish Godfather. Meyer Lansky. His hotel — right on Havana's seafront . . .'

'The Malecon.'

'Yes. The Riviera opened on the Malecon in fifty-seven. The biggest and most tasteless place Cuba had ever seen, they say. And that's saying something in pre-revolutionary Havana.'

'And your mother?'

'She liked to be called an artist. On tour with a troupe from Paris — from the *Folies Bergère*. They were famous in their day, I'm told.'

'And?'

'And? And what?'

'They married, went back to England?'

'They didn't marry. I was born the year after they met — the end of fifty-seven. My mother went home after my father died in some street shoot-out in sixty-one — the year of the Revolution. He copped a bullet when I just turned four. Incidents like that were common.'

'I see.'

'No, you don't,' Farr muttered.

'I'm sorry.'

'Why should you be? Bodies were turning up on street corners with alarming frequency. Faces slashed with knives, throats cut. Batista's secret police were very, very busy and didn't care who knew it.'

'You went back with her?'

'I didn't have much choice, did I?'

'You liked it in England? Croydon, I mean.'

'No. Not at all.'

'Why?'

'It was cold, wet and very dirty. The food was terrible. We had no money. I loathed it. The British are racists, far more than they know. It's a disease with them. Only there's no known cure. No pill. They are particularly nasty towards someone who is like them but at the same time not one of them. Children can be 'specially cruel.'

'You came back.'

'When I was fifteen. As a cabin boy on a Dutch freighter out of Liverpool. I ran away.'

'And your mother?'

Farr shrugged. He had said a lot more than he had intended, but it seemed to do the trick. The confidence seemed to unlock something in Garcia, for he now switched subjects.

'You know my wife's brother?'

Farr didn't lie. Not because he wasn't an excellent liar, but because he could too easily be caught out. There were lies worth telling and lies that weren't.

'Yes. A secret policeman.'

'Captain Gomez. You know him?'

'I've met him.'

'Felipe talked about me?'

'He asked me to persuade you to be sensible.'

'Sensible!'

'Exactly that.'

'You think that's being sensible?'

'What he said made perfect sense to me, doctor, but then of course I didn't know—'

The neat little man in the white coat was shaking with fury, or nerves, or both.

'Get in, doctor.'

Garcia got into the front passenger seat.

'I must get back to my patients.'

'Yes, you must. But first I think we should talk about this, don't you?'

There was a gentle onshore breeze. Farr could smell the sea, mixed with the fragrance of jasmine that grew in profusion along the hospital wall – one of the benefits of having no traffic to speak of and no air pollution, either.

'When does the trade show open?'

'Thursday.'

'Three days.'

'From tomorrow morning, seventy-two hours.'

'Tell me what Felipe said.'

'Gomez thinks you're making a mistake. So do I.'

'I'm doing what I think right.'

'For whom?'

'For Cuba.'

'For Cuba.' Farr almost choked on his disbelief. The arrogance of the man! 'There's only one person who decides what's good for Cuba, doctor. And that's the President.'

Garcia shook his head as if he were dealing with a child.

'It's simple. Cuba's main foreign currency earner is the sex industry. Have you seen the planeloads of foreign men arriving? Taking girls to their rooms? So young, some of them. Don't think I don't see what goes on in Cespedes Park. So far, only one of Cuba's twenty-nine municipalities is affected by the epidemic. This one, right here. But how long is that going to last? When a sixteen-year-old opens her legs for a pair of jeans and a glass of rum and Coke at a hotel disco? How long before it reaches Havana, Mr Farr? Then the other towns.'

'Ricardo.'

'And how long before the news gets out, Ricardo – to Miami, and the rest of the Americas? It could be on the news tonight for all we know. Just think what they'll make of it in the States.'

'Only if you tell them, doctor.'

Garcia opened his arms in a gesture of helplessness.

'Okay! You tell me what to do then!'

'You're an educated man, doctor. I'm illiterate. Or very nearly. I didn't have the benefit of a Cuban education. I'm certainly not one to give advice.'

'I think you are.'

'Why? because I'm a hustler? Because I've got the clap?'

'What would you do in my place?'

'I'd do what Captain Gomez suggests. I'd listen to your brother-in-law very carefully. He cares. After all, you are family. So go ahead and write your report. You sign it. You keep a copy for yourself. You hand it to the hospital administrator personally. You wait while he reads it. As soon as possible. Make your recommendations, but otherwise stick to the facts as you know them. No politics, no polemic, no histrionics, no futile gestures. Just facts and a couple of simple recommendations. Medical steps. That's all.'

'That's all?'

'Sure. You've reported the matter. You've brought the authorities' attention to the problem. You've upheld your responsibility as a doctor and a head of department. You're an expert in your field. You're respected. They'll listen to you. And you've been professional. What the hell else is there?'

'It's not enough.'

'For whom? For you? For me? Of course it's not for me . . .'

'It's not enough to deal with the problem with the time left to tackle it.'

'That's not for you to judge, is it?'

'They want to hush it up. They want to keep it quiet because they don't want to admit they don't have the antibiotics to deal with the problem. They want to wait until the trade show is over. After all – who's going to know it started here, in Santiago de Cuba?'

'They?'

'You know who I mean.'

'That's a good point, isn't it? Who is going to know?'

'Everyone's going to know, Ricardo. Sooner or later.

Imagine how that will make Cuba look in the eyes of the international community when we send a couple of thousand foreign businessmen and journalists home to their wives with a new and virulent dose of the clap.'

Bad for business, Farr thought. That's what it would be.

'How does Cuba look now? It doesn't exactly have a glowing reputation – not that it's really your concern. Right?'

Garcia's face was set.

'I'm calling a meeting of our committee tomorrow. I'm going to propose we issue a statement on the Internet. Calling for the postponement of the trade exhibition and urging international aid to combat the outbreak.'

Farr banged his hands on the steering wheel in frustration.

'Your committee? Your committee?'

'An independent medical committee for the city. I'm the chairman.'

'You can't be serious!'

'It's the only responsible thing to do.'

'And what about your family?'

'They'll have to cope as best they can.'

'Will your wife understand when they take away the family ration cards? And what about your kids? Will they understand it when they take their father away? Have you thought about that? And Amelia – they'll take her in for questioning too, you know. Or when Gomez is demoted and transferred to some eastern shithole? He won't be able to protect you even if he wanted to . . . Jesus, how I hate people with ideals!'

Dr Garcia's head dropped to his chest. He muttered something.

'What did you say?'

'I said I've thought about precious little else. And that I will pray for them.'

'That'll be a big, big help.'

'You're not Catholic?'

'No, doctor. I'm not.'

'It's good to pray at a time like this.'

'Be sure to tell your family that. And your patients.'

'You don't understand. I'm no hero.'

'No, I don't think you are, either. A fool more like.'

'You don't approve.'

'Of suicide? No, doctor.'

'That's not what I mean.'

'Isn't it? I'm sorry. I mean you no offence. But what your brother-in-law said was right. You are crazy. Or self-righteous. It's all very well playing the hero, but not polishing your ego at other people's expense.'

Garcia looked hurt, almost as if he might burst into tears.

'I'm sorry,' he said. 'I thought you'd be pleased. After all, it's in your interest to find relief from the infection as soon as possible . . . I have to go.'

Why did people who'd been wronged or insulted insist on saying they were sorry? The English always said 'sorry' when they meant anything but. Farr waited a few moments, watching the doctor's slight figure move away and wearily climb the steps of the hospital, putting his hands on his knees as if trying to push himself up. There was something in that slight figure Farr hadn't noticed before. Something unbending.

A stubbornness.

The stuff martyrs are made of.

Maybe he would feel different after a few hours' sleep, Farr thought. He hoped so. Cuba already had more than its quota of martyrs. If they melted down all the heroes' statues in all the parks and in front of all the public buildings in all the plazas in all the towns and villages across the island, they would have enough bronze to build a six-lane road bridge all the way to Miami.

Farr started the Lada.

chapter seven

(Capricorn, October 13–14. If you aren't in love,
you soon will be. People misunderstand your
intentions, but stick to what is right.)

She startled him.

'Damn – you gave me a fright!'

Amelia put a hand on his arm and squeezed it.

'I'm sorry, Ricardo. I shouldn't have come.'

The perfume she wore identified her long before he could
make out her features in the gloom of the stairwell. It was the
Chanel he'd given her the previous month, one tiny bottle out
of a large consignment that had sold out within days, mainly to
the wives and mistresses of Farr's acquaintances among the city's
black marketeers.

'How long have you been here?'

'I waited downstairs, but it was too hot. The stairs were
cooler. Anyway, you know what it's like for a woman on her
own. A couple of hours, I suppose.'

'Well, you better come in.' Farr unlocked his door, swung it
open and waited for Amelia to go in ahead of him.

She was wearing a plain black dress and red sandals.

'You don't seem happy to see me.'

'It's not that . . .'

'I'll make an appointment with your secretary next time.

Okay, Ricardo? Anyway, it's that time of month.'

Farr ignored the sarcasm.

'That never stopped us before.'

'Still——' She turned to look at him.

'Please. Make yourself comfortable.'

Amelia looked around curiously.

'So this is where you live. Quite bourgeois – for a pimp.'

There was none of the usual pleasantries lovers display; no kisses, no hand-holding or hugging. As for the jibe, Farr ignored it. There was nothing bourgeois about a one-room apartment with peeling paint, a hole in the floor for a toilet and no air-conditioning. But then comfort, like everything else, was relative.

'Are you all right?'

'Shouldn't I be?' She turned and looked at him.

'I mean your health . . .'

'I'm fine.' She frowned, eyes searching his face.

'No problems. Women's problems, I mean.'

She sat down carefully on the sofa as if afraid it might collapse. It was large, a little lop sided, with a fringed yellow cotton rug thrown across it to hide the wear and tear. It matched the yellow-wash walls.

'No. Should I have? Ricardo, are you okay? Why the sudden concern for my well-being? You look different, somehow. Bothered.'

'Disappointment is my constant companion, a legacy of the zodiac,' Farr said, but he couldn't keep a straight face when he said it.

'Ah, of course. I forgot.

'I talked at some length to your husband today.'

'That's it. I knew it. After my brother saw you.'

'Felipe. I passed on his advice.'

'And?'

'Dr Garcia's mind seems pretty well made up.'

'You tried to convince him, though, didn't you?'

'Of course.'

'Didn't he listen?'

'Oh, yes. Your husband listened. Amelia, I wish you'd told me you were going to drag me into your family squabbles.'

'It happened so suddenly. You were the only one I could think of. I wanted to talk to you first, but I couldn't find you. You weren't in your room at Las Americas . . .'

'Would you like something to drink? Rum, perhaps . . .'

She shook her head impatiently. 'Anyway, it isn't a family squabble. It's a fucking crisis. We could lose everything if that crazy son-of-a-bitch of a husband of mine goes ahead with his plan. Oh, God, Ricardo – I don't know what to do.'

She put her hands over her face and gave a muffled sob.

'We have two kids, you know.'

Farr sat down on the sofa next to her.

'I'm sure it won't be as bad as all that.' He put a hand on Amelia's shoulder and immediately regretted it when she leaned against him. Her touch was enough. Just her voice over the phone could excite him. Trouble was, he only ever thought of her in a blatantly sexual sense. Amelia was his fantasy, the sole focus of his priapic daydreams. The only temporary solution was to make love to her, but the fantasies only returned stronger than ever.

'And you don't even like me any more.' She mumbled the words behind her hands.

It was just an act, Farr thought.

'That's not true,' he lied. 'Of course I do.'

She gets her brother to threaten me, he thought, then she accuses me of not liking her.

'Then why don't you want to make love to me?'

She looked up at him. Her mascara was beginning to run.

'I do, but not here. Not now. Anyway, you made it clear you didn't want to because it was your period.'

'It's one of your tarts, isn't it? One of your whores!'

'It never bothered you before.'

'No. As a matter of fact it amused me.'

She opened her purse and took out a mirror to inspect the damage.

'It did?' Farr was genuinely surprised.

'That's what you like about me, too, isn't it? That I'm married, that what we're doing is wrong. You like that. You're downright perverse.' She sniffed loudly.

What was this, Farr thought. True confessions? Well. Two people could play that game.

'It gives it an edge of risk, certainly.'

'Do you like to think of me fucking my husband? Does it excite you to think of Ernesto sticking his thing in me?'

'If you must know—'

'You like my small tits, too, don't you?' Amelia touched them with her hands. Caressed them through the thin, satin-like cloth of her black dress. 'You like to suck them, no?'

She pulled down the straps of her dress.

She wasn't wearing a bra.

Amelia pouted. 'My big baby,' she said.

'It's something you always liked.' Defensive.

'Sure. But answer the question.'

'Yes, I do like them.'

'Say it.'

'What?'

'Say it. Tits. I want to hear you say it.'

'I like your tits.'

'For a pimp, you're very prim and disapproving.'

'I am?'

'Maybe that's why you are a pimp – you're incapable of having a normal relationship with a woman.'

'I wouldn't know, Dr Freud.'

'You like the way I cut my hair short.' She tossed her head and ran her fingers through her hair so it caught what little light there was coming through the shutters. She dropped her voice. 'You like to do it doggy-fashion.' She put her right hand on his crotch. 'I think it's because I'm like a boy to you, Ricardo. Maybe you're a repressed homo. You like my white skin, too, don't you? You've found a way of repressing your desire to conform with Cuban machismo, no? By fucking other men's wives or whores – when you'd really prefer to be in bed with the husbands or johns . . .' She pressed hard with her hand.

'Maybe.' Farr shrugged. He was retreating. He wasn't going to let her provoke him.

Farr wasn't going to do the other thing, either. No.

She unzipped him. Put her hand inside.

Amelia laughed. She took her hand away.

The pain hit him again.

He grunted involuntarily, but she didn't seem to notice.

'What is it, Ricardo? You're agreeing with everything I say today. You're like a nurse in a psychiatric hospital. Avoiding a fight with the mental patient at all costs. Humouring me. But it's my husband who's crazy, not me!'

'What do you want, Amelia?'

'Fuck me.'

'No.'

'You love it.'

'I do, yes.'

'Then do it.'

'No!'

'Do it!'

'No!'

'Bastard!' She had put her right hand behind her back to unzip her dress, but now she whipped it out and hit him clumsily with the fist, a wild swing that connected more by chance than deliberation, the knuckles striking the bridge of his nose. Immediately it began to bleed.

'Oh, shit,' Farr said. He stumbled to the bathroom, palm to his face like a cup to catch the blood.

'There's no water, Ricardo!' Amelia giggled, loudly enough for him to hear as he bent over the basin, watching the blood drip from his nostrils. He twisted open both taps. She was right. There wasn't.

'I hear your American friend has brought you lots of goodies,' Amelia said, raising her voice.

'Goodies?'

'Don't play dumb with Amelia. Amelia knows. All kinds of goodies. Batteries. Toilet tissue. Contraceptives. Let me see. Oh, yes. Sanitary towels. You can spare me some of those . . .'

'Who told you this rubbish?'

'There are no secrets in this town, Ricardo. Not for long, anyway. And it's not rubbish. As you well know.'

'Who told you?'

'Ricardo.' She said it reprovingly. 'Who else? My omniscient, omnipotent brother. Captain Felipe Gomez. He told me he'd overlook the stuff you keep under the floor just as long as you persuade my asshole husband to act sensibly like a normal human being, and not some sort of self-appointed saint who likes nailing himself to crosses.'

What else did Gomez know?

Farr put his head back. The bleeding had stopped.

Act sensibly, he said to himself. Sensibly.

'And if I don't manage to persuade him?'

Farr thought, why me?

Amelia had found a pack of Popular and was lighting up.

'Then, sweetie, you go down with the rest of us. In your case a long spell in prison.'

'You're making this up.' Farr came back into the living room. He was far from sure about that, but tried not to betray his uncertainty. He touched his nose gingerly. It was sensitive, and seemed to have swelled up a little.

'Am I making up your secret haul under the floor, Ricardo? Well? Tell me. Am I? Eh?'

Farr could see Amelia was enjoying herself. He had never been able to reciprocate her feelings for him, and she knew that all along, only with increasing bitterness. He had been sexually obsessed by her and she had used that for all it was worth. She had been content with that at the start, but now that too was fading (they were both getting a little bored in the apparent immutability of their relationship), so she grabbed whatever means she could find to hold him. She was tapping her red sandals on the threadbare rug now as if to indicate that she knew exactly where his treasure was hidden. His strategic asset was turning into his oppressor, Farr thought, and he recognised the pure, heady stuff of hate stir within him, uncoiling like a small, venomous serpent.

James T. Plush Jr wanted to eat out and in one of the new, private restaurants, the *paladares*, where the covers were limited to twelve. Somewhere authentic but nothing fancy, he decreed. Whatever that meant to a man in a stetson hat and hand-tooled leather cowboy boots. Did he mean inexpensive? Farr had turned up at the hotel to find the two of them waiting for him, sitting side by side on a sofa in the foyer. Holding hands. Plush talking. Wearing his hat and boots and a cowboy shirt, blue with lots of fancy white embroidery around the shoulders and chest. Maria half-turned towards him, gazing into the pink, fleshy face with its prominent and very sunburned nose. Well, Maria was earning her keep, Farr thought. If every word Plush uttered earned Maria a peso, she'd be a dollar millionaire by now. He couldn't ask for more, Farr told himself. She's playing her part to the full. Doing all she's supposed to. Nevertheless, Farr couldn't entirely dismiss the feeling that something was wrong, slipping out of his control. So much seemed to be escaping his grasp – just when things had seemed on track, when the big money was within reach.

He glanced up at Maria's expression in the rear-view mirror.
Saw her smile. Not at him. At something Plush said.

Farr thought, she's actually listening to the prick!

A look on her face like a cat that's got all the cream.

Plush said, 'I didn't know you were famous, Ricky.'

'Notorious in a small sort of way,' Farr said. 'Certainly not famous.'

'Maria tells me you write the one column in *Diario* that everyone reads without fail every day.'

'Oh, that.'

'C'mon, Rick. Here's today's paper. Translate mine for me.'

'If I must. What's your sign?'

'Guess.'

'Taurus – or Capricorn.'

'Capricorn.'

'Okay, let's hear it, Rick.'

Farr cleared his throat. 'If you aren't already in love, you soon will be . . .'

Maria clapped loudly and enthusiastically.

Plush beamed.

He gave Maria's shoulders a squeeze with his arm. 'Hey, now didn't we have fun today, Maria?' He laughed. 'Ricky, you sure got somethin' going there, son.'

Farr drove them to a garden restaurant which Plush's guidebook described as 'intimate'. Plush had insisted on sitting in the back of the Lada with Maria. He said there was more legroom back there. Farr didn't argue, though he knew it wasn't true. On the way, Plush – sitting directly behind Farr with his knees pushing against the back of the driver's seat – described their day; he did so at great length and in minute detail and all for Farr's benefit. He cracked what Farr thought were bad jokes, and Maria tittered at them. Farr switched off after a few minutes. He needed those antibiotics, and he had to figure out a way to get Plush to obtain them – without giving away the reason. Driving helped him think. He told himself it wasn't because of any special embarrassment over having a dose of the clap. Plush was supposed to be a professional journalist with many years' experience. Farr thought that if he wasn't exceedingly careful, Plush would smell this epidemic story a mile off.

That would wreck everything.

Farr recalled news of Plush's Cuban assignment, and how upset he had been when he heard he was going to be upstaged by one of the *Chronicle*'s own Stateside staffers. Initially he had thought they'd let him cover the trade show. To begin with, Farr had imagined his own byline in the paper, and a regular flow of dollar payments.

By Our Own Cuba Correspondent Ricardo Farr.

Respectability, Farr had thought – and a real job at last! At first he was quite excited by the idea. This would be his chance to prove himself, to gain a reputation abroad as a professional. From there it would only be a short step to a visa and, finally, escape . . . to Florida! At that stage, Farr hadn't grasped the significance of the trade exposition, and he came to realise as the weeks passed that Plush's presence would mean more cash, not less – and without the exposure and political risks of a local filing the stories and having them printed under his own name in a US newspaper.

By the time Plush arrived, dragging his suitcases through the arrivals section, Farr had persuaded himself it was all for the best. Face it, he said to himself, you're no writer. He had to admit he found it hard to string just a single, workmanlike sentence together. He could think it up all right, but he found it hard to write down on paper. As fixer, driver, horoscope provider, stringer and finally supplier of girls, Farr knew no equal for sheer diversity, and he had finally persuaded himself he would keep both a lower profile and make a lot more money this way.

Now he wasn't so sure.

Plush, with Maria's help, chose *arroz con pollo* — chicken with garlic, orange and green peppers along with saffron rice. Maria followed suit, smiling and holding Plush's hand. Farr decided on *mojo criollo* — the special orange, oregano and garlic sauce he loved with slow-roasted pork.

When Maria left the table to go to the ladies' room, Plush leaned forward and put a large, plump hand on Farr's arm.

'Don't think I don't know, amigo.'

He winked, exaggerating it by squeezing up one side of his face.

'What, Jim? What don't I think you know?'

Farr was finding it hard to maintain the pleasant smile.

'I may be many things, Ricky, but I'm no fool. Regardless of what you think. Maria's not your cousin, buddy, and she ain't no damn dance student, neither.'

Farr said nothing. He kept his face and eyes blank.

'She's one of your girls. But I don't care. I really don't. I don't blame you. In fact, I admire your business instincts. You've done me a real big favour. I'm grateful to you. We both are. You can't know what this means to us both, buddy.'

Plush sat back in his chair and took a long pull from his beer as Maria reappeared, smiling at both men. Plush, looking relaxed and happy; Farr tense, bemused, trying not to show it.

'Having a good talk, you two?'

'Sure we are,' Plush said, winking again at Farr.

Farr thought, this is her doing.

Plush's eyes suddenly narrowed.

'Say — is that blood on your shirt, Ricky? His nose looks kinda swollen, don't it, Maria? What happened, Rick? Get into a bar fight, did you, huh?'

Plush threw back his head and expelled a bellow of laughter that turned heads at the other tables. Farr looked down at his own shirtfront and as he did so, a large drop of blood splashed right onto his lap.

72

chapter eight

(Capricorn, Oct 14–15. Sometimes a colleague may
act strangely. Don't be impulsive. Your mood could
make all the difference.)

'Hey, you see that?'

'What?'

'Soldiers. In the trucks.'

Maria said something from the back.

'What was that you said?'

'Maria says they don't use the military. They didn't during the Pope's visit. They deploy police and party cadres.'

'Yes?' Farr glanced into the rear-view mirror but he couldn't see anything at first except the top of Maria's dark head. He could see Plush's face, though, flushed and sweaty from the beer and the heat. 'Well, maybe it's different this time. This isn't exactly the Pope now, is it?'

There were more military vehicles, lights blazing, blinding Farr in the dark. He had to put a hand up to adjust the mirror. When the trucks rumbled past, engines roaring, scattering dirt, Farr saw they were open at the back, benches running down the centre with the soldiers sitting back to back, facing out. Farr had to move quickly to one side again as a big, six-wheeled armoured troop carrier rushed up behind them.

'That's fourteen I've counted so far,' Plush was saying. 'Let's say twelve fully equipped soldiers to each truck. That's—'

'One sixty-eight,' Farr said.

'They're not going to the park,' Maria said.

'Maria's right,' said Plush. 'Did you see 'em, Ricky? Helmets, AK-47s. And there were a couple of Russian-built armoured vehicles riding shotgun with the first lot.'

'BTR-60 bringing up the rear and in the lead a BRDM command car,' Farr said. He liked detail, exactitude. He added: 'Armed with DhSk 12.7s.'

'Hey, the man knows his shit,' Plush said.

He had taken out a notebook and pen.

'What's happening, Ricardo?' Maria sounded nervous.

'How should I know?'

'You will find out, won't you, buddy?'

Plush had leaned forward. Farr smelled his beery breath and felt its warmth on the back of his neck.

'Course, Jim,' he said.

'If it turns out big, buddy, call me. Any time.'

Showing off in front of Maria, Farr thought.

It was only the trade show. Farr told himself that by morning, Plush would have forgotten all about it. The Command Council would issue a short statement and it would be carried in the papers. Maria could translate it for him over breakfast. Farr knew how these things were worded. The People's Army had taken protective steps in case of provocations by the Revolution's imperialist foes. And so on.

Nothing like a few troops driven around in circles after dark to help take people's minds off their empty bellies and titillate the surviving brain cells of visiting hacks, Farr thought. Seven trucks drive round town twice and become fourteen trucks. Twice more, and they're a column of twenty-eight. Another hour of the same, and Plush and his cronies would have totted up not a hundred and sixty-eight soldiers, but lead elements of a three-thousand-strong brigade. The US networks would lap it up in a dull week. Cuba's army on alert . . . warns of plot . . . tanks on the streets. The first rule of journalism, Farr thought: never let the facts get in the way of a good story.

Ouch! There it was again. Another twinge.

'Can we talk?'

'This is not a good place, Jim.'

It was bandit country, in fact. Cespedes Park was nowhere to roam at night unless you wanted to lose your wallet.

Plush turned to Maria. 'Go on ahead, hon. I won't be long.'

Farr had stopped the car right outside the front of the hotel. He had no intention of getting out and opening the door for his passengers. He sat there, watching people coming and going. The place was filling up. He saw businessmen in suits, carrying briefcases. He recognised the television types; the crews with their pigtails and casual clothes, the big metal boxes covered with airline labels, the correspondents with that blow-dried, tight-assed prima donna expression. Look at me, their faces said. Prime-time celebs swaggering about in brand-new khaki duds bought from New York safari shops as if this was a photo shoot in the Serengeti, their combined incomes comparable to the gross national product. The moment anyone stepped out of the revolving doors, they were set upon by the crowds of *jineteras* and self-styled 'guides'. Like flies clustering on rotten meat, Farr thought. He watched Maria go on up the steps, moving carefully in her spiked heels and tight miniskirt. He watched that shapely bottom of hers, the way it moved from side to side, shifting sinuously under the thin material. Cuban girls had pert bottoms, and Maria was no exception. Her ass jutted like a shelf. It was her single most important asset. He felt an ache of regret, saw the heads turn, the uniformed doorman check her out, hesitate, uncertain whether to challenge her. Maria was saying something, a word.

Abrupt. Lifting her chin. Confident. I'm no street hooker, her expression said.

Don't mess with me.

She turned, raised a hand.

She looked almost regal.

Not waving to me, he said to himself. Farr was already the past, a forgotten episode. He felt a sudden rush of bitterness. All he'd done for the bitch . . . She didn't need him. Plush got her into the hotel. She didn't need Farr as her passport. All that crap about love, he thought. The only thing Maria ever loved was the mighty dollar. As for Plush, he was beaming like a fool, waving frantically back, flapping a hand jerkily like a wind-up toy cowboy.

'Let's take a hike, Ricky.'

'Okay.' Not said with any enthusiasm. 'On second thoughts, Jim, maybe you'd better call the newsdesk before you turn in.'

'C'mon. Last deadline's long gone.'

Farr shrugged, opened his door.

'Shows you're on the story. At midnight.'

'Uh-huh. Maybe you're right.'

Plush was already standing there, waiting for him, hat back on his head. Plush touched the brim with his fingers to make sure it was set at the right angle.

Farr tried again. 'Maybe give them a paragraph over the phone while you're at it. Ask the night editor to put you over to the copy-taker. It looks good. Something for the morning news conference. Something you can follow up.'

'I underestimated you, Ricky.'

'Something along these lines: witnesses reported troops on the streets of Cuba's second city only seventy-two hours before the world's last bastion of communism opens a sanctions-busting trade show on Thursday . . . stop para . . . Several hundred helmeted soldiers clutching AK-47 rifles were driven through Santiago de Cuba after dark, escorted by armoured vehicles, the witnesses told the *Chronicle*, stop para.'

'What was that last bit?' Plush had his notebook out.

Farr repeated it, slowly, looking past Plush and watching a group of hustlers break away from the throng around the hotel steps and head straight for Plush, drawn by the stetson, the loud voice and the Texan's sheer size.

'Jim . . .'

Plush didn't hear the warning.

A moment later they were all around him, like American Indians whooping it up around Colonel Custer at the Little Big Horn. Hands pawing him, all talking at once, circling, dancing. Offering him their sisters, very clean, their brothers, very handsome. Or themselves. Five bucks, mister. Three.

Hand-relief only one dollar, mister.

Fifty cents.

Farr stepped forward.

It would be Plush's last stand, too.

Farr picked out the most aggressive, a sharp-faced kid in his teens. Taller, quicker than the rest. Seventeen and already made mean by the hunger gnawing at his belly.

One hand sliding into Plush's back pocket.

Then Farr saw the blade, just a brief glint.

Farr slammed his right foot down on top of the kid's right trainer.

Put his weight on it, anchoring him.

Pivoting, Farr brought his right elbow up fast. Connecting with the boy's jaw. Farr's shoulder behind it.

The boy dropped the knife or whatever it was and brought both hands up. Farr heard a click as the jaw snapped. The youth started to lose his balance, and Farr hit him again, this time with his left; a short, street-fighter's jab with his fist to the side of the head. The boy's legs gave way completely.

Largely for the benefit of the others, Farr slammed the heel of his left shoe into the youth's kidneys. Swung again with the other foot, changing the angle and using the toe this time, aiming for the groin.

Farr stepped back, hands open, knees bent.

Ready for the next punk.

But they were scattering in all directions.

'Cocksucker!'

It was another teenager in black leather, looking back at them, a ring through her bottom lip, black make-up around her eyes, her mouth a scarlet scream of fury.

'C'mon, Jim. Let's move!'

Farr was angry. He hadn't wanted any of that.

'Christ! What did you do to him?'

Plush didn't move. Stood there, staring.

'Not much. Nothing he didn't deserve. He had his hand in your pocket and he had a blade. He'll be fine. Now let's get moving.'

'You haven't killed him, have you?'

'Of course not.'

Who the hell cared about a seventeen-year-old cockroach with a razor or knife?

No one.

Plush said he had prepared three features. The fourth was ready and he would file it the next morning, real early before setting out. The *Chronicle* was going to run a feature every day of the trade show, calling it 'A Letter from Cuba', with pride of place right there on the op. ed. page. Together, of course, with spot coverage of the show itself. Had Farr remembered what they had talked about on the phone the week before Plush's arrival?

Farr frowned. He vaguely remembered there had been something. Something that wasn't quite right, something he'd hoped Plush would forget or drop as too impracticable.

What was it?

They were walking through the trees, in the direction of the fountain. Instead of getting darker, the place was getting lighter and now Farr could see why. The lights showing through the trees were fixed to the top of the ten-foot wire-mesh fence that ran round the area set aside for the trade stands. There were workmen still hammering away, and armed police were sauntering around in pairs. A few tourists were there, too, just looking.

There were also lights set around the foot of the cathedral, illuminating its graceful spire.

'Hem's car,' Plush said. 'You remember. I asked you about it. You said I should talk to the last owner, in Miami. Well, I did. Gutierrez.'

Farr remembered now.

They followed the fence.

'I don't think you appreciate what a helluva story it is to Americans, Ricky. Hemingway was one of our greatest writers, maybe even the greatest . . .'

'What did Augustin Gutierrez say?'

'The usual. How he was offered a Lada for it, got fed up and hid it someplace and went to Miami. How he'll come back to Cuba some day and make his fortune out of it.'

'If it hasn't fallen to pieces, or been sold off.'

'Well, he didn't tell me where he'd hidden the damn thing. I mean, I'm not exactly the first American correspondent . . .'

'I imagine not.'

'He's been offered a fortune for that car, amigo. Can you imagine? A fifty-seven Chrysler. A collector's dream classic.'

'So?'

'It's my feature tomorrow.'

'But you don't have a clue where it is.'

'No, but there's that old standby, "mystery shrouded the whereabouts . . ."' Plush laughed.

'So what are you going to do?'

'We're taking the early flight. Maria's taking me to see the

Hemingway memorial at Cojimar. We'll have lunch there. I hear the seafood's really great. Then we're going to pay a courtesy call on Gregorio Fuentes, Hem's fishing guide and friend. Maybe he can give me a quote about the car. For some colour we'll check out Finca Vigia. They got his old Royal typewriter and his Mannlicher.'

'And me? What do you want me to do?'

'Well, you're going to earn your keep as a stringer and help me with the trade show, Ricky. In fact, as you've got the lingo, you're going to do most of the legwork. We'll need a solid story for Thursday's early editions – so why don't you check out the latest? Maybe talk to some of those delegates at the hotel?'

'Is this what you wanted to see me about?'

'Not exactly.'

They were retracing their steps. Farr was thinking that Plush was a good deal more complex than his ridiculous clothes and eccentric manner might suggest. The American was difficult not to like, and at that moment it occurred to Farr why this was so. Plush treated Farr like an equal. There was an unassuming generosity, a disingenuous side to Plush that was difficult not to warm to. It was a new experience for Farr. Plush, meanwhile, was putting a hand in his shirt pocket. He produced an envelope with the name of the hotel printed on the front of it.

'Take it.'

'What is it?'

'Maria wanted me to give it to you.'

'Why didn't she give it to me herself?'

'She was embarrassed, I guess.'

Farr opened it carefully, saw the dollar bills.

'What the fuck is this?'

'It's what she says she owes you. From her money. The money I pay her. She says you usually take half. She says most pimps take a lot more. She holds you in high regard, Ricky. That's two weeks' worth. I paid her in advance. So we're all square.'

'Bitch!'

'Hey! That's no way to speak of the lady—'

'No? The *puta* makes me lose face. She can't even pay me herself. She has to get you to do it.' Farr suddenly realised he was speaking fast in Spanish.

'You don't get it, Ricky, do you?'

'Get what?'

Farr found himself trembling with humiliation.

'When this is over we're going back. Together. Maria and me. Didn't you see the ring?'

'Ring?'

Farr stopped and stared at Plush. His mind felt sluggish, slow. He was like a diver with the bends. Everything moving slowly, weighed down, distorted by oxygen deprivation.

I don't believe this, he thought. What's he telling me?

It just wasn't possible. It couldn't be.

'I bought her an engagement ring this morning, Ricky. First thing after breakfast. She chose it. We're engaged. I popped the big question last night in our room and Maria accepted. She was too shy to tell you herself. She thought you'd take it badly. C'mon, Rick, be a sport and congratulate me!'

chapter nine

(Capricorn, Oct 16–17. Your moral support matters
more than your credit. See things from another's
view and the world will seem a better place.)

Farr did the only thing he could do in the circumstances. He took
the proffered hand, shook it and forced himself to smile.

'Congratulations, Jim.'

'Thanks, buddy.'

Farr suppressed an urge to spit on those pretty cowboy boots.
But he had just been given an envelope full of dollar bills –
possibly the last he'd ever get from Maria. Accept it with
good grace, he told himself. Then there was his fee as fixer
and stringer – and the expenses on top of that. He couldn't
afford to be anything but pleasant towards Plush. They needed
one another and he certainly needed Plush more than ever.

'Well, I guess that's it, Ricky. I'm going to hit the hay. See
you tomorrow night when we get back from Havana. Around six
or seven.'

'Jim?'

Farr went up the steps with him.

'Yeah?'

'I need your help this time.'

'Why, sure.' Plush stopped, turned, noticing the different
tenor of Farr's voice, the edge of desperation.

'Do you know anyone heading this way in the next day or so? To Santiago? Before the trade show starts?'

Plush rubbed his chin. 'I might. Why?'

Farr glanced round; too many people were doing a whole lot of nothing in front of the hotel.

'Can we talk? This won't take a minute.'

Farr reminded himself that this wasn't in the Gomez plan. It was going a whole lot further.

'Okay, Ricky. I could do with a nightcap. Why don't you come up to the bar? Maria will be asleep by now, I reckon.'

'I got this blood on my shirt.' Farr looked down at it.

'Man, no one's going to notice a little bitty blood.'

Some of it wasn't his, though. Some of it belonged to the kid in the park. The pickpocket.

Plush was saying they had a photographer coming in from Mexico. Costas, a tough Greek who'd done a lot of good work in Croatia and Bosnia and before that the Gulf and Lebanon. He wasn't a staffer, but the newspaper guaranteed him so much work a year. He had been shooting some feature stuff in the Chiapas for a news magazine and had gone on to Peru to cover the demise of the Shining Path guerrillas. He wouldn't be in Santiago long. Just the opening crowd scenes, really. Capture the mood, get some pictures to go with the stories . . .

'Have you got his number?'

'Yeah. If he's not there, the newsdesk will have it.'

'Anyone else?'

'Let me see. Well, there's this Canadian lady I know from the AP coming in from Puerto Rico.'

'Know where she is right now? Got her number?'

'Sure. Look, Ricky, what is this? Part of your smuggling racket? I don't think you can recruit the entire goddamn US press corps to help bust the embargo for El Presidente. Christ, do you know what you're doing, son? Just because I brought in that suitcase for you—'

Farr thought, I was wrong about you. You may look a fool, Plush, but you're a lot smarter than that idiotic hat and vacuous grin would suggest.

Tomas came over, nodding to each in turn.

'Good evening, sir – Mr Farr, good evening.'

When he'd taken their order, Plush said, his eyes following the waiter's back: 'You know that guy?'

'He's a professor of imperialist history at Santiago University.'

'You don't say. The expert on imperialism turns out to be a capitalist waiter, huh?'

'To feed his family, yes. The tips are pretty good. He'll make more in a good week here than he would in a year in his university job.'

'I'll be damned.'

'Which reminds me, Jim. Would you hold some cash for me?'

'Sure.'

Farr passed the bankroll over, pressing it into Plush's hand.

'How much is there? Feels like a lot of green.'

'Two grand. Count it later. In your room.'

'Okay. No problem. I take your word for it.'

'No, don't. Just count it when you get a chance. Keep it safe until I ask for it. It's my savings.'

'That's it, Ricky?'

'Can we call these people tonight? Costas and the Associated Press woman? From your room?'

'Rick, you're a greedy little son-of-a-bitch, you know that?' Plush said it with a smile, but his eyes narrowed, a glitter above the round cheeks.

Farr balled his hands tight into fists. Let it slide, he told himself. Let it go. Hang onto the British side of your nature. Lock the angry Cuban away where he can't do harm.

Farr took a deep breath.

'This isn't my racket, Jim. What's more, I'll pay for it. Out of my own pocket. What would you say if I told you that this is one hell of a big story? A human interest scoop – of international proportions. That you can have it, take all the credit for it. That it will be the biggest thing this trade show will produce? It's front-page stuff, Jim – only you've got to help me, and not go off at half cock.'

Plush's eyes gleamed, as Farr knew they would.

'What do you mean – half cock?'

Tomas was back, with cognac in a balloon glass for Plush, *canchanchara* – rum, honey, lime juice and ice – for Farr.

'Thank you, Professor,' Plush said, ostentatiously leaving a dollar tip on the tray.

Tomas gravely took the note, crumpling it up in his hand and keeping his eyes averted, and backed away.

Farr said in a low voice, 'You've got to help me find the mules. Mules willing and able. And then wait until the job's done before you file the story.'

'Got to?' Plush said it with a mocking grin.

'If you want the story.'

'And if I don't?'

'Then there won't be a story.'

'I don't make the news, Jim. I report it.'

Farr fought to control his irritation.

Fucker chooses this moment to go all ethical on me, he thought.

'You keep confidences, don't you, James? You protect sources, don't you? You agree to hold information under embargo at the request of those sources, right? You time your copy to have the maximum impact? C'mon, Jim. What I'm asking you to do now is no damn different.'

Plush stared at him, a hard, calculating look. 'And what's your angle on this, Ricky? Where's the profit in this for you, huh?'

*   *   *

The Garcias lived in a cobbled backstreet, tucked away to the east of Avenida Manduley, in a yellow wash terraced cottage with ochre tiles on the roof and white paint around the doors and windows. Ornate Spanish-style courting grills, painted black, kept out thieves and an old lantern hung above the door, adapted for electric power seldom seen these days.

Anywhere else and the area would be seen as trendy, snapped up for second Caribbean homes and horribly gentrified by wealthy foreigners while the locals moved out into prefab estates.

The Blockade was not without its merits.

Farr stood on the step. He thought they'd never wake up. He imagined he could feel the entire neighbourhood's eyes on his back as he kept hitting the door until his knuckles hurt. Then he used the flat of his hand, slapping the wood, pounding it until his palm tingled.

Farr began to think he had the wrong address.

'Who is it?'

The doctor's voice was muffled.

'Ricardo Farr.'

'Who?'

'Farr!'

'One moment.'

Once inside, Farr was suddenly at a loss for words.

He heard Amelia's voice from the bedroom.

'Who is it, darling?'

Darling.

Dr Garcia cleared his throat. 'It's Farr,' he said over his shoulder, as if that surname explained absolutely everything.

'What is it, Farr? What do you want?'

His tone was neutral. Neither friendly nor hostile.

'I'm sorry, doctor. But I need your help. I think I've found people to bring in what you need, but I need a contact to get hold of the right drugs. I'm not sure that without a prescription . . .'

'Wait here. I'll get a pen and paper.'

'What are you doing here?' Amelia was standing in the doorway. How long she'd been there, Farr couldn't tell. She was barefoot, hugging herself and dressed in a simple white cotton shift.

'I need a name,' he said.

'A name?'

'A name and a telephone number or address.'

Dr Garcia was back.

'Here,' he said, holding out a slip of paper.

'Who is he?' Farr looked down at the name.

'He's our committee's contact in the States.'

'Can you trust him?'

Garcia nodded.

'He won't go to the newspapers or tip off any of those crazy expatriate Cuban groups, will he?'

'He'll tell your people where to get what they need. I've written down the antibiotics again for you with two additions. The top three are administered by injection. The other two are more modern and can be taken orally.'

'Fine.'

'What about money?'

'That's taken care of,' Farr said.

'There's dried blood on your shirt,' Amelia said.

You know all about that, Farr thought.

The Garcias were standing next to one another. There was a closeness, a familiarity that Farr detected, something that despite their best efforts he and Amelia had failed to destroy in their repeated acts of adultery. The house itself, even at night and in the dark, had its own smells – polish, the evening meal now long finished, soap, flowers, coffee, her perfume.

Farr felt awkward, clumsy. Out of place. This was a family. Regardless of what had gone on between him and Amelia in that room at Las Americas, this was alien emotional territory.

Unfamiliar. Ties of blood, interdependency. Not somewhere someone like him belonged at all.

'Thank you—'

Farr stumbled backwards, found the door, groped for the handle.

Dr Garcia opened it for him.

He whispered, his face close to Farr's ear: 'I'm being watched. They watch this house. I noticed it for the first time last week. I think they follow me, too.'

'They've probably been keeping an eye on you for a lot longer than that, doctor. Ever since you formed that committee of yours.'

'You took a risk coming here.'

That pain again. Garcia couldn't see the grimace of pain it prompted because it was too dark. Farr needed those bloody antibiotics before the clap reached his heart and brain.

It didn't bear thinking about. Any risk was worth taking to stop that happening.

'Good night, doctor.'

It was as black as Hades out there on the street.

'Good night, Señor Farr . . . and God bless you.'

chapter ten

(Capricorn, October 18–19. Romance is in the air.
Be patient, and problems might evaporate without
you having to act. Listen to a friend.)

It was Tuesday morning; the moment Farr managed to pull himself upright and focus on his surroundings he saw something wasn't right. He couldn't spot it at first. Things just looked different yet nothing appeared to be missing or broken.

Nothing out of place, either, but after a few minutes, and just as Farr was beginning to think he was imagining things and putting it down to the paranoia inherent in his irregular way of life, he realised the rug on the floor had been turned right around, the simple Chinese pattern facing the wrong way like a compass needle pointing due south instead of north. No, despite his painful head, it wasn't his imagination. Similarly, in what passed for a bathroom, the contents of the little cabinet where he kept his shaving kit and toothbrush had been taken out, minutely examined, or so it seemed, and everything carefully put back – in reverse order.

Hell!

He dropped to his knees, levering up the floorboards and getting a small splinter in his right hand in his haste. To his immense relief, he found everything was in place under the floor. He counted it all twice, just to make absolutely sure.

Not a tissue box, toothpaste tube or condom missing.

Farr, who had had previous experience of searches, was puzzled. Normally Vice would have left everything in chaos, deliberately, taking away anything they fancied or of value and causing as much destruction and mayhem to the rest of his possessions as they saw fit, slashing up clothes and bedding for good measure.

From their point of view, he knew, it was quicker and more effective than going through the courts. Wreck the class enemy's means of earning a living, take away his wealth and if he doesn't take the hint, break his legs.

Not this time, though. Why?

It obviously wasn't Vice.

They're playing cat and mouse with me, Farr thought, playing the long game. That was the Gomez style.

There was a trickle of water from the taps and Farr splashed his face, ran his fingers through his hair. He pulled on a clean vest, a short-sleeved shirt, then jeans and sandals. He filled a shoebox with painkillers and condoms, tucked it under one arm and tottered down the stairs, wincing from the sudden, strong sunshine.

There were two of them, the younger man with his hands in his pockets, feet apart, staring at some of the neighbours' kids kicking a ball about before being herded off to school. The first was dressed like an office worker, in *guayabera* shirt, short-sleeved with a breast pocket and cotton slacks. His middle-aged companion, unshaven and with grey hair showing at the temples, wore a string vest and patched blue jeans. He leaned casually against a lamp-post, smoking a cigar, a straw hat on the back of his head, facing the door of the decrepit old pre-Revolution mansion, now subdivided into a dozen homes and where Farr lived most of the time. His official residence.

Neither man moved when Farr appeared, throwing a hand up to shield his bloodshot eyes from the hot sun, then striding with what he hoped was a sense of purpose across the street to his car, his head thumping away from all the rum he had consumed in the bar with Plush the previous evening. Oh, and it hadn't ended there. It came back to him now. When they went up to Plush's room – it was really a small suite – to use the phone, Plush had produced another bottle.

It had taken ages to get through. While they waited, they toasted one another. Plush assured Farr that Maria was sound asleep in the adjoining bedroom.

Eventually they gave up, and Plush sent a fax to Costas and the AP.

How did he ever manage to get home?

Farr could feel their eyes on his back, watching him put the box on the floor in front of the passenger seat.

He drove past the watchers slowly, in second gear. He didn't look directly at them. They wouldn't have liked it at all if he had. They would have taken it as an insult. The last thing he wanted to do was give these people an excuse to go back into his place and rip it apart and steal his cache. They could if they had a mind to. They didn't need a warrant or a magistrate's permission. They could do whatever they wanted, at any time. Without reference to anyone. They were the law.

And Farr? Farr told himself that in their eyes he was a criminal of the worst kind, a profiteer – and hence a counter-revolutionary standing in the way of history, trampling on the rights of the proletariat, taking the very yams and pork scratchings out of their mouths.

How they must hate him, he thought; for his car, his clothes, the dollars in his pocket. It was the ancient enmity between gamekeeper and poacher, dressed up in ideology. His father had known what it was like. He was smart enough to know, as Farr did, that there was nothing admirable about being poor. The old man had paid the ultimate price for it.

When Farr looked back in the mirror, they were still there.

What would Warren Buffett have done in his shoes?

He would sell, that's what, Farr thought, fantasising furiously that he was being driven to work on Wall Street in a stretch limo, smelling the real leather interior and wearing red braces, a mohair chalk-stripe suit and handmade brogues. Warren would take his profit, that's what. Way to go, Warren. Of course we'll do it nice and slow, Farr said to himself, so as not to attract the attention of other big traders and turn negative sentiment into a general free fall. Farr's mouth moved as he tried out the phrases. Hi, Warren, how you doing? In his mind's eye he could see the floor of the stock exchange, as he'd seen it on CNN. He was being given the VIP tour, and people like George Soros were coming up and pumping his hand. Mr Farr from Santiago de Cuba. A big-time player, a venture capitalist.

It was one hell of a dream.

Lydia was usually to be found on Jesus Menendez during the week, on the lookout for stray male tourists in the port area. Her spiel was simple; she'd produce a street map, offer to help them find their way to wherever they were going, ask if they had a guide, suggest a restaurant or a place to stay, talk about the history of the place, fall in with them and – bingo!

A single john could provide a week's work.

Lydia too was a student, but what she was reading depended entirely on her mood or her estimation of the client. Farr knew that while resting between tricks, Lydia particularly favoured a private café, a new one, that served her favourite – batidos, made of condensed milk, ice and fresh fruit whipped up in a mixer. Farr knew of only one other place – Coppelia Ice Cream Parlour in Vedado, Havana – that still made them. The ingredients were hard to find, and expensive. It was Lydia's one indulgence. As far as Farr could tell, fancy clothes, make-up and jewellery didn't interest her. Lydia didn't do drugs or have a thirst for rum.

Outside, a dozen passers-by had gathered around the morning edition of the local paper pasted up on the wall. There was a shortage of paper, like everything else, and Cuban newspapers were put up in barber shops and cafés.

No one spoke. There was just a little genteel pushing and shoving to get close enough to read the small print. No one said much – it wasn't wise to comment on official news. When an old man grunted and turned away, his expression inscrutable, Farr squeezed into his place and read the lead item splashed across the front page.

PUBLIC SAFETY ANNOUNCEMENT

The Revolutionary Council announced public safety measures have been adopted as a precaution ahead of the All-Americas Trade conference opening in Santiago on Thursday.

One thousand extra police and five hundred party cadres have volunteered for duty to ensure foreign dignitaries, businessmen and other visitors are protected from petty crime, and that this all-important event takes place without interference from foreign imperialist circles that seek every opportunity to besmirch Cuba's good name and upset its friendly relations with brotherly American nations.

Military reinforcements drawn from the Martinez Villena mechanised infantry brigade have been flown into the province in support of the civilian authority. The Council said in a statement released shortly after midnight that a special investigative team was already set up and functioning in the city. Reporting directly to the Council, its task was to target antisocial, anti-revolutionary elements . . .

'Ricardo!'

Farr felt someone cannon into him.

'Lydia . . .'

She kissed him on both cheeks, twice.

Lydia put a hand up to his face, touching him gently, her expression turning to one of concern.

'What's happened, Ricardo? Someone hurt you?'

'That bad, huh?'

'Your nose is swollen and you've got a shiner coming up a real treat around your left eye . . . have you been fighting, Ricardo? It's not like you to get physical.'

'You know me, Lydia,' Farr said. 'It's the other guy who gets physical. I always run away.'

That got her laughing. She was pulling his arm impatiently. 'It's so good to see you. C'mon. Have a *batido*. On me. I was just going in to order one when I spotted you . . .'

'How are you?'

Farr was thinking about that stuff about the special investigation. The reinforcements.

'Can't complain. Things are fine, really. Which reminds me . . .'

She started to open her purse.

'Not here, sweetheart. Later.'

Lydia shrugged.

She was the only girl on his books who didn't hold back on him when it came to money, make excuses, cry and make up all manner of sob stories.

They took a table at the back, both of them facing the door, though for very different reasons; Lydia to inspect potential clients, Farr to see if he had a tail.

Farr wanted a café *Cubano* – strong, black and very, very hot.

'And Inez?'

'She's fine,' Lydia said.

They were holding hands like lovers.

'I haven't seen her for a week at least.'

'You know Inez. Keeps to herself.'

'How would you like to work the Casaverde?'

A slow smile spread across Lydia's face.

'You've got to be kidding, Ricardo.'

'No. Not if that's what you want.' Farr adopted a phoney American accent in imitation of Plush. 'Time to graduate, kid, and get off the streets.'

'What about Maria?'

'She's retired.'

'She has?'

'She's hoping to get married . . .'

'No!' Lydia's mouth dropped open and stayed that way.

'It's someone she met here in Santiago. An American.'

He didn't say they'd been together for barely a week.

'I'm happy for her. Really. It was her dream.'

'You still prefer days?'

'My mother expects me home at night – is it a problem?'

'How many you supporting at the moment, Lydia?'

She lifted her face from the milk shake. Ticked them off on her fingers like a schoolgirl doing her maths homework.

'Let's see . . . there's my mother, her sister. My two sisters and younger brother. Two uncles, both out of work. My maternal grandparents.'

'How old are you now?'

'Eighteen. Nineteen in February.'

'You don't want to stay in this business too long, Lydia.'

'I don't intend to, Ricardo.' She frowned, looking down at her glass. 'Are days going to be a problem?'

'At the hotel? No. Not at all. You can work the pool and the bar. Maybe I can set up a few afternoon appointments for you. Inez can take over in the evenings. Do you think she'll go for it?'

'Oh, yes. I'm sure she will.'

'You double your charge to ten dollars a day. More if you can get it. The usual fifty-fifty split. I pay all expenses, tips. I grease the wheels. Make sure reception and the barmen give you no hassle. They know me pretty well now, so there shouldn't be a problem.'

Lydia leaned over and kissed Farr on the cheek, then wiped away the lipstick, taking care not to touch the sensitive part of his cheek and nose.

'It's wonderful news! I won't have to do all this walking. I'm getting corns on my poor feet. Also, Vice is giving me a hard time round here.'

'Why didn't you say so?'

'It's only in the last few days. I think it's this trade fair. They kept me for one night.'

'That's what I'm here for.'

Lydia put her head on one side and looked hard at Farr.

'You're not like other pimps, Ricardo.'

'No?'

'You don't beat your women. You don't make them work more than they want to. You don't take all their money . . . you never ask me to go with you.'

'Do you think you'd be better at what you do if I did all those things?'

'No!' She looked shocked, not quite sure if he was joking.

'There you are, then. I'm an enlightened employer.'

'I'm going to have another of these . . .'

Lydia and Inez were so different. Lydia had golden skin, dyed blonde hair most *jineteras* seemed to think foreigners liked and a smile that stretched from one side of her face to the other along with very white, even teeth. Farr thought she was quite plump in a shapely sort of way. She wore cut-off jeans and a flower-patterned halter top. Youthful, healthy, fun to be around. Easygoing. Inez, by contrast, was skinny, dark-haired, serious with huge eyes and a rather intense expression. Very Spanish. If Lydia liked to play the cuddly, outgoing girl, Inez preferred the role of femme fatale and the subdued light of the piano bar.

'You'll need some new clothes.'

'For the pool?'

Their heads were together, and they spoke in whispers.

'You've got to look the part.'

'Oh.'

'A decent beach wrap, a couple of new swimsuits. Beach bag, towel, shades, some nice sandals, protective cream.'

'Ricardo, I don't need all that.'

'Yes, you do. And there's something else. You know what these are?' Farr pulled a handful of condoms out of his pocket and dropped them in Lydia's lap.

'Course I do.'

He added another handful.

'You split them with Inez. Use them. Never agree to go with a client unless he agrees to use them. You know how to put them on?'

'Some men don't like them.'

'Then don't do it with them.'

'You can say that, but it's not so easy . . .'

'You want to get very, very sick?'

'No!'

'There's a sickness spreading through town. If you don't feel you can safely use these, then maybe you should go home for a while, take a holiday for a couple of weeks.'

'No way! I need the money, Ricardo.'

Farr shrugged. 'It's the Latin guys, I know. They don't think it's macho. Tough. Keep to Westerners. Whoever it is, you've got to bring it up pretty early on so there are no misunderstandings once you're in the john's room. Right?'

'If you say so, Ricardo. I never go with Cubans, anyway.'

'There are some rich pickings out there, Lydia. Especially with this trade show. I want to get you started as soon as possible. Tomorrow, if possible. Can we meet later?'

'Sure.'

'Say the cathedral? Six o'clock?'

'No problem.'

'I'll have your clothes and other gear for you then, and you can pass me the cash.'

'Ricardo?'

'Yes?'

She was watching a young man with blond hair wander in, his eyes searching the tables for a place to sit; uncertain of himself, clutching an English-language guidebook. Farr thought he looked Dutch or German, and his clothes suggested he was better off than the average European backpacker.

'Maria said to me she had four ambitions. You know?'

She was still watching the foreigner, trying to catch his eye. That would be the trigger to spring one of her dazzling smiles on him. That was very often quite sufficient.

'What were they?'

'American Express card with no credit limit. Number One.'

'Number Two?'

'A foreigner who was too old to be demanding. She said she was tired, wanted a rest from that.'

'She never really enjoyed that part of it, did she?'

'None of us do, Ricardo. Or we couldn't do what we do if we did. You know? But some of us are so good at acting that we sometimes fool ourselves – no?'

'I guess so.'

There was a pause. Above their heads a speaker oozed the syrupy love song '*Reloj No Marques Las Horas*'.

'How old is her fiancé?'

'Around fifty – but I'm not sure.'

'That's old all right!'

'What was her ambition Number Three?'

'A US passport,' Lydia said.

'Four?'

'Her own home and her own car. In her name.'

Lydia squeezed Farr's knee. 'Maria like you a lot, Ricardo. I know. You made her cry so much because she love you and she think you don't care for her. You know that, I think. But maybe her dreams come true now . . .'

chapter eleven

(Capricorn, October 19–20. Your word is as good
as your bond. People rely on you. Try to shed your
mask of indifference and show your feelings.)

Farr sold the contents of the shoebox to Mr Patel, a pharmacist
who appreciated Farr's business acumen and readily paid in hard
currency. Born in Uganda and unofficial banker to Santiago's
criminal class, Patel added everything up twice in the back room
of his shop, pointing out in a patient and courteous manner that
he was taking most of the risk as he saw it, and deserved as a
consequence a double-digit profit.

Farr didn't haggle. Nothing was ever written down, of course.
No records, no evidence. Patel's handshake was safer than most
bank vaults, Farr thought.

'That'll be four hundred and eighty dollars in your account
including accumulated interest, Mr Farr.'

'I'd like to draw all of it, Mr Patel.'

'Very well.'

Mr Patel opened his safe. 'You like some whisky, Señor Farr?
Johnnie Walker and Black Label. The real thing. Special price.'

'No thank you, Mr Patel. Another time, perhaps.'

Farr spent the rest of Tuesday afternoon preparing his story to
kick off Thursday's opening of the trade show. He doorstepped
the hotels where the delegates were staying, patrolling bars and

restaurants and lobbies and flashing his worn press card at his prey, standing four-square in front of them to force them to stop, and refusing to be shaken off until they agreed to speak to him. Farr's technique was to stand very close, almost touching, and then, like a loyal hound, stay glued to his target's side wherever he or she went: into a lift, a meeting, a restaurant, keeping station until he got what he wanted. He resisted the temptation to offer other services. A translator, perhaps, sir? Would you enjoy some pleasant company, perhaps? *Una chica para tu habitacion?* Or perhaps the famous Tropicana on tour? These well-worn phrases passed through his mind all afternoon, but he succeeded in ignoring New Business Opportunities and concentrated on the matter in hand. It was easy, Farr told himself: a matter of knowing what you wanted and shaping two or three questions to get the answers you needed. He already had the headline in his mind's eye before he started out:

CUBA TRADE VISITORS URGE SPEEDY END TO US BLOCKADE.

He asked the same things of everyone he met: would you like to see an early end to the embargo against Cuba? Do you think this trade show will help bring that about? By five p.m. Farr had a dozen quotes from the seven delegates he had managed to ambush. He decided to write it up that evening and show it to Plush. Only two quotes didn't fit the consensus. He'd ignore them, a minority view that would only complicate matters.

'Mr Farr!'

As he was crossing the lobby of the Casaverde, Farr was accosted by a tall, languid figure who hailed him loudly, arm raised above his head as if he was trying to catch the attention of a cab driver just after the bars have shut during a tropical downpour.

Farr stopped.

'Crispin Delaware, Canadian consulate.'

'Mr Delaware . . .'

Farr was momentarily taken aback. He took Delaware's hand, and looked up into pale northern eyes, paler than his own, a long, thin face and white hair that grew low down on the side of his long head and was carefully folded over the top like a silver wool blanket.

'Alison's a great admirer of yours, Mr Farr.'

Who was Alison?

'She is?' Delaware had placed his arm across a very puzzled Farr's shoulders.

'Time for a quick one? Alison will be thrilled to hear that we've met. Just a few minutes of your valuable time.'

The arm was compelling him forward.

Alison. Who the hell was Alison?

'You're consul here, in Santiago?' Farr said it for something to say more than anything else.

'Good heavens, no. In Havana. I'm the counsellor for commercial affairs, Mr Farr. Came down last night to help shepherd our Canadian delegation around the provinces. I'm delivering a paper myself at the trade show. Like a copy?'

Delaware didn't wait for a response but snapped open a leather briefcase, plunged his hand into it and pulled out a bulky typescript, which he shoved at Farr so that he was obliged to take hold of it.

'There you go,' Delaware said. He raised his arm again, vertically, in an effort to summon a waiter. 'I'm going to have a daiquiri. I love the damned things. What'll you have, Mr Farr?'

'A beer. Thank you.'

Did 'Beyond 2000: Cuba's Role As An Emerging Market' have any cash value other than toilet tissue? Probably not.

Tomas appeared, and while Delaware was giving the order, Farr checked his watch. He told himself he would have to leave in twenty minutes.

When Tomas had gone, Delaware said, 'To be frank, I'm puzzled how you get away with it.'

J. W. Diaz

'Get away with it?'

'You're not an astrologer, but Alison says you have real talent. How come the authorities let you do it?'

Farr felt immense relief.

Oh, that.

'It's harmless. I make a point of always being positive. I like to give people hope, you see. It's not religious – rather the opposite. It doesn't go against anything our leadership says or does . . .'

'No, no.' Delaware looked impatient, even irritated that Farr hadn't grasped what he was saying.

'I mean, you don't use charts and plot the astrological planets, do you?'

'No, of course not. I make it up, or most of it. I'm sure the editors at *Diario* know that, too. I thought everybody did. The women I know read it and tell me each week what they think of my column, but they think it's just a joke, too.'

'Well.' Delaware was trying to get something out of the pocket of his suit jacket. 'Alison will be disappointed to hear that. She loves the damn things. I mean astrology, tarot readings and so. Personally I think it's all rubbish, and a poor substitute for religious faith.'

It was a section from the last weekend edition.

'Don't worry,' Delaware went on. 'I won't tell her.'

He unravelled the page and straightened it out.

'Now where is it? Oh, yes. Here's the horoscope.

'Aries: the arrival of strangers in great numbers will mean change – hopefully, change for the better. Warm-hearted though you undoubtedly are, you should not overlook warnings.'

The drinks arrived.

Delaware paid.

'And then again, in Aries – you really will have to be prepared to put a shoulder to the wheel if you want enjoy the harvest you dream of.'

It's awful, Farr thought to himself.

Delaware raised his glass.

'To better times, Mr Farr!'

'Yes, indeed. Better times.'

They drank.

'Damn, that's good!'

Delaware put his glass down and leaned forward.

'Now tell me how you do it.'

'Do what?'

'Compose your astrological messages.'

'Well.' Farr paused. 'It was like this. I happened to find an English astrology paperback for 1979 in a hotel room a long time ago. It was out of date even then. I think it must have been left behind by a visitor who'd taken it out of a ship's library. I remember it had SS *Strandloper*, Walvisbaai stamped on the spine and the inside cover. I think it was one of these big deep sea trawlers, you know. Maybe a Cuban soldier brought it back from the *aventura Africana*. Though Walvisbaai isn't in Angola, after all. Anyway, where was I? Yes. I just copy some of it, you see. Rewrite it, swap things around.'

Farr shrugged. Picked up his glass and drank, his eyes on Delaware, who was shaking his head.

'Oh, I know what you're going to say, Mr Delaware. Please. I do. You're going to say it's not very honest, and of course you're right, it's not. But then this is Cuba. We have to survive. A businessman has to make do with what he has. In this case, humanity's infinite appetite for hope, for certainty in an uncertain world. I don't get paid much for it. Pesos, not dollars.'

Delaware's face said he wasn't interested.

'Farr, you can tell all that stuff to Alison. She'll love it. She might put you in one of her human interest stories. She's always on the lookout for human interest. But don't give me all that nonsense, laddie. Just between us. I want to know how you do it.'

'I've just told you.'

'Is it a book you use? A particular page? Perhaps the astrology book you mentioned—'

'I don't follow . . .'

Delaware was leaning even further forward, right on the edge of his chair.

'It's a code, though, isn't it? A one-time pad, maybe?'

Delaware sucked the last drops out of his glass.

'I'm sorry, Mr Delaware, I think there's a misunderstanding . . .'

'But you do communicate with those people. How else could you possibly manage it? I know you do. There's no other way. Alison told me that you . . .'

'People? What people?'

Farr stood up. Whatever was going on, he didn't like it. It was unsafe. Talking like this was unsafe, never mind anything else. Delaware seemed pleasant enough at first, but he was either deeply disturbed or playing a game Farr couldn't begin to understand, and which he wanted no part of.

Farr gave a short bow. He stood very still, hands at his sides and spoke loudly, in a formal voice, aware that they might be watched or overheard. 'Mr Delaware. Thank you. I enjoyed our chat and I'm glad we met. I must go – I'm late for a previous appointment. Goodbye, sir.'

Minutes later, Farr was walking towards the cathedral, Cespedes Park to his left, figuring out in his mind the lead paragraph, the most important part of any newspaper story – delegates arriving for Cuba's first-ever Americas trade show opening on Thursday declared overwhelmingly their determination to seek a quick end to the United States' economic blockade of the island – when he heard a hiss, the distinctive and faintly annoying Cuban way of trying to attract someone's attention.

Another hiss, only louder.

Farr looked up.

'Tony?'

His fellow pimp didn't slow down. He had a curious way of walking. He flapped his arms and took huge strides, keeping his head well back, a frantic march. Tony wasn't more than about twenty-two, very skinny and tall. He wore a maroon T-shirt and a pair of dirty light blue jeans, split at the knees, and sandals made out of car tyres. His black hair was long, down to his shoulders, his cheeks scarred from some childhood skin ailment. To Farr he had the jaded good looks, the questionable charm of the rock star, the premier-league footballer gone bad. Tony was striding along, heading straight for Farr, as if deliberately setting a collision course.

'Tony—'

Farr and Tony were never friends, not since he had turned Tony down for a line of credit. Tony ran a stable of young, inexperienced girls from the eastern provinces. It involved a high drop-out rate and a quick turnover. They operated at the lower end of the market; the out-of-town flophouses or 'love hotels' which rented rooms by the hour. Tony had wanted seed money for a big expansion, but Farr objected to Tony's penchant for violence, the knife he always carried and the fact that he also had sidelines as a small-time drugs peddler and loan shark.

Worse, he had a long sheet of petty convictions.

Tony was the kind of citizen the President was only too willing to pay to emigrate to the States. He simply wasn't a sound investment opportunity.

'Don't go in there, man.'

Tony was right in front of him, pupils hugely dilated. Sweating furiously, damp patches on the T-shirt.

'What—'

'Don't go in the park.' Tony dodged at the last moment, his shoulder brushing Farr's chest. Then he was gone.

Farr turned. 'Tony – what's happening?'

Tony fired his last warning back over his shoulder.

'Get out of here, man!'

But Farr didn't turn back. Something – instinct, the sense that he should behave normally, naturally, and never show panic – kept him going. Partly because he didn't trust Tony. Farr slowed right down, whistled tunelessly between his teeth, put his hands in his pockets, lowered his eyes.

A man out for an evening stroll, oozing insouciance.

Another twinge, a nasty one. He told himself he should have used the hotel bathroom before he came out.

Farr heard them before he saw them. The deep rumble of a truck, hydraulic brakes wheezing, tailboard crashing down, shouted orders, the sound of hobnail boots tumbling onto the street, the tell-tale jingle of rifle slings and ammunition clips.

Farr walked right past the entrance to the park. Past the cathedral. Not looking up.

They were sealing off the entire park.

He searched with his peripheral vision.

Boots, a blur of uniform as they ran past.

Farr didn't need to see or hear any more; armed police, plainclothes state security and party cadres in blue shirts.

Inez and Lydia were in there, waiting for him.

chapter twelve

(Capricorn, October 20–21. There are setbacks,
but show you mean well. Self-discipline is fine, but
don't keep looking at your watch.)

Farr kept going, holding himself in check and forcing himself
to saunter, until he felt sure he was out of sight of anyone in
the park. He went straight to his car, half running, half walking
the last hundred yards.

He could lose everything, Farr told himself; his secret
cache, his girls. He was sure the tourists, painters, buskers,
domino-players, shoeshine boys and young lovers who usually
hung around the park would be allowed to go immediately,
but Lydia and Inez would be swept up in the dragnet along
with the money-changers, ticket touts and rent boys, taken
away in paddy vans to be fingerprinted, photographed and
questioned.

Questioned.

The Lada wouldn't start at first. On the fourth turn of the
key it coughed into life.

The speedometer showed a steady 45 kph, but once he
turned off into the quieter residential streets, streets with
virtually no cars, not even parked, he had to slow down to
get past groups of boys playing football and again when the
road was blocked by teenagers on bicycles.

What would he do if he were Gomez?

Repeat the action elsewhere, he told himself, at all the foreign-currency hotels and throughout the city. Vacuum up all the flotsam and jetsam that coalesce in the backwaters of the trade show and tourist hangouts. Frighten off the *jineteras* and clients alike. Lock up pimps like himself.

That would include El Rancho, close to the university.

Farr had two other girls working that beat. Both students, genuine students this time. Marta and Celia worked evenings and weekends when they weren't studying. His amateur enthusiasts.

If they were lucky, all four would be held overnight and released. If Gomez decided to play hardball, on the other hand, Farr's most important source of hard currency could dry up.

Conviction on the antisocial charge of *disobedienca* could put them away for quite a while, months at least. It didn't bear thinking about.

If he were Gomez, he would impose a curfew every night while the trade show was on. That way he could curb the activities of Santiago's tarts still at large and their clients, all in the name of public safety and protecting Cuba's foreign guests – and not a word in public about the epidemic. Gomez couldn't stop the sex trade entirely, of course; there were always the mornings and afternoons as every adulterer knew and as Amelia and Farr himself had already discovered – but it would certainly reduce the level of business and, presumably, slow the rate of infection.

That wouldn't solve Farr's problem, though.

Farr parked at the back of the tenement building, then walked round to his place, past the blackened balconies, the peeling paintwork, broken roof tiles and cracked plaster, the rhythm of salsa pumping out on the street from the cassette recorders in the little one-room homes above his head. He didn't so much as glance at the watchers. They would be there, almost certainly. He took the stairs two at a time, kicked the rug aside, dropped to his knees and started flinging the remaining condoms, the rolls of tissue, the painkillers and aspirin, the sanitary towels and toothpaste and batteries back into Plush's big suitcase.

He hauled the suitcase down the stairs, using both hands to lift it down from step to step. He left it upright in the darkest corner of the foyer, right at the back, hoping the two men outside wouldn't come in and spot it sitting there.

Three minutes. That's all he needed.

The sweat dripped off the end of his nose and chin. He slicked it away with his fingers, and stepped out onto the pavement again, trying to look nonchalant and forcing himself to keep to a leisurely pace.

When he brought the Lada up to the front, lurching to a halt directly outside the entrance, he left the engine idling and opened the rear door from the inside. This time he made no effort to conceal his haste; Farr jumped out, ran around the front of the Lada and disappeared into the building. In less than eight seconds he was back with the suitcase, half dragging and half carrying it. With a supreme effort he heaved it into the back, slamming the door and throwing himself behind the wheel once more, and with a nasty grinding of gears the Lada lurched into motion.

His heart felt as if it was beating faster than a humming-bird's wings.

If they saw him, well and good. But they couldn't stop him now unless they followed him, and that would mean leaving their post. Farr was counting on that.

Another five minutes and he was turning into the Casaverde. He drove right up to the steps, left the car where it was and ran up to the front door. Through the big sheets of plate glass he recognised one of the uniformed porters, and pushing his way in, went up to him, grabbed a gloved hand and shoved a ten-dollar dollar bill along with the Lada's keys into the man's palm and curled his fingers over the money.

'Mr Farr . . .'

Farr held his fist closed with the money and keys.

'My car's right outside, Hector. There's a suitcase in the back that belongs to Mr Plush, one of your American guests. It's full of his stuff. Take a trolley down there and get the suitcase up to his room before it's stolen, okay? Then park the car for me, will you?'

'Sure . . .'

Hector looked down at his hand, then at the bruise on Farr's face.

'Now, Hector . . .'

Farr turned away, his eyes getting used to the gloom of the hotel foyer after the hard brightness outside. He started to move away from the concierge's desk, the sweat cooling and drying on his back. He was intending to go over to reception to see if Plush and Maria were back from Havana, when he saw two men push themselves up out of their armchairs.

There was no mistaking these two, Farr thought. They were both dressed for hotel duty, in jackets and ties, trying (and failing) to look like business guests. They had that carefully cultivated manner of looking the other way. The bigger of the two secret policemen had carefully folded the newspaper he was pretending to read and put it aside, the second man patting his hair and self-consciously checking the knot of his tie.

They didn't want a scene, Farr knew, and he could use that to his advantage.

In his mind's eye his rapidly decreasing options presented themselves in a series of images: Farr pictured his Lada, the rear door open, two porters in white gloves struggling with the heavy suitcase. Hector was there, holding the car keys. The driveway was otherwise empty. The park, crawling with cops and busybody party cadres, lay beyond.

They were closing fast. The big one had his right hand in front of him, fingers as thick as bananas playing with the buttons of his check jacket – inches from the tell-tale bulge at his waist. His companion, much shorter with a pugilist's broken nose, had a rolling walk like a sailor, his hands open and held away from his sides. He looked like a wrestler.

Farr knew this hotel better than some of its employees. Entrance behind him, coffee shop and newspaper stall to his left, centre and ahead the nests of chairs. Behind them, glass doors leading to the outdoor restaurant, veranda, pool and bar, and moving right the lifts, the reception desk and cashier . . .

Between him and the advancing plain-clothes security officers stood a dozen or so Austrian tourists, elderly men and women in new holiday clothes obediently waiting for their tour guide to allot them rooms, their neatly tagged bags at their feet. The luggage included several golf bags, Farr noted.

They formed a perfect obstacle.

Farr pivoted to his right – and ran.

He sprinted down the short leg of the L-shaped lobby towards the stairs and the washrooms. He ran silently on the thick, patterned carpet.

Past the row of telephones Maria used to call her clients.

He swerved abruptly to the right again, hitting a plain cream door with his shoulder, crashing through it and running flat out down a service corridor to a another pair of fire doors at the far end. There was no carpet here; the sound of his feet hitting the linoleum seemed to him like pistol shots and his own breathing roared like a hurricane in his ears.

The images kept coming. The two agents barging awkwardly through the Austrians then coming around the corner, breaking into a run, separating, one heading for the stairs, the other for the men's lavatories.

He watched her carefully, then stepped out of the shade.

Amelia had a straw basket over her arm and was moving down the line of stalls, inspecting the vegetables. There wasn't much to choose from. Farr watched her negotiate for green peppers, waited while she handed over the money and received change in return. Every now and then Farr would turn his head, first one way, then the other – trying to look casually interested in his surroundings as he watched his own back.

The traders knew her. It was the regular Wednesday fruit and vegetable market and Amelia shopped here regularly. Farr could tell it by the way they called to one another across the trestle tables, smiled and joked, the familiar way she joshed with them and haggled over the prices.

Farr moved parallel, keeping one row of stalls between them and watching his own reflection in the glass windows of the shops lining the little plaza.

Now and then he lost sight of her behind other shoppers.

He came up behind her, drew parallel, then touched her arm.

'Those tomatoes look good,' he said quietly.

If she was surprised, Amelia didn't show it.

'Yes, don't they.' She turned to the trader. 'How much?'

Farr waited, turning round, hands in pockets.

'Come on,' she said once the tomatoes had joined the peppers and parsley. 'Take my arm.' She gave his hand a reassuring squeeze between her arm and side. 'Let me buy you a coffee. You look as if you need one.'

'Then I'll carry your basket.'

'What a gentleman!'

They crossed the cobbled street together.

'You want to know about my Ernesto.'

'Yes.' Farr knew he should have said no. He should have said he wanted to know about her. He told himself she wouldn't have believed him anyway, but would have liked to have heard him say it nevertheless. He thought women preferred lies to the truth as long as the lies were more palatable. Men did too, but wouldn't admit it, even to themselves.

'You want to know about the committee and whether he made his appeal on the Internet.'

'Yes.'

They stopped just outside the café.

'You look terrible,' she said. 'Have you been in a fight?'

'I spent the night in the back of the Lada,' Farr said.

They didn't speak again until they were sitting on either side of a small table, Amelia with her back to the wall and Farr facing her, the window to his right giving him a clear view of the square beyond. Their coffees were in front of them. Farr didn't wait for her but sipped his eagerly.

'Well,' Amelia said, 'I don't have the answers.' She went on to say that the night before last a dozen student activists had gathered in the street outside their home and thrown stones at the windows and broken them. Just to let the Garcias know that they were officially disapproved of and on the state's shit list. She paused and then added, almost as if it were a sudden afterthought, that the previous afternoon her husband had been taken away for an interview.

'Did they—'

She knew what Farr meant.

'No. They didn't touch him. He was terribly calm. They took him from his office at the hospital – just to let everyone there know too, I suppose – to a house in the suburbs. There's a name for such a place—'

'A safe house.'

'He said it looked as if no one lived there. A modern bungalow, quite small, with a swimming pool that was empty and had dead leaves in it and lots of old books on the shelves in the living room.'

'Then?'

'They questioned him. They accused him of being a terrorist, of trying to import something they called Semtex into Cuba.'

Farr knew what Semtex was. It was a specific brand of plastic explosive made by a company in the Czech Republic. If Farr had lived anywhere else, he would have bought shares in Semtex. Like sex and astrology, the market for plastic was always growing. Warren Buffett would surely have approved.

'They asked him about you. They said you were a member of the terrorist group.'

'Oh, God.' Farr passed a hand over his face.

Amelia said her husband returned home two hours after he was picked up at his office.

'What did you say to him?'

'I told him to drop the whole thing. I told him what you told him. We both told him what my brother wanted us to say – to do his duty as a doctor by reporting the matter, and then button his lip.'

'Go on.'

'He listened. He said nothing. That's his way.'

'Did he mention someone called Delaware?'

'No. No, I'm sure he didn't.'

'Have you heard of a Canadian called Delaware?'

'No, Ricardo. I don't think so. Who's Delaware?'

There was a pause. Farr finished his coffee. Amelia hadn't touched hers.

'They came for him again last night,' she said, adding that there must have been six or seven of them in their home with more outside. In civilian clothes, she said, but carrying guns quite openly. Actually, she was wrong. She corrected herself, it wasn't last night. It was that morning, at four a.m. The agents told them Garcia was going for another interview, this time at state security headquarters. He would be back very soon. They kept telling him to hurry. They said he wouldn't need anything because he would be home so soon. They watched him dress. He had to leave the bathroom door open when he went to the toilet. Amelia said she thought they were worried he might try to kill himself.

'They wouldn't leave us alone even for a moment to say goodbye. We had to say our goodbyes in front of them.' Remembering, Amelia looked close to tears.

She took a tissue out from the front of her dress and blew her nose with it.

Amelia said, 'Of course you don't believe it when they say that someone won't be long – but you want to believe it, desperately. That's why they say it. Of course he isn't back, and I've no idea where he is. Damn him! He's so stubborn!'

Amelia was pulling distractedly at the skin on her wrist.

'And your brother? We both kept our side of the bargain . . .'

'I tried to call Felipe. I went to his office. I sat there and waited. He either wasn't there or he refused to see me. Nobody would tell me anything. But I had to do some shopping . . .' Amelia looked anxious, as if she wanted to get home quickly in case there was news.

There won't be, Farr thought.

Unusually, he noted, Amelia wore no jewellery. Just a simple black dress of stretch-type material and low-heeled shoes. Her hair was loose.

She seemed to read his thoughts.

'You see, I'm ready for prison myself. I keep a little bag packed near the front door. The children's things are packed and my mother will look after them.' She shrugged.

Amelia born under Leo, Farr remembered. The sign of control, organisation.

'Did he leave any message? Did he say anything about—'

'About the epidemic? No. And he said nothing about you. No message. I'm sorry.' Amelia looked away, out of the window at the square, drenched in sunshine. It was as if, he thought, she was trying not to show her feelings – feelings not for him but for Garcia.

She loves him. She must. Farr told himself a man and a woman couldn't marry and live together, share the same home and bed and not feel something for one another. It wasn't possible. Farr found he didn't really mind. Rather the contrary – he wished there was someone who would feel that way about him when his turn came. It would come, of that he had no doubt whatsoever.

'Amelia.' Farr paused, trying to choose his words carefully. 'I want to say something to you. Something personal. They've got my place watched too, and yesterday they tried to arrest me. I may not get this chance again, not for a while.'

Amelia looked at him now, curiously.

'I wanted to say to you that we – that what we did – our meetings, you know, in the afternoons . . .' His voice trailed off in his confusion.

'Go on, Ricardo. Say it.'

'It wasn't just the sex. It meant a lot to me, that's all.'

Amelia suddenly seemed to find her coffee interesting and lowered her head over it, hands folded and forearm lying on the Formica-topped table.

'You once told me, Ricardo, that your mother drank heavily, and that your father beat her. You said your first memory of your mother was her sitting on the bed crying and your father hitting her.'

'Yes.'

'That's true, is it?'

He nodded.

'You weren't making it up?'

'No.'

'You don't mind if I ask you something personal, do you? About your mother?'

'No – go ahead.'

'Was your mother – did she . . .'

Amelia's voice trailed off, but Farr knew what she was asking.

'Was she a whore? Is that what you want to know?' Farr sighed. 'The answer's yes. She was. She had a liking for the nose candy, too.'

'She was an addict?'

'She had an expensive habit.'

It was Farr's turn to feel emotional. He put it down to fatigue and the stress of the last two days.

'Your father ran girls in the hotel, too, didn't he?'

Farr nodded, speechless.

'I used to think, Ricardo, that the way you dressed, the way you behaved, was an act of rebellion. I liked it. It seemed so . . . reckless. It attracted me to you. Here's a man who's got real balls, I told myself. Someone who wants to be himself and gives a finger to the one-party state. Now, after all this time, I realise that you're living your father's life, treating people – and especially women – the way he treated them.'

'I don't beat women.'

'No. But if anything, you're trying to live his life for him. It's not rebellion, Ricardo, but convention. You want his approval. Even now, even though you hardly knew him and he's been dead all these years and you're forty years old . . .'

'Forty-one next month.'

Farr turned his head away and stared at the window, but he wasn't really looking. Amelia put her hand on his arm.

She asked, 'How do I reach you?'

'You can't. I don't think it will be long before they pick me up. That's why I followed you here, Amelia. I have something to ask of you.'

Farr hesitated. He felt her watching him.

'I look a mess,' he said. He laughed. He turned the other way and caught his own reflection in the mirror above the counter. It seemed funny for some reason. Ridiculous, even.

'I wanted to ask if you have somewhere you can hold some money for me. Somewhere safe they won't know about even if they do make a thorough search . . .'

Amelia's dark eyes held his, studying him intently.

'I think so.'

'Then look in your basket.'

Amelia looked, then turned back to him.

The fat bankroll, held together with two thick elastic bands, was tucked in among the vegetables. 'How much is there?' she asked in a hushed voice.

Farr leaned forward, their heads almost touching.

He had to trust someone. He had to jettison everything he had before they took him in.

'My savings,' he said. 'Three grand.'

Amelia was shaken by the sight of it.

'Ricardo, I never saw so much money before!'

chapter thirteen

(Capricorn, October 21–22. Live more for the
moment and you will enjoy the company of others.
A good time for financial movers and shakers.)

Plush was talking when he opened the door and for several
seconds he didn't recognise Farr. All he saw was a stranger
in a house painter's grubby white overalls and cap. Plush was
about to shut the door again when Farr took a step forward and
put a hand out to stop the door being slammed in his face.

'Jesus H. Ker-ist,' Plush said.

Farr put a finger to his lips and slipped past into the suite.
Plush, who was wearing nothing more than a white bath towel,
had the presence of mind to poke his head further out and look
up and down the corridor.

They stood and stared at one another for a few moments.

'Where did you get that outfit?' Plush was grinning at
him.

Farr didn't answer. He had rented it for a small consider-
ation from its owner, but he didn't want to get into all
that. He unbuttoned a pocket and pulled out some papers,
folded twice.

'It's the piece you wanted. I'm sorry I didn't get it to
you before.'

Plush was pacing, lips moving as he read. Farr stripped off

the cap and overalls. The wall opposite was all window, floor to ceiling, and it provided a panoramic view of the downtown area of Santiago, the harbour with its ships and cranes, and beyond that, the curve of the bay itself.

'Good stuff,' Plush said, still reading. 'We've still got time.' He checked his watch. 'I think we should get this off straight away. Smart move, Ricky – it's controversial in the States, but they'll love it here in Cuba. No reason not to put your byline on it . . .'

Farr wasn't listening. He looked round for the suitcase. The room was all soft and inoffensive pastels; pale green, pale beige and even paler pink. As for the carpet, it was so thick his feet seemed to sink right into it. He had a sudden urge to take his shoes off and feel the carpet between his toes.

Plush seemed to know at once what he'd come for. 'Don't worry, son. The suitcase is in the bedroom. Quite safe.' Plush studied Farr, giving him a lengthy sidelong look. 'You're in trouble, aren't you?'

Well, Farr thought, I'm not ordinarily in the habit of turning up in hotel rooms in fancy dress.

Plush picked up bits and pieces of diaphanous clothing from an armchair, so ephemeral they looked as if they might float away by themselves. He kicked aside a shoebox and a bright red plastic carrier bag. Maria had been shopping again. Lydia must have been right about the plastic and no credit limit.

Farr almost felt sorry for Plush.

'Take the weight off your feet, big man. Like a drink?'

'Don't think so, Jim, thanks.'

'Maria's taking a bath. She told me about the arrests. Do you know how many?'

'At a guess I'd say a couple of hundred.'

Farr sank slowly down into the chair. It felt so good. He could hear the air-conditioning humming away softly. Only people who could never afford a room like this and had never spent a night in one would really appreciate it, he thought.

He kicked off his shoes, finally, and put his bare feet up on the coffee table with its scattering of foreign fashion magazines, presumably Maria's.

Plush had finished reading Farr's story. He folded it up again. 'There's a curfew from midnight.'

'I didn't know, but I'm not surprised.'

Plush perched on the arm of the settee. Farr thought he looked like a big pink whale that had somehow beached itself in the hotel suite. A beluga, perhaps, almost hairless except for a little reddish fuzz on the chest and the ponderous belly.

'Why are they after you, Ricky?'

'Lots of reasons, Jim.'

'Uh-huh.'

Plush was waiting for more, but Farr wasn't going to elaborate. He was having trouble keeping his eyes open.

'We'll be out for an hour or two – you're welcome to sleep here on the couch tonight. Order anything you want on room service. Or I can do it for you – if you're worried about being recognised. Hey, Maria will be pleased to see you. She was getting pretty worried.'

'She was?' Farr found that hard to believe. After the envelope, he thought she was probably hoping she wouldn't see him again.

Plush held his towel in place around his waist with one hand and bent forward. He beckoned to Farr and spoke in a whisper as Farr pushed himself forward so their knees were almost touching.

'Costas gets in late tonight. Around eleven. The AP woman at breakfast time.' He winked at Farr and tapped the side of his nose, a gesture of conspiratorial complicity, Farr guessed.

Farr nodded. Clearly Plush thought the room was bugged. Or else he didn't trust Maria.

The door to the bedroom opened.

'Ricardo!' Maria rushed in and threw her arms around Farr's neck. 'Oh, I was so worried, Ricardo. I thought you'd been arrested. I'm so pleased to see you!'

She planted a wet kiss on his cheek.

'How are you, Maria?' Her perfume, a powerful and sweet scent Farr didn't recognise, swirled around the room. 'I'm fine, Ricardo. Wonderful. James is so sweet. So generous.'

She exchanged glances with Plush.

'Except . . .' Maria put her hand to her mouth to suppress a giggle. Farr noticed she had painted her long nails black to match a black off-the-shoulder dress covered in little shiny things that caught the light whenever she moved.

'Except,' Plush said, 'Maria sat up practically the whole night watching those damn ads on satellite TV. You know the stuff they sell, buddy.' Plush turned his voice up into a high-pitched, high-speed parody of a television salesman. 'It really, really works. Call now and save money! Call this number toll-free . . .'

So that's what they do at night, Farr thought.

'James, you're horrible,' Maria said, pouting.

'I had to explain to Maria the toll-free calls are only free inside the United States.'

'What kind of stuff?'

'Jeez, Ricky,' Plush said. 'You wouldn't believe it!'

'The nut-gun,' Maria said proudly. 'I really liked the nut-gun. It would make a great Christmas present!'

Plush explained. 'Looks and sounds like a Kalashnikov rifle, only it's made out of plastic. You sort of cock it and let go, and with a loud smack it smashes your nuts. Can you imagine passing that damn thing around the dinner table, showering your guests with walnut shrapnel?'

'What else?' Farr asked.

'The meat feet,' Maria said.

Plush put both hands over his face, momentarily forgetting the towel. 'Oh, yeah. Sure. Don't let's forget the meat feet so the meat doesn't swim in its own fat in the oven.'

'How about the food glamouriser?'

'Or the cap-snaffler,' Plush said, shaking his head.

When the hilarity died away, Plush glanced at Maria, then turned to Farr, his face suddenly grim.

'Ricky my son, they came looking for you. Couple of hours ago.'

'Who did?'

'Guy in a suit. Two others with him. The two gorillas waited out in the corridor.'

'I don't know any suits.'

'He said you knew each other pretty well. That you had a long talk the other day. A family matter, he said.'

'Did he have a name?'

Maria was listening, saying nothing and staring out of the window.

'Yeah. What was it again, Maria? Captain Somebody-or-other from State Security . . .'

Maria, all dressed up for a night out, shivered visibly.

It was the word security, Farr knew.

She turned her back, folding her arms.

'Gomez,' she said. 'Captain Felipe Gomez.'

When they'd gone, Farr settled back in his chair. He must have fallen asleep immediately for when he woke – it seemed an instant later – the room was quite dark except for the lights from the city and a half-moon suspended above the bay, turning the sea into dark, cold silver. His watch told him it was 9.04. Farr remembered a strangely awful dream: there was a parade down the pink and yellow streets, the hulks of the old mansions like ancient ruins, worn down by neglect and the action of salty, damp winds and blazing summers. He knew everyone in the parade; he was walking towards them, going the wrong way, greeting them in turn and intending to join them. They each wore huge tarot cards several feet high, back and front like the sandwich men of old, the signs coming right up to their chins and only their feet showing below. Fidel himself was there in the lead, his grey beard whiter and longer than ever, and flanked by Gomez on one side and Plush on the other. Behind them the women – Amelia and Maria, Lydia, Inez, Marta and Cecilia. Fidel wore the arcanum of the Magician, symbol of free will and originality. Gomez was the Emperor, the man of moral power, certainty. Plush was the Hierophant, representing stability and experience. Amelia wore the card of the Hermit, figure of discovery, Lydia the Star for pleasure, Inez the World for ambition.

Farr was angrily pushing his way through the figures, turning from one to the other, banging on the huge cards with his fists as if fighting his way through a phalanx of Roman shields and feeling terribly anxious because he had no card at all, no placard. They bounced and jived and twisted in time to a loud and obnoxious cha-cha that made his head hurt.

'Where's mine? What's happened to me?'

Maria was smiling at him, showing him her card as if proud of it, opening her mouth and speaking – but he couldn't hear a thing. He looked – it was the Chariot, symbol of audacity.

Dr Garcia was last, a straggler. He carried the image of Death around his neck, the skeleton and the scythe representing radical change, an ending – and a beginning.

'What about me?' Farr heard himself cry.

He looked down at himself and all of a sudden there it was.

The Hanged Man. Desertion, lack of awareness. Letting go.

He turned to Garcia to remonstrate, but he had already moved on, following the others, leaving him behind on his own in the street. People on either side of the street were laughing at him. The two security men he'd seen in the hotel earlier had the painted faces of circus clowns. They were doubled up with mirth, howling at him, their eyes running and mouths gaping, their guns showing under their cheap jackets.

That was when he woke, a sharp pain pinching his testicles.

Someone was banging hard on the door of the suite. Tremendous knocks, well spaced out, as if they'd been trying to get his attention for ages. Then the telephone rang, all three extensions simultaneously. For several moments Farr sat quite still, hands clamped over his ears, hoping it was all part of his tiresome nightmare and that it, too, would pass.

chapter fourteen

(Capricorn, October 23–24. People respect you
for what you are, not what you have. Follow your
heart and everything will turn out for the best.)

'Who is Warren Buffett?'

'A great man.' Farr added quickly, 'Along with Fidel and
Che, of course.'

'Is he a member of your organisation?'

'I told you. I have no organisation.'

'Tell me about this Warren person.'

Lieutenant Martinez had taken over the afternoon shift. A
lanky man with grey stubble and a cheroot sticking out from
an untidy grey moustache, he seemed almost bored by the
proceedings. Unlike the brute in the morning, he wasn't given
to sudden temper tantrums. He didn't look like a bully. He had
a lined, brown face set permanently in an expression of anxiety,
like a man nagged by toothache or a disappointed wife.

'Warren Buffett is the third richest man in the United
States,' Farr said. 'He became rich because he's smart. He
picks undervalued shares in growth companies.'

'So?' Lieutenant Martinez turned at the wall and paced back
again, turned the other way.

'So I've tried to follow his example.'

'In Cuba?' Martinez took the cigar out of his mouth.

'There's no stock market in Cuba. There are a few joint ventures between the state and foreign firms and that's it.'

'There isn't a stock market yet, but I'm sure there will be, and when there is I hope to be ready for it.'

Farr smiled encouragingly. He wanted to get on friendly terms with Martinez. His expression suggested it was all a misunderstanding that could be cleared up eventually.

'So? Tell me more.'

'It's all about cash flow and earnings per share. It's about finding a product or service that everyone wants or needs and which can be endlessly replicated, and buy into it when it's undervalued. Cheap, in other words.'

'Such as?'

'Sex. Or in Buffett's case, Coca-Cola.'

'Sex?' Martinez had come to a standstill in the centre of the room, right in front of where Farr sat on a plain upright chair in front of a battered table, a single lightbulb suspended from the ceiling. Martinez puffed furiously on his cheroot.

'Lieutenant.' Farr bent forward, pressing the tips of his fingers together, trying to find the words that Martinez would understand, perhaps even sympathise with. 'There are only two kinds of people when it comes to sex in Cuba. There are people who sell it and people who buy it. I sell it. It's a growth industry. Myself, I've never had to buy it, at least not yet. Maybe when I'm older . . .'

'You're a pimp is what you're saying. We know that.' Gomez put the cheroot back in his mouth.

'I don't see it quite like that. I provide a service in a growth industry. If I had the capital—'

Martinez had resumed his pacing.

'Go on.'

'Eight hundred thousand people came to Cuba as tourists last year, mainly Canadians and Germans. The tourist business is worth one and a half billion dollars to this country.

The government's ambition is to increase the number of holidaymakers to a million next year. That's a twenty per cent rise right there.'

'Where'd you get those figures?'

'They're official statistics, published in Cuban newspapers. In *Granma*. You can check them yourself.'

Martinez was frowning, still pacing.

'What's this got to do with your pal Warren Buffett?'

'Ah! Lieutenant, can you imagine what's going to happen when the Americans lift their Blockade, finally? Tourism's going to take off! Not twenty per cent. More like fifty or sixty per cent annual growth. This is the time,' Farr said, hearing his own voice getting louder in his excitement, 'to get a foot on the bottom rung—'

Farr found himself slapping the table with his palm for emphasis, his own predicament quite forgotten.

'I don't know what the hell you're talking about, Farr.'

'By the way, Lieutenant, how did you know I'm one of his admirers?'

'I'll ask the damn questions.'

Farr remembered where he was. He had been knocked off his chair three times in the morning session and kicked all over once. His nosebleed had started again. He did not want to repeat the experience. He was tired and sore and thirsty. He wanted a bath and clean clothes, something to eat and a good night's rest in a comfortable bed, but he knew he was in a place where all that counted for nothing. He was back in the nether world of the people-without-shoes.

Martinez put both hands on the table and leaned forward, his face inches from Farr's nose. Farr could feel the heat from the burning end of the cheroot and the smoke made his eyes run.

'You're lying, Farr. You're making this up. Warren Buffett is one of your people in the States, a member of your organisation. A terrorist like yourself. Tell us about it. From the beginning. How he recruited you.'

Farr shook his head. The smoke was getting to him. It was Martinez's third cheroot and there was a layer of smoke just above Farr's head. He couldn't even see the ceiling of the interrogation room, despite the harsh white light.

'Warren Buffett invests in franchises.'

Farr shut his eyes and wiped the tears off his cheeks.

'Franchises?'

'Let's say I have a brand name like Coca-Cola. You pay me a lump sum in return for a licence to use the brand name Coca-Cola here in Cuba, and set up a bottling plant and distribution network. I get a small percentage of the profits. In return, you get use of the brand name and I ship out the Coke concentrate for you to put in your bottles. That way we both make money, lots of money, and we're both happy. You just need partners to provide start-up capital.'

'Uh-huh.' Martinez was looking at Farr suspiciously, holding the stump of his third cheroot between thumb and forefinger. Was the prisoner trying to make a fool of him?

'Apart from sex, what other activities do you engage in?'

'I invest in hope, in the appetite for it.'

'Did you say dope?'

'Hope,' Farr said. 'Hope.'

'What the hell are you talking about?'

'I write "Farr's Stars" in *Diario*. The daily horoscope. People need to be told they're okay, that everything will be all right eventually. It's hope I'm selling, the feel-good factor – not that I get paid properly for it, I can tell you.'

Martinez stared.

'Well I never! My wife reads 'em every day.'

'She does?'

'Course. Now come on, Señor Farr, guess my sign.'

Señor, now. The celebrity astrologer.

Farr cupped his chin in one hand and looked hard at Martinez, narrowing his eyes. 'I can tell you worry a lot about your job, Lieutenant. You're a modest man. You don't boast about your achievements.'

Martinez waited, trying to not to give anything away, but Farr could tell he liked what he had heard.

Farr crossed his fingers under the table.

'I'd say you were born around August–September.'

'Maybe.' Martinez looked away, trying not to smile.

'Virgo.'

Martinez clapped in mock applause, each clap like a pistol shot in the confined space.

'Not bad, not bad at all. August the twenty-eighth, in fact.'

'Didn't I tell you?'

'And what kind of franchise would you set up . . . a chain of massage parlours, perhaps? Short-time hotels?'

Farr chose to ignore the sarcasm. He took the question seriously, as he did all questions of a financial nature.

'Nightclubs, singles beach resorts, motels. Farr's Friendly Inns. They would be very friendly. Cubans start with a big advantage because we're a very friendly people.'

'We?' Martinez said. 'We? You're surely not trying to suggest you're one of us, are you, Farr?'

Lying on the cement floor of his isolation cell (lying because there was nothing on which to sit and lying was more comfortable – or not quite so uncomfortable), Farr tried to imagine the world, his world, going by while he was in the tiny room with steel plates over the barred window. Time was hard to measure. It must be evening, though he had no way of knowing. That very morning, he told himself, the trade show had opened. In the States the *Chronicle* had hit the streets with his name on a story for the first time (he imagined the paper boys cycling past big colonial homes, flinging the papers across immaculate lawns). And where were his workers? Had they been released? Or had they been charged, convicted and sentenced by one of Gomez's tribunals, specially set up to try antisocial cases? What had become of Amelia? In his mind's eye he tried to imagine Plush, sticking out with his stetson above the other media people behind the crush barriers, while party cadres marched and countermarched with their red flags and posters of the beloved Che and Fidel. And what of Costas and the AP correspondent? Had the mules arrived? Would Plush know what to do with the supplies they brought in? How would they contact Garcia − if they could contact him, that is? Perhaps Maria would help Plush find a way to get the stuff to the hospital.

When they came to get him he asked if he could go to the lavatory. He was led to an open stall and his minders fidgeted impatiently and muttered to one another while he shut his eyes and braced himself for that first, stinging spurt. How long would it be before the clap got into his veins and travelled to his heart and brain?

How long did he have? Days? Weeks?

Garcia never said.

He was put into the back of what seemed to him to be a Russian-built jeep with hard seats and a hard suspension. Three soldiers kept him company in the back, peasants with blank faces clutching Chinese SKS rifles, the kind with the folding bayonets. It was dark outside, and the streets − streets he failed to recognise − seemed utterly deserted.

Of course. There was a curfew after midnight. That was why he had the military escort − they were the only ones who could move about with impunity. He could smell the sea and once he thought he saw waves breaking on a beach. He felt a small victory. It was after midnight, though how much after he couldn't tell, and he was fairly sure they were moving south.

He still had some grasp over reality, some sense of where he stood in the passage of time.

'Look, Farr. It really is very simple. You must help yourself and us – by talking. You can only help yourself in this situation by helping us, and you only help us if you talk. You follow?'

Farr nodded.

'So talk, amigo.'

'I don't know anything.'

'The name of the organisation. Let's start with that.'

Gomez took out a cigar.

'There isn't an organisation. Not one that I know of.'

'And the name of your contact in the States?'

'I don't have a contact in the States.'

'Oh, but you do. Garcia wrote it down. You passed it on to the photographer and journalist. Or at least the American spy James Plush did, using the hotel fax.'

'Spy?' Farr almost choked on the word. 'Did you say spy? Plush can hardly do up his own shoelaces, let alone spy on anything.'

'He'd like us all to think so.'

'It's all an act? You've got to be kidding, captain.'

'We arrested them both, you know.'

'Who?'

'Your Greek friend. Costas. And the Canadian girl. Your mules – on arrival at the airport. Costas was picked up in customs last night, and the señorita this morning. Or I should say yesterday morning as it's Friday already. I thought you'd want to know.'

Farr groaned inwardly. There goes my cure, he thought to himself. What was there to say?

'Tell us about the plastic.'

'Plastic?'

'The Semtex.'

'I don't know anything about any Semtex!'

'All right.' Gomez sighed. He looked so different, Farr thought. He wore a cream jacket, grey trousers and shiny black shoes. He looked formal, stiff with self-awareness as if someone had starched him as well as his shirt. They sat in armchairs. The place was a little dilapidated, uncared for, but it was comfortable enough, with the moths chasing each other around the single lamp on the side table next to Gomez's chair.

'I thought we had a deal, Farr.'

'We did and I stuck to my side of it.'

'Well?'

'I tried hard to persuade Garcia that he was making a mistake. I told him he had his duty to do. As a doctor, and as head of a department. That meant writing up a report, making his recommendations and ensuring he handed it into the hospital superintendent personally, taking care to keep a copy for himself. Just as you said. I told him to keep politics out of it. State the facts, I said, and make a couple of strictly medical recommendations. Isn't that what we agreed? I told him he had his duty as a father and husband not to abandon his family out of some stupid idea of sacrificing himself on some petty local issue. That's it.'

'You saw my sister?'

'Yes. Amelia and I agreed on this as a plan of action. She told him more or less the same thing, in essence. To be sensible — but not stick his head out, not to make a hero of himself. But she told me he'd been arrested. Is that true?'

Gomez said nothing. He sat in his chair, quite still, for perhaps as long as two minutes.

'If that was all there was to it, you wouldn't be here now. But you went further than our deal, didn't you? Much further.'

'I wanted to help, that's all.'

'A sudden rush of altruism, Farr? I don't buy that.'

'I acted on impulse.'

'Not like you. What's your sign?'

'Capricorn.'

'And what should that tell us?'

'That I'm ambitious.'

'Cold. Like the English.'

'Something like that.'

'Not that I believe any of it, mind you. It's hocus-pocus.'

'I understand, Captain.'

'Are you thirsty, Farr?'

'Very.'

'What will you drink?'

'A beer.'

Gomez spoke to someone else in the room, another plain-clothes agent perhaps, sitting somewhere there in the dark. 'Make it two, take one for yourself,' Gomez ordered.

When the man had shuffled off to the kitchen, Gomez leaned forward.

'Why did you go further than our agreement?'

'What do you mean?'

'You asked Plush for help.'

Farr hesitated. Much as he might dislike Plush – no, it wasn't dislike so much as irritation – he wasn't going to implicate him.

'You asked him to contact people he knew coming into Santiago and you gave him a contact name to collect some materials to bring in with them. Right?'

'You make it sound like a conspiracy, Captain. I'm not a terrorist, and neither is your brother-in-law. As for Plush, he's guilty of nothing but being a harmless fool.'

'I believe you, but that's how it looks in Havana.'

'Havana?'

'Careers in State Security are made and broken on cases like this. Havana wants to get its hands on you. You and the others. They can build a big fat case. This is a conspiracy against the state involving foreign intelligence officers from the United States and locally recruited agents.'

Farr was silent.

It wasn't a matter of what was and what was not true. He knew that what he should say, what he should have said right at the beginning in fact, was that he had a dose of the clap – the new, virulent strain – like all those other people, and that all he was trying to do was get hold of the antibiotics to fix it. It wasn't ideological. It wasn't right or wrong. It was all about saving his own skin.

He started to speak, to try to explain, but a shadow slipped between them, carrying the beers. He was an old man, bent forward and silver-haired, but Farr couldn't make out his face. Farr gratefully took the icy bottle and raised it to his lips. He didn't need a glass.

The shadow retreated.

'Enjoy the beer, Farr,' Gomez said. 'It may be the last you'll taste for a very long time.'

chapter fifteen

(Capricorn, October 25–26. Do what you do best,
and try not to think too far ahead. Spend more
time with family, especially the children.)

'How do you do it?'

'I'm glad you like it, General.'

'It's really excellent. I never learned to cook, I'm sad to
say. My wife was the one who spent time in the kitchen;
and now she's gone—' General Reyes shrugged and forked
another mouthful of chicken into his mouth. While he chewed
he kept his eyes on Gomez. He wanted to ask another question.
Something made clicking noises while he ate, and Gomez
thought it must be his Russian dentures.

'I am sorry to have treated you like a subordinate just now,
General. With the drinks.'

'Not at all, my boy. It was quick thinking. It gave me a
chance to get a good look at him, too.'

'And? What did you make of him?'

The general grunted. 'He's venal, streetwise, an extrovert.
Impossibly vain, of course. Those clothes! He's of absolutely
no use to the Revolution, that's clear. A criminal beyond hope
of rehabilitation. He has no family, I think.'

'That's right.'

'An advantage. No one will make a fuss.'

General Reyes was gnawing at a chicken leg.

'Why haven't you married, Captain?'

'I married the Revolution, General.'

'I understand. It's like the priesthood. But now you're senior enough to take a little time for yourself?'

'Perhaps.'

'Forgive me — is this your home, or a safe house?'

'It's where I live. It's dreary, I know.' Gomez was embarrassed.

'It feels like a place that's never lived in, Felipe. I can smell the dust on those books of yours. Even the pool is empty and full of leaves.'

General Reyes was far too thin for his old uniform, Gomez noted. He seemed to be shrinking in old age. His collar was several sizes too large and his neck protruded from it like a tortoise's, the sinews sticking out against the loose, scaly skin.

'I sleep in my office most nights. And for that reason I do use the place for certain sensitive jobs.'

'See much of your sister?'

'Not really.'

'She's married to that doctor — what's his name?'

'Ernesto Garcia.'

'The difficult one.'

Gomez didn't answer, but found the general smiling at him. A smile that said he knew he was right, and that he knew Gomez would have liked to change the subject. A state security officer needed to be above reproach, and so did his family — even the in-laws.

'You should relax more, my boy. Take up a hobby.'

'My work is my hobby.'

Their glasses refilled, the general pushed his empty plate away and loosened his stiff uniform collar. He belched appreciatively.

'Delicious! Now — to business. What do you make of this fellow? And what are you going to do with him?'

'He's obsessed with making money and terrified of being poor. He despises the proletariat. He thinks of himself as an entrepreneur.'

'Odd name,' the general said. 'It's not Cuban. He doesn't look particularly Cuban.'

'His paternal grandfather came to Cuba from Caracas. His mother was English . . .'

'And he's a pimp?'

'Of the superior sort. He organises call-girls for clients at the more expensive hotels. His foreign looks help him get a foot in the door. He uses his mother's name for the same reason.'

General Reyes snorted. 'Scum floats, Felipe. And he writes a horoscope in *Diario* . . . I think my granddaughters mentioned something of the sort the other day. It's degenerate rubbish.'

Gomez got up and went over to where the general was sitting and offered him a cigar. He waited while General Reyes made his choice, then clipped it for him and struck a match and helped him light it.

'He's what they call a stringer or part-time correspondent. He's not someone we can simply disappear without there being repercussions.'

'What are you going to do with him?'

'Let him run.'

'Havana won't like it.'

'We have no evidence.'

General Reyes threw up his bony hands. 'Evidence? In my day state security officers were expected to use discretion—'

'It's not that easy any more, sir. We need our friends overseas. I've got a Greek and a Canadian in police cells at the airport, but I have no reason to hold them much longer. We can't afford the adverse publicity, not during the trade show.'

'Dammit, Felipe! Fifteen years ago I would have had Farr shot. A call to the Villa Marista would have been sufficient . . . afterwards, of course.' The old man chuckled, a phlegmy rattle in his throat.

Gomez knew all about the Villa Marista and its reputation. He took his orders from there. 'When we arrested the foreigners we found nothing, nothing at all. No drugs, no explosive, no weapons. Not even a copy of *Playboy*.'

'And the American? Plush?'

'My orders are to leave him alone unless we have lawful reason to do otherwise . . .'

'He's CIA?'

'There's nothing firm. Not yet.'

'And this fellow Delaware?'

'A meddlesome diplomat, all piss and wind.'

The general sighed.

'You'll free Farr and the others.'

'We'll see which burrow our rabbits bolt down, General.'

'Then you'll let loose your ferrets?'

'Once we're sure.'

General Reyes seemed reassured.

'Have you ever seen a ferret snap a rabbit's neck, Felipe?'

'No, General, I can't say I have. I don't think there are ferrets in Cuba.'

'It's a European animal, Captain, domesticated for specifically that purpose.'

The two men rose as one and stood facing one another. General Reyes, the taller of the two, stretched out his right arm and put his hand on Gomez's shoulder, giving it a squeeze. Gomez tried not to wince. The general was a relic of the Revolution, a guerrilla all but mummified in rum and tobacco, but his bony fingers were still immensely strong.

'I may not appreciate all this newfangled rubbish about upsetting the wrong people,' Reyes was saying. 'In my day, a good beating on the bottom of a man's feet with a two-by-four would work wonders. But I still have some influence with El Comandante. If you need a word in the right ear, Felipe . . .'

'It's appreciated, sir. If I need help, I certainly will ask.'

Farr said nothing at first. He was taken out through the prison gates while it was still dark and left there by his escort, alone, bewildered and unable to see anything.

'Over here!' Gomez flicked his car lights on and off, and leaned out of the window to call him.

'I thought there was a curfew,' Farr said when he reached the Chevvy.

'There is. It'll be light in a few minutes. Just get in, will you?'

'Where are you taking me, Felipe?'

'Home. I'm taking you home.'

While Gomez drove Farr was content to let his mind wander, watching the light spread across the sky to the east.

In the streets of downtown Santiago, Farr woke from a doze and turned to Gomez.

'Who was that man?'

'What man?'

'The one who brought us the beers in that house.'

'Oh, him – he helps me out.'

'He was very old.'

'He is, yes.'

'He was wearing a uniform.'

'Some people feel happier wearing uniforms, especially if it helps them remember better days.'

When they got to Farr's tenement building, Gomez followed Farr inside, then walked around the room, hands on hips. He stopped at three enormous piles of paper in one corner.

'What are these?'

'Newspapers – what else?'

'Foreign newspapers.' Gomez said 'foreign' as if it was a dirty word.

Farr was sure Gomez had been there before, probably leading his men in searching the place. It was on the tip of his tongue to ask, but he thought better of it. A more pertinent question was surely why Gomez pretended not to know what they were if he had led the search party.

'They're mostly copies of the *Wall Street Journal* and the *Financial Times*,' Farr said. 'I pick them up in the hotels. People just leave them lying around. Sometimes I sell them. Occasionally I manage to get hold of a copy of the *New York Times*. That's worth a dollar or two to some people.'

'What do you do with the ones you don't sell?'

'Read them, of course. I read them before I sell them. I learn about commerce. About markets and companies. I only keep the business pages that interest me.'

'You don't throw them away?'

'After a few months. I like to go back and read the interesting bits again.'

Gomez inspected the kitchenette and then the bathroom, such as it was, then came back and watched Farr take his shoes off and lie down on the sofa and shut his eyes.

'This doesn't look like the home of a capitalist,' he said.

'I hate spending money, and I think the cops would spend a lot more time on my case if I did live it up.'

'Your girls will be freed tomorrow. The Greek and Canadian will be released today without charge.'

'You didn't confiscate any of their things?'

'We found nothing at the airport.'

'Nothing at all?'

'Should we have?' Gomez looked closely at Farr, who still had his eyes shut, his hands folded across his stomach.

'What happens now, Felipe?'

'Nothing,' said Gomez. 'What did you expect?'

'And Dr Garcia?'

Gomez shrugged. 'What about him?'

'You arrested him too, didn't you?'

'He was questioned.'

'You mean he's been released?'

'He took your advice. And his wife's. That part of our deal held up well.'

'He did what?' Farr sat up.

'He wrote his report. That's all.'

'And the committee? The stuff on the Internet?'

'He was the only one who turned up to the meeting. We made sure none of the other members did. We had a word with each of them and they found all sorts of reasons not to attend.' Gomez smiled at the thought of Garcia finding himself alone.

Farr groaned and sank back on the sofa.

'So what's going to happen about the epidemic?'

'What epidemic, Farr? I don't know anything about any epidemic and it will stay that way until after the trade show.'

'But that's another six days!'

'Six days? No. Two days. I can see we managed to disorientate you quite effectively.'

'What day is it?' Farr was alarmed, looking for his shoes and struggling to his feet. It was true. They had disturbed his sleep and kept mixing up the meals, bringing him breakfast in what he was sure was the evening and dinner – if a corn-meal mash usually fed to cattle can be called dinner – at first light.

'It's Tuesday,' Gomez said.

'You mean I've been in that cell for five days?'

'Four and a bit.'

'And nothing's been done – about the gonorrhoea?'

'The curfew and the arrests have discouraged some of the more promiscuous among our visitors. Even the pimps still at large are keeping their heads down. I'm doing what I can. The rest is up to the authorities in Havana.'

'And what happens to me?' Farr was in pain and anxious to get to the lavatory. He was also tired, terribly tired, and he badly needed to wash. He knew he stank. He could smell himself and it sickened him. He stank of prison smells – shit and piss, sweat and ammonia, a distinctive sourness on the skin and in his hair; a stink every guest of state security knew only too well.

Gomez looked away from a cupboard he was examining. 'You, Farr? I'm afraid I don't follow.'

'You don't get it, do you? I've got the clap. Not just any old dose of the clap – but the special bug. Garcia gave me the test and told me what would happen if I didn't get the right antibiotics. I need the medicine, Captain, and I need it quickly. Now do you understand?'

Farr couldn't wait for an answer. He fled the room, unfastening his trousers as he went and slamming the lavatory door behind him in his haste.

chapter sixteen

(Capricorn, October 26–27. Someone has your
interests at heart. Be ready for a nice surprise.
Show appreciation and others will pitch in.)

Farr didn't bother to undress. He woke once during the night
to relieve himself, but all told he slept for fourteen hours;
when he woke he could feel the heat of the sun despite the
jalousies over the windows; from the angle of the bars of
light, like bright throwing-knives tossed onto the wall above
his head, he knew it must be close to noon. As he pushed
himself up off the settee motes of dust danced around him
like fireflies in the white-hot beams. There was nothing to
eat in what passed for a kitchen save for a wrinkled apple.
Having devoured that and drunk a cup of water, spilling
much of it down his chin, Farr rubbed himself down under
the dribble of cold water from the rusty shower-head to try
to get rid of the prison odour and the dullness brought on
by prolonged sleep. He shaved, squinting at himself in the
mirror, slapped his cheeks with aftershave, found his last clean
shirt, an outrageously yellow and red affair, pulled on rumpled
khakis and a pair of sandals and stumbled down the stairs with
breakfast on his mind. He imagined the smell of coffee, the
taste of bread and oil and salivated; there was so much to
do, to think about, but as Farr stood momentarily blinded on

the street, fumbling for his sunglasses, it was his hunger that preoccupied him.

He didn't notice what had happened to the Lada until he almost bumped into it; he knew where it was without having to think about it. It was where he always parked it. Entirely wrapped up in himself and trying to cope with an odd sense of vertigo he put down to his brief imprisonment, it seemed to take him several seconds to realise why the boxy little car seemed so much higher off the ground and oddly tilted. He stepped back. Yes, he could see – yet somehow his mind refused to absorb the information his eyes provided. Anyone who drove a car on Santiago's streets, and had the petrol to keep it going, was someone. It was a status symbol, and Farr had enjoyed the sense of accomplishment and the mobility the Lada had provided for the best part of a decade. Its eccentricities and ugliness infuriated him, but when all was said and done, he loved that car in a way he loved nothing and no one else. It went with the fake Rolex – now adorning the wrist of a prison warder.

The Lada was perched unevenly on four piles of bricks; it had no wheels. It had a derelict, apologetic look. Farr felt a surge of unreasoning sorrow and anger; how was it, he asked himself, that a bunch of teenage hoodlums could come out and take his wheels right under the noses of the state security men who were watching his place day and night? He resisted the temptation to turn around and give them the finger (he knew they were there, he didn't have to look), and he knew the answer as he asked himself the question – state security wasn't interested in petty crime or protecting their quarry from theft; that wasn't their job. They might even have organised it as part of a campaign of harassment. Farr would have to spend several hours finding those tyres and buying them back, and he would be a lot poorer than when he had started out.

He started walking, feeling the sun's heat on his back.

He would have to act quickly, otherwise tonight they'd be back for the seats and the battery.

Breakfast first.

An ugly thought crossed his mind. Gomez, the smarmy bastard, was deliberately playing with him.

He made straight for the men's room. He took the same route he had when pursued by the two state security agents. He stood in front of the urinal for what seemed like ages. Nothing happened. Farr whistled to himself. Still nothing. More curious still, there was no pain. What had Garcia said? He couldn't remember exactly, but it occurred to him that if he was feeling no pain it was because the initial symptoms had gone. If that was true, it surely meant he was entering the secondary phase of the disease. Right now those bacteria or whatever they were were seeping into his bloodstream, gathering strength to attack his joints, his heart. Even his brain. Instinctively he put his free hand up to his head, his fingers coming away damp with sweat. Everything in his nature rebelled against the notion of radical action; he had never liked taking the initiative. He would be the first to admit he was not a courageous man. As long as Farr could remember, he had always been happy to encourage someone else to try out his ideas and, if they worked, he would follow the stalking horse to profit and pleasure. If the result was less than desirable, well, he would melt away with the rest of the crowd to live to fight another day. Now it was different. There was no one else to cajole, to persuade into the role. To save himself he must act. No one would do it for him.

Farr had the place to himself. He washed his hands vigorously, deep in thought. He splashed water in his face. Combed his hair. Smiled at himself. Tried again, this time with the shades on, pulling his facial muscles into a broad and humourless grin. The savoir faire seemed to be slightly off-centre, like a drunken whore's lipstick, but it was better.

He retraced his steps, enjoying the air-conditioning which seemed set not far above freezing and the deep carpeting under his feet. God, he thought, it was good to be back. He missed the luxury of the place and the fact that he wasn't paying for it. Not a single cent. By the bank of telephones he paused, put a receiver to his ear and dialled Plush's suite. He waited for twelve rings. No answer.

At reception he smiled, laying both hands on the counter, palms down, fingers loosely laced together; it was the action of someone at ease, confident in his own authority.

'Yessir – what can I do for you?'

'Hi.' Farr whipped off the shades and smiled. 'I'm looking for Mr James Plush of the *Chronicle*. Suite number—'

'Mr Plush checked out yesterday, sir.'

'He did? Are you sure?'

There was a flurry of whispered conversation between the young desk clerk and a suave junior manager Farr knew as Sanchez.

'Mr Plush took the airport shuttle bus at three-thirty yesterday afternoon,' Sanchez said, coming forward to the desk and wearing the faintly supercilious smile of the man who knows he has all the answers. 'I believe he was booked onto a flight for Havana that connects with a Nassau flight.'

'Did he leave any message, Señor Sanchez? My name is—'

'No, Mr Farr, he left no message.'

'Was he alone?'

Farr removed his hands and forearms from the counter.

Sanchez paused at this point. Farr could see he was debating with himself the limits of Farr's influence, and his own responsibility in not acknowledging certain information that wasn't strictly his business. Or perhaps he was assessing the size and likelihood of a hard-currency tip.

Sanchez switched to English.

'No, sir. There was a young lady with him.' Sanchez lowered

his gaze and moved the visitor's registration book, a huge affair grandly covered in blood-red leather, an inch to the right, then back again.

He added, in Spanish this time: 'His fiancée, I believe.'

Farr tried to wipe the expression of shock off his face. He replaced the sunglasses, though in the subdued lighting of the foyer it would be all too easy to bump into the furniture or the odd tourist if he wasn't careful. His mouth twitched in an effort to rediscover the jauntiness of the affluent man-about-town he liked to adopt with hotel staff. It didn't quite come off this time, so he nodded to Sanchez and turned round. He took a few steps away from reception. His hand was in his pocket, separating out the notes and coins, but in his not inconsiderable confusion the idea of a tip for the balding, middle-aged Sanchez escaped his mind.

He needed to eat.

'Mr Farr—'

It was Sanchez calling him. He turned, and the manager was holding up an envelope. Farr walked back to the counter.

'Sorry, Mr Farr. No one told me. Before I came on duty this morning a Ms Alison was asking for you. She left a note.'

'Miss—'

'Alison.'

The name only vaguely registered. There was too much else on Farr's mind. He looked down to make sure the banknote he had in his hand was a single dollar, then he held it out, thumb keeping the note pressed into his palm. When he took the envelope, he contrived to push the note into the manager's hand.

'Thank you, Mr Sanchez.'

'Thank you, sir.'

Farr pushed the envelope into the back pocket of his khakis. He was ferociously hungry, but Farr always wanted to spend money when he was in trouble. Specifically he had an urge to gorge himself. Whether it was nature — the instinct to hoard resources in time of danger — or something to do with his sojourn in wet, grey Croydon as a child, he had no idea. He made a beeline for the coffee shop. En route he discreetly checked how much cash he had on him — twenty-three dollars and thirty cents. That was plenty for what he had in mind.

He was going to spoil himself. He didn't want to think about money. He walked into the mock-Spanish-style coffee shop and looked for a table that would let him face the door and keep his back to the wall. The morning buffet had long since been cleared away; it was far too late for breakfast, but there were pancakes with seven different fillings, freshly squeezed orange juice and real Italian coffee listed on the plastic-covered, all-day menu decorated with drawings of women with narrow waists, their hands over their heads clutching castanets and wearing flamenco dresses.

Farr thought he saw a discarded newspaper on another table.

By the time the waiter brought his order, Farr was deeply engaged in the Lex column of the *Financial Times*, one of his favourites. His lips moved as he read, and a forefinger traced the tiny words on the pink paper. If only for thirty or forty minutes anxiety had been subdued the way an aspirin can dull the edge of a headache. The issue of gonorrhoea's secondary symptoms, the whereabouts of Plush and the plight of his Lada seemed to recede into the background. Farr had also forgotten all about the envelope in his back pocket.

chapter seventeen

(Capricorn, October 27–28. It isn't luck that matters. When people leave, it's sad, but that's no reason to feel resentment.)

Varga was cutting the cards, concentrating, looking down at his own fingers. He was a sharp-featured man in his sixties, someone very aware of his own appearance, wearing a black knitted shirt under a black jacket of what looked like shot silk with padded shoulders, a combination that Farr thought was altogether too fussy to be merely elegant. Varga's hair was carefully combed back from his forehead. The clothes and the narrow features gave him an edged look – like a cardboard cut-out, Farr thought, a gangster with hunched shoulders and a predatory profile.

'No money tonight, boys.' Varga's voice was husky, almost soft. He raised a hand slowly over the table like a priest giving the blessing.

Hernandez, sitting to Varga's left, scowled in what Farr took to be incomprehension or disappointment or a combination of the two. He took his cigar out of his mouth and pitched his chair forward. 'Whaddya mean – no money?'

'Fine by me,' Farr said. He had never been especially fond of gambling, and he lacked the necessary attention span to make a consistently good card player. He couldn't afford to waste his cash. Not now.

The view from the top of the mountain was thrilling, but Farr noted that neither of his fellow card players seemed to notice. They were sitting outside a cabana, one of twenty-five log cabins let out to guests and part of the Gran Piedra hotel.

'What is this — no money?'

Hernandez was looking first at Farr, then Varga in search of an explanation. What was the point of doing anything if money wasn't involved? Hernandez had very dark, curious eyes, pale skin and very little hair (except for wisps which stuck out at the sides and over his ears), while his nose appeared absurdly small, as if a cosmetic surgeon had tried to craft the perfect shape, only to make it smaller and smaller. As for his mouth, it was a perfect bow, fleshy and soft like a girl's. He wore *Santeria* bangles on his right wrist. Did Hernandez believe in the *Santeria* god, Olofin, who lived at the bottom of the sea? Farr looked away. Hernandez made him feel uneasy.

'You use Patel to hold your bundle?' Varga had snapped the packs together, a faint smile on his lips, the big gold ring on his right pinkie flashing in the late afternoon light. He held out the cards, splayed like a fan, offering them to his fellow players. 'Take one for dealer.'

'Sure I do.' Hernandez shrugged his shoulders, suspicion on his face.

'That's all the cops wanted to know. Did I give Patel money — that's all they asked. They must have asked it a hundred times and when they realised I wasn't going to talk to them they just left me alone in the cell until they let me out.'

Varga helped himself from the bottle of rum next to him.

'Patel's been picked up. Held on suspicion of illegal association. Bail was set at a million pesos.'

'You gotta be kidding,' Hernandez said, his voice muffled by the cigar now back in his mouth. They had each drawn a card. Farr had the ace, and flipped it face up on the table.

Lucky in cards—

'I start, you deal,' Farr said, addressing himself to Hernandez.

'Fuck,' Hernandez said with emphasis, shaking his head and squinting through the smoke so he could see to pick up the cards and deal thirteen to each of the three players.

'See, the only people who can pay that kind of money are Patel's relatives,' Varga said in his soft voice. 'He lends them our money with interest, naturally, and they use it for their various enterprises. That's what he gets for holding. It's like a commercial bank Stateside. He gets interest for the risk from his people and our investment, plus a small return is guaranteed. Right, Hernandez?'

Farr was watching the cards.

'So?' Hernandez was almost finished. Nobody touched his cards until Hernandez was done.

Varga explained. 'So the only people who can come forward with that kind of bail are his brothers and cousins and as soon as they do, they get arrested, too. Right now they are keeping well away.' He gave a short wheeze of laughter, screwing up his face as if a fly was sitting on his nose. 'Can't say I blame 'em. I'd do the same.'

Farr sat back, making the wicker chair under him creak. He sorted the cards swiftly, high ones to the left, low to the right. He watched Hernandez put the rest of the two packs face down in the centre of the baize table.

He was thinking that he'd withdrawn his cash from Patel's safe just in time. It left Plush and Amelia each holding cash on his behalf. Plush had left him in the lurch without so much as a message. He had to find Amelia – fast – so he could pay for the tyres.

Varga shut his eyes and made the sign of the cross over the table with an exaggerated sweep of his hand. 'For what

we are about to receive, may the Lord make us truly grateful.'

Pick up, Farr told himself. Nice — a jack of hearts. Don't
look at it too long. Now discard. A five of clubs. The key
to this game was to remember everything that went into the
discard pile, count everything in one's hand and figure out who
held what. A player didn't have to be clever, Farr told himself.
It was a matter of practice. He poured two fingers of rum into
his glass, then added a splash of Coke.

Hernandez took the bottle. 'What the fuck do they want
to pick on Patel for?'

Varga picked up, discarded, and it was the turn of Hernandez.

'It's Captain Gomez,' said Varga. 'He's running the show,
and the name of the game is putting the squeeze on Patel to
hurt our pockets, put us out of business. Gomez heads this
new investigative unit with special powers and reports to an
ex-general, a crony of the President's.'

'General Reyes,' Hernandez said.

'The show ends today,' said Farr.

Varga glanced at Farr. 'No guarantee our Captain Gomez
will let Patel go at all, though, is there?'

'No,' Farr said. 'There's no guarantee. There's no guarantee
that he'll let our girls go, either. They were supposed to be out
today—'

'Shit,' Hernandez said. 'Pimping's all I got.'

Hernandez was indeed the main source of girls in the city, the
number-one player. He exported them all over the Americas,
the Middle East, even Japan. He didn't let them keep their
money, except for tips. He took it all. He did it by charging
them for accommodation, medical check-ups, taxi hire, clothes,
electricity and food. They just had to work that much harder
and be that much nicer to their clients. Farr was aware that
it wasn't true that pimping was his sole trade, not if the
street talk was to be believed. Hernandez had powerful party

connections, so the gossips said, linked to Cuba's growing role in the international drugs trade.

'You know him, Ricardo?'

'Who – Gomez?'

Varga waited.

'Yeah – I met him.' Farr kept his eyes on his cards.

Varga smiled his shark's smile, showing his teeth.

'Gomez know you're banging his sister, too?'

Farr felt the sweat pop out of his skin on his upper arms and chest as if he were being squeezed.

Varga leaned forward, still smiling. 'Let me see – yes, every Tuesday and Friday afternoon at Las Americas? You didn't think you could keep something reg'lar like that going for very long and not have people know about it, did you? I seen you both comin' and goin' there. Sure our friend Hernandez here knows it, too. You shouldn't be so reg'lar about it, man. Ring the changes.'

'Asking for trouble,' Hernandez muttered, shaking his head from side to side.

Varga was watching Farr closely for any sign of reaction. 'She's got that married look, Ricardo. Hey, you listening to me? I said she looks married, you know? She's got that furtive, hungry look that women have when they're getting it someplace else they know they shouldn't.'

Varga chuckled. Farr was doing his level best to show no sign of torment. He watched Varga draw a card out of his hand and tap the table with it.

'Is that why they haven't charged you for that kid – the one in the park? You got some special protection, friend? Huh?'

'What kid?'

Varga put the card down face up in front of him. Then he took another, like its predecessor a modest seven, and put that down too, one slightly overlapping the other and both in a neat line at right angles to the edge of the table. He added a joker and took a seven off the top of the discard pile – the seven Farr had discarded, thereby having unwittingly made Varga a present of the pile and an almost sure win of this round. Damn, Farr thought. He wasn't to know. It was luck and bad luck. His bad luck and Varga's good luck. Four cards in all now lay in a line on Varga's side of the table, soon to be joined by other 'melds'. Then Varga picked up the entire discard pile. He did this all slowly with almost ritual deliberation so his opponents could see every move. He was enjoying this, too. Farr ground his teeth together. That must be worth a good five hundred points. Damn!

'What kid?' Varga mimicked the surprise in Farr's voice. 'What kid? C'mon, Ricardo, it was only last week, for Chrissakes.' Varga was busily absorbed in adding to his hand, sorting out the cards, knowing he was well on the way to winning this first round of canasta. 'I'm talking about the juvenile thief in Cespedes Park. You hit him. You hit him hard. You must have been real mad. I'm not saying he didn't deserve it, mind, but you broke his jaw. You broke his jaw and took out some teeth. You knocked him cold and he choked in his own blood and he died.'

Farr ran up the steps of the hospital. It was getting dark. He hoped he wasn't too late. On the envelope in his back pocket he now had the name, thanks to Hernandez, of the man in Santiago who ran two *pancheros* or tyre bars. Hernandez had also offered to put the word out that Farr was willing to pay the going rate for his tyres back and no hard feelings. As for Varga, he knew where a brand-new – well, almost brand new – set of wheels could be had.

Until that happened, Farr thought, life would move from the slow lane of the Lada to the extremely slow lane of the bus, bicycle and his own two feet.

He must get hold of his money.

The nurse or whatever she was – the one who had called his name that first time he had seen Dr Garcia – now barred his way as he rounded the corner and headed into the urinary section.

'Dr Garcia's surgery is closed. It's after six.'

'Is that right?' Farr smiled, stepped around her and was through the first door, heading for what he thought he remembered as the right curtain.

'Get out of here!'

It was Dr Garcia's voice. The first thing Farr saw when he swept the curtain aside and stepped into the cubicle was a large and bare backside. A hairy, male bottom. Garcia was sitting in his roller chair, presumably doing to the patient what he had done to Farr, the light from his desk lamp angled towards the patient's genitalia. The stranger turned his head, not daring to move any other part of his anatomy, looking over his shoulder at the intruder, his pants around his ankles. His expression said it all; a mixture of sheer fright, pain and deep humiliation ranged across his face.

'Dr Garcia. It's me – Farr.'

'I know who you are. Can't you see I have a patient?'

'I'll see him when I've finished,' Farr heard Dr Garcia say as he took a seat on a plastic chair in the now deserted waiting room. 'This is the last, isn't it, sister?'

'Yes, doctor.' She glared at Farr as she emerged from Garcia's cubicle, her arms folded across her ample chest.

Garcia called after her. 'Then go home, nurse.'

'Good night, doctor.'

As the nurse bustled past on her way out, Farr looked around him to see if there were any interesting-looking foreign newspapers or magazines lying about. There weren't.

'All right,' Farr heard Garcia telling the anonymous patient. 'You can get dressed now. Come back in a week – this time next week. And please, no unprotected sex . . .'

A figure slipped past in the gloom, face averted.

'Well, Farr? What can I do for you?'

Dr Garcia put out his light. Farr could hear him locking his desk. Now Garcia emerged, standing before him in his white coat, hands in the pockets, the features of his face indistinct in the gloom.

'I wanted to know how things went, doctor. Your committee meeting, and so on. Whether you—'

Farr felt compelled to stand up for some reason.

'I followed your advice, Farr. I hope you managed to get hold of the antibiotics we so desperately need. Did you bring any with you?'

Farr was on his feet. 'I'm really sorry, doctor. Both mules arrived, but both were arrested at the airport and the authorities say they found nothing on them. I was questioned myself—'

'So was I.'

'What—?'

'I said I was taken in for questioning. I caved in, of course. I'm not brave. I never was cut out for that kind of thing. I'm just a doctor. No one turned up for the committee meeting other than myself, and I know why now. They were all informers or provocateurs, all of them.'

Garcia's bitter voice of betrayal trailed off.

Farr couldn't restrain himself any longer. 'I'm sure you did the right thing. Really. It was the only sensible thing to do. Of course it was.' Farr spoke quickly, trying to find the right words before he got on to what he really wanted to talk about – himself. 'Doctor, I don't have any pain any more. The symptoms have gone. What are we going to do?'

'I told you this thing has stages, Farr.'

'How long have we got?'

'We?'

'Well. I meant the, er, germs or whatever they are. They go into the bloodstream—'

'*Neisseria gonorrhoeae* attack the heart and brain. Yes.'

'So—'

'I can't help you. I have seventy-eight new cases, and by the end of the week I shouldn't be at all surprised if I have double the number. I'm really sorry.'

'And your report?'

If Farr wasn't mistaken the outline of Dr Garcia gave a slight shrug of fatalism.

'And Gomez?'

'Captain Gomez did his best according to the way those people work. He locked you up. Locked up all the pimps and prostitutes he could find, I guess. Locked me away too, so I couldn't make a fuss while the foreign press was in town.' Garcia gave a bitter little laugh.

'Amelia?'

It was now quite dark. All Farr could see was the vague white blur of Dr Garcia's hospital coat.

'Amelia. Yes. I knew you would ask about my wife, Farr.'

Farr thought, he knows.

'She's left.'

'Left?'

'Left. She left. She walked out.'

Farr's mind summoned up the image of a roll of dollar bills nestling comfortably in the bottom of Amelia's straw basket, among the green peppers and parsley.

Farr felt he knew what was coming, like an episode of déjà vu.

'You know better than I, Farr, that you can buy a legitimate exit visa if you have the hard currency and know the right official. That's what Amelia did. I don't know where she got the money or how she knew whom to pay. They say it costs thousands of dollars. At any rate, she had enough change left to buy a one-way ticket – to Montreal, I believe, with an onward connection to Los Angeles.'

'And the children?'

'She's taken them, too. Can you believe it – they flew business class.'

chapter eighteen

(Capricorn, October 28–29. Your mood
should be greatly improved. Your efforts
are paying off. Make sure you spread a little
happiness, too.)

— May I speak to Mr James Plush, please?
  —Would that be Editorial, sir?
  —Yes. Editorial.
  —Thank you, sir. Hold, please.
  —National desk.
  —May I speak to James Plush?
  —Who shall I say is calling?
  —Ricardo Farr. Calling from Cuba.
  —Sure. Hold on a moment.
  —Thank you.
  —Hey, Ricky! That you? How are you, man?
  —James, I need your help.
  —You want I call you back?
  —It's okay. This won't take long.
  —Go ahead, buddy. What's the problem?
  —You got some money of mine, right?
  —You haven't spoken to Alison?
  —Alison? Who's Alison?
  —The AP correspondent. The one I mentioned to you

before – before you were arrested. Ricky, I gave her your cash because she was handling, you know, the other thing—

—No, Jim. I haven't spoken to anyone called Alison.

—She's still there, Rick. Staying at the Casaverde. There was some problem at the airport but that's solved now. Costas has already left . . .

—I'll ask for her. What did you say her family name was?

—Rick, I'm real sorry I didn't get to say goodbye. You did real well, you know, and I'm sorry you got arrested. We were kind of worried about you here at the *Chronicle*.

—It was nothing. They arrested a lot of people during the trade show. You know how things work around here, Jim . . .

—Uh-huh. Is there anything else I can do?

—What did you say the name was?

—Alison.

—Alison who?

—Alison Delaware. You got that?

—I got it. Alison Delaware.

—Anything else we can do, Rick?

—A new set of tyres would be good . . .

—What was that?

—I was kidding. I got the wheels of my Lada stolen.

—Hell, I'm sorry, man.

—Everything's fine, really.

—You want to hear about the story I did today, Ricky?

—Jim, I got to go.

—Aw, Ricky, let me read it to you.

—Sorry, Jim. No time. Really.

—You sure? I can call you right back.

—No, Jim, thanks. Everything's fine.

—Those were some nice pieces you did. Stay in touch, son. You take care now, you hear? Maybe . . .

—Same to you, Jim. Bye. Bye for now.

*　　*　　*

'That's it?' Martinez took the cigar out of his mouth and inspected the end of it close up, like an entomologist counting the spots on the back of a small and rare South American wood-louse. 'Sounds to me like Mr Plush wasn't overly enchanted to get a call from his paper's Santiago de Cuba stringer. That's the way it is with those Americans. All over you when they want something. Next day, when they've got what they want, they don't know you, cut you dead in the street.'

Gomez threw the transcript down. He wasn't listening. He was leaning back, hands folded behind his head, his feet up on his desk. Martinez leaned forward and picked up the printed sheet and started to read.

Gomez asked, 'What was that bit – you know, where Plush says Alison was dealing with the other thing?'

'Right.' Martinez had the cigar between his teeth again and answered out of the side of his mouth. 'It says – here we are – I gave her your cash because she was handling, you know, the other thing—'

Gomez expelled his breath sharply. 'We found nothing when we picked her up. I watched them search her and her luggage. And the Greek, too. Aggressive little sod, he was.'

'I know, boss.' Martinez was still holding the telephone transcript in case Gomez asked him to go over any more of it.

'Alison. Alison what?'

'Delaware,' said Martinez. 'D-E-L . . .' He was starting to spell it but Gomez interrupted.

'Daughter of that Canadian asshole diplomat.'

Martinez said nothing.

'If only they were Americans, not Canadians. We could sew this up if they were Americans, but it's kid gloves for Canadians. Christ, how I hate interfering politicians!'

'Captain, if this conversation tells us anything at all, it's that there is something we still haven't found or figured out. There's money. Instead of Plush paying his stringer, here we have Farr giving money to the American. Now that don't make any sense, at least not to me. And there's this "other thing". What "other thing" can they be talking about?'

'Might be a newspaper story they're cooking up together. I have to say that Farr did produce a couple of very sympathetic articles — maybe they're working on something.'

The expression on the face of Martinez said he didn't believe it.

'Or?' Gomez swung his legs off the desk and lurched upright, the front legs of his chair crashing like two simultaneous gunshots on the floorboards, startling the occupants of the other three desks.

'Or?' Martinez repeated, smoke swirling up around his face. 'Or we simply didn't find it. We missed whatever it was because we weren't looking in the right place.'

'In which case we better find it before our friend Farr does, right? Even better — let's turn up when he gets his sticky little pimp's paws on it.'

Farr wore his tuxedo over an open-necked red silk shirt, tapered black Italian pants, shiny black pumps. His hair was gelled and carefully combed. He had shaved. He had sprayed an expensive French cologne over himself. He had on a second pair of shades. They weren't as good as the fake Raybans, but he thought they looked all right. He felt good, very good, despite the fact that he was down to his last dollars and so far had failed to make contact with the woman named Alison Delaware. His right hand played with the notes in his trouser pocket as if they were a talisman, the equivalent of a comfort blanket. Lydia took up position on his right flank, slipping her hand under his arm, Inez clung to his left with the fingers of both hands, fingers tipped with black nail polish. He walked slowly because they both wore high heels and dresses they must have shoehorned themselves into, Inez in her spangly little black number, her face a mask of inscrutability, a veritable sphinx of illicit sensual promise; Lydia beaming and fidgeting with excitement like a happy puppy with a walk around the park in prospect. She wore a yellow dress that showed off her tan and peroxide hair and threatened to expose pretty well everything else, too. It was the first of two tours Farr had planned, because he felt it was important they meet his contacts on the afternoon shift as well as the evening.

'Tomas, how you doin?'

'Fine, thank you, sir. Ladies.' Tomas, although he was carrying a tray of drinks, succeeded in bowing as their paths crossed, Farr guiding both women out onto the veranda. The professor seemed genuinely pleased to see them. Farr thought he knew why. Sure, Tomas knew all about imperialism. He also knew what was good for business, and what was good for Farr's business was good also for Tomas. How did that *Wall Street Journal* article put it? The trickle-down effect. Oh, yes. There was another term he liked. Revenue stream. Well, Farr's cash trickled down all right. More like the damn Niagara Falls! He said the terms to himself, feeling the unfamiliar shape of the English words with his tongue like a man trying an unfamiliar dish. Farr felt the heads turn, the eyes of the foreigners, tourist touts, security men and staff following their steady progress. Yes, he thought. You look all you want. You want to touch? Go ahead – but you pay. He knew some looked with resentment, others with scorn. It was only envy, he thought. Farr told himself he had learned a long, long time ago that he needed no one's permission to be anything he wanted, and this was just what he wanted, or at least he was on the way to being and having what he wanted. Everything else was unimportant. Everything. Everything else, all the moralising and sanctimonious crap about socialism and history and Revolution and religious faith

and this 'ism' or that 'ism' were just an excuse – an excuse
for being afraid.

'Mr Farr. Good evening.' Assistant manager Sanchez inclined
his head, his bald scalp looking like a huge polished egg in the
subdued foyer lights.

'Mr Sanchez, may I present two young friends of mine, Lydia
and Inez. You'll be seeing more of one another, I'm sure.'

'Enchanted,' said Sanchez, his mouth twitching into something resembling a smile, his fingers more enthusiastically and
effectively grasping hold of the crumpled dollar bill.

Noise, hot air, a wave of chatter and bright lights hit them
as the automatic doors slid open with a sigh.

'Ooh!' said Lydia, and gave a little hop of pleasure.

She tugged Farr's arm.

For her part, Inez gave no hint of interest, but her eyes
scanned the bar beyond the dinner tables set with white
tablecloths and little candles and bunches of flowers. Past the
tourists, the hovering waiters, the young couples cooing at one
another. The mascara-rimmed radar of her glance honed in on
a dishevelled and portly foreigner on his own. He seemed to
notice, for he shifted his fat thighs awkwardly on his stool to
try to see the three newcomers more clearly.

Farr walked his companions around the pool, his arms now
around their waists. They stopped momentarily to admire the
unruffled surface of the dark water, and then they returned full
circle to the bar. By now every male, accompanied or single,
would have noticed them, Farr knew. They all sat down on
stools, Farr on the edge so he wouldn't get in the way of any
action that might develop. He ordered two *cuba libres*, intro-
duced Lydia and Inez to Camillo, the barman, and folded a ten-
dollar tip inside the bill and pushed the saucer over to him.

'I won't be long, darlings. Be good.'

'Don't go,' Lydia said with an exaggerated pout, tugging at
his arm as he began to move away.

'You won't forget what I told you—'

'The condoms? Don't worry.'

Inez hopped off her stool and pecked him on the cheek, then dabbed at the lipstick with a tissue.

Farr strolled away, back to the hotel.

Yes, he did have a temporary cash-flow problem, but if Lydia and Inez did their bit it would be over by morning.

Humming a serene number from the *Havana Flute Ballet* to himself, Farr turned back once, swivelling round on his heels like an infantryman at the tail-end of a foot patrol, and was pleased to see femme fatale Inez was already talking to the lone visitor.

We're back in business, he told himself.

At last.

chapter nineteen

(Capricorn, October 29–30. Don't be so hard to
please. Make an effort to be pleasant. Money is
tight, but not for long.)

An unfamiliar face behind the reception desk appeared before
Farr, but he kept going nonetheless, the casual saunter of a
foreigner entirely at his ease. In fact, it was all to the good
that the clerk didn't know him. He had expected Sanchez, and
the deception had been planned accordingly.

Farr spoke in English.

'I'd like to speak to Alison Delaware, please.'

'Certainly, sir.' The man looked down to check the room
number.

'Think it's three-twenty-two.'

The receptionist looked up, smiled.

'Four-twenty-six, sir. You can use the house phone around
the corner. Just dial nine first.'

'Thanks.' Farr gave the clerk a big smile and walked away.

'Sir?'

'Yes?' Farr swung around.

'Miss Delaware's key is still here, sir. Don't think the lady's
in. Do you want me to page her? She might be in the bar or
having dinner.'

'That's okay, thanks.'

He walked right past the phones and into the men's room. He had no pain, but he still wanted to pee all the time, only now he could only squeeze out a few miserable drops after standing at the urinal and staring at the white tiles for what seemed like ages. He washed his hands carefully, and while drying them on paper napkins from a dispenser above the basins he inspected his own face in the mirror. Already he had a few grey hairs above his ears (Farr called them the outriders of middle age), and little curls of pale hair were actually peeking out of his ears — another recent indication of his four decades. Farr twisted his head sideways, first one way then the other: in the harsh white light the broken veins in his nostrils stood out; nothing to do with middle age this time, but Farr's thankfully brief but near-catastrophic flirtation with Colombian marching powder.

Farr still wanted to pee.

He imagined the gonococcus swimming around in his veins, being pumped through his system by his heart like a miniature Mongol horde heading straight for his brain, divisions peeling off from the main force to assault his joints, his heart valves. Just thinking this way made him feel a little nauseous.

He stood straight, smoothed his lapels, jutted out his chin and winked at himself. He mimicked a black African-American accent and muttered, 'You lookin' good, bro.' He winked ferociously at himself. For good measure he hunched up his shoulders and bent his knees, putting his right foot well back. He started to weave, ducking his head and bouncing on the balls of his feet. He held up his right hand in an imaginary glove close to his face, his left fist leading. In this southpaw stance he threw a couple of quick punches at his own image, a straight left from the shoulder and followed up with a jab with the right.

Back at the phones he dialled nine. Then four-twenty-six. He let it ring a dozen times just to make sure. He turned round so he could see anyone coming around the corner, or anyone watching the corridor from the central area of the lobby. No one paid him the slightest attention. People were coming and going all the time, but none looked down the corridor to where he stood. No one came near him all the time he stood there, in fact, receiver pressed to his ear. He counted the rings.

Farr took the service stairs two at a time.

The corridor was quiet, empty.

It was a corner room, which was a good thing because he couldn't be seen at the door by anyone emerging from the lift or stairs. He had the pass key – actually, it was a copy of a pass key he had 'borrowed' several months ago – in the palm of his right hand. He told himself the only risk was of a guest suddenly emerging out of the opposite room. If that happened the best thing would be simply to smile and say 'good evening' and keep his face averted.

The key went in smoothly. Farr turned the knob gently and pushed the door. It swung inwards easily, silently. No one saw him. Farr stepped inside.

He was careful to close the door behind him, and pocketed the pass key. He turned round again, taking off his shades and facing into the room. He didn't move, but let his eyes get used to the dark.

'Miss Delaware?'

His ears picked up the sounds – laughter from a balcony somewhere above, on another floor, and the quick tapping of a woman's heels above his head. Then a series of grunts and gasps from the room next door. A man's voice, then a girl's cry, muffled but unmistakable and not in anguish, but pleasure – real or simulated Farr couldn't tell.

Alison Delaware had a room, not a suite. The windows were open, the net curtains billowing back and forth in the sea breeze. To Farr's right was a row of walk-in cupboards, to his left the bathroom, the door slightly ajar and the interior quite dark. Farr took two steps forward so he could see the rest of it – the low table, minibar, dressing table and television against the wall to his right, the armchairs and coffee table under the picture window, the double bed to the left. The colour scheme just like Plush's suite – beige, pink and pale green – the carpet thick and deep.

He could smell Alison Delaware's perfume.

White Linen, if he wasn't mistaken.

Farr went back to the door, slipped the 'Please Do Not Disturb' sign on the external doorknob. He locked it from the inside and put on the chain. He strode quickly over to the windows and drew the curtains, making sure there were no gaps between them. Then he put on the main room lights. He had no idea how long he had. He had to assume the worst – that she would be back in minutes.

First the bathroom. Bottles of shampoo, conditioner, skin moisturiser, a bag of make-up, toothpaste and toothbrush in a glass – Farr touched each item with a fingertip. He stirred the contents of the make-up bag with his finger, peering into it. Packets of cream, anonymous bottles full of pink stuff. Nothing. Wet towels underfoot, the tiles above the bath itself still moist with condensation, the plastic shower curtain and white towelling robe behind the door damp to the touch. Farr felt reassured – she couldn't have been out of the room long, and that gave him hope the mysterious Alison was out for the entire evening. Journalists were late-night people, and they liked to hang out in bars long after closing time. They liked to drink. Good.

He stood on the lavatory seat and checked the cistern, behind it, and put a hand in the water itself.

The room was a mess. The bedlinen had been thrown back in a tangled heap. Clothes lay everywhere, mostly T-shirts, skirts and jeans. A suitcase was open, more clothes spilling out of it. Magazines, a hairbrush, a bottle of mineral water and a travel alarm clock coexisted on the bedside table. Farr lay down gently on the carpet, lowering himself like someone doing press-ups, but there was nothing at all under the bed. He went through the bedside cabinet. Nothing. Then the drawers on either side of the television; he drew them open quietly, peered into the back, then slid them shut.

He went over all this territory again, checking the underside of all the horizontal surfaces, from the coffee table to the underside of the drawers. He lifted the mattress on one side, peered underneath, then went round the bed and tried the same thing there.

Guidebooks, empty notebooks, pens.

A Spanish–English dictionary.

A half-empty bottle of Polish vodka.

Farr lifted up the single picture on the wall – a clumsily executed and garish oil painting of Cuban fishing boats at Cienfuegos.

It had to be the walk-in cupboards.

Underwear and stockings in the drawers, flimsy things neatly folded in contrast to the rest. Farr ran his fingers through them searching for – what? A wallet, a notebook? He looked down; two pairs of shoes. He put his hands in the shoes; nothing.

He used both hands to shift the sliding door so that it made no noise on its rollers. Below the clothes and hidden by them – two dresses, a skirt, some lightweight women's pants – there was a big metal suitcase. The kind with reinforced corners that television crews used for their audio-visual equipment. Farr's heart thudded away – this was surely it. Why was it that whatever he was looking for was always in the place he looked last of all? It was immensely heavy . . . Farr altered his stance, turning sideways, one shoulder actually pressing against the dresses inside the cupboard, bending his knees, and tried to lift it a second time, succeeding in getting it up an inch or two, just enough, then swinging it out of the cupboard and into the narrow passageway.

Red-faced, Farr grunted as he set it down. His fingers seemed on fire the moment he released his grip. He got down on his knees, careful to lift up his trousers by pinching them at the crease between thumb and forefinger. He shook his fingers to get the circulation going. He put both hands on either side of the locks. It looked like a well-made combination. He had to decide now. He had a choice. It couldn't wait. He would have liked to have gone down to the bar to see how his girls were doing and have a quiet drink and think about it. Farr, he told himself, you're a procrastinating, cowardly bastard.

The truth of it was that the fastest method was the noisiest; forcing it, in other words.

They were still at it next door. Farr could hear the bed springs twang in rhythmic accompaniment through the party wall.

He took a deep breath. Choose now, he told himself.

The loud knock, behind him and no more than four feet away, made him jump.

There was the briefest pause. Farr was on his feet, swinging the case back into the cupboard.

A coat-hanger snapped under his shoulder and a dress slithered to the bottom of the cupboard.

Another series of loud, impatient knocks followed on the heels of the first.

Farr heard a key slide into the lock and he watched, fascinated, as the doorknob began to turn.

chapter twenty

(Capricorn, October 30–31. There's a new love in
your life – only you're too busy to notice. Make
savings this week.)

Farr curled his right hand firmly around the tumbler of vodka
and orange. It was mostly vodka, a triple or perhaps a quadruple
measure. The first sips had steadied him sufficiently so he could
sit in one of the armchairs under the window and watch the
battle unfold with something approaching dispassion, despite
his being both subject and object of an increasingly heated
dispute. On the face of it the fight seemed an uneven affair,
with two members of the hotel staff and Lieutenant Martinez
of State Security along with his subordinates ranged on one
side against a lone hotel guest, a woman – but what a woman!
She wasn't tall or broad or in any other respect physically
imposing. On the contrary, she was slim, with thick blonde
hair down to her shoulders and in normal circumstances –
and Farr could imagine nothing less normal than the present
situation – a face that would have been both sweet and kind,
the eyes quizzical, interrogative. Now those same blue eyes
were bright with anger, the cheeks flushed, and her voice rose
above everyone else's. She's a Visigoth, Farr thought; perhaps
one of those Teutonic woman warriors straight out of the pages
of *Asterix*. Everyone was speaking at once, Alison Delaware in

fluent Spanish, her arms akimbo, her legs — yes, admit it, Farr said to himself, the legs were really quite exceptionally long and shapely (for a foreigner) — planted well apart like a sailor holding station on a pitching deck.

'I must ask Mr Farr to accompany us.'

'He'll do no such thing.'

'Mrs Delaware—'

'Miss Delaware, if you please.'

'Excuse me, Miss Delaware. This is a criminal matter. It does not involve you. Please.'

The walk-in cupboard was shut, but Farr's attention was on what lay there under the dresses, and the life-saving medicine he presumed the suitcase contained. Just two metres away from him — if he could just take enough pills, slip them into his pocket, this whole mess would be over.

'It does involve me. This is my room. Mr Farr is my guest.'

'Your guest?' Martinez was taken aback.

'You heard what I said. My guest. I asked him to meet me here, and here he is.'

'He is wanted for questioning in connection with a serious crime. The hotel staff said he broke into your room and was in the process of stealing something.'

'I made no complaint. The staff are mistaken. Nothing is missing. That's hardly a serious matter even if it was true, and I know it isn't. Mr Farr and I are friends and colleagues. In fact it isn't anything to do with you at all. Please leave. Now.'

Martinez recovered quickly. He stroked his moustache and adopted an expression of extreme gravity. 'Mr Farr is wanted for something far more serious, Miss Delaware.'

'Then I suggest you question him later. When we have finished. And when Mr Farr has obtained the services of a lawyer. He is entitled to legal representation, is he not?'

'Of course. In Cuba, the justice system—'

'And naturally I will call my father at the Canadian mission in Havana and inform him that my hotel room was invaded by members of state security who harassed me, threatened me—'

Farr took another sip. The father. An image of a man with white hair growing out of the side of his head and plastered carefully over the scalp entered his mind. Delaware. Of course. Why hadn't he made the connection earlier?

'We're not threatening you, Miss—'

'No? You hold me at the airport, you empty my suitcase on the floor, you have me stripped and body-searched. You call this a welcome for a member of the foreign press?' With each rhetorical question, Alison Delaware's voice rose in pitch and volume. 'Mr Farr is a respected journalist, accredited to a leading US newspaper, and you're threatening to drag him off to God knows where without proper authority? Where's your arrest warrant?'

Martinez lost his temper. With a curse he tried to push past Alison to reach Farr, but Alison was having none of it. She deliberately stepped to the side, directly into his path, and put out a hand like a cop nonchalantly stepping out onto a highway and halting rush-hour traffic in mid-flow. Martinez was caught off balance. In trying to avoid the hand and failing to do so (for his chest slammed into it), his knee struck the edge of the bed and he almost fell. Behind Martinez Farr could see the ashen faces of the cleaning lady and the desk clerk. They were trying to tiptoe backwards, to reverse back out of the room into the corridor and make good their escape. Their stratagem failed. They reappeared again, somewhat more rapidly than their exit and more terrified than ever this time, for they had been promptly and roughly propelled back into the room by two plain-clothes heavies guarding the door.

Alison's voice rose to a battle-cry – Farr thought it loud

enough to be heard right down the full length of the corridor, in the adjoining rooms as well as the floors above and below.

Farr was impressed.

'You're assaulting me, Lieutenant. These people are my witnesses. You attacked me! You pushed me and put your hands on my person. I shall file a news story about this incident, and it'll be all over the Spanish-speaking world by morning. In Washington and New York, too. Is that what State Security really wants, Lieutenant? More bad publicity for Cuba? Haven't you people already done enough?'

Martinez let out a low growl of frustration.

He ignored Alison. He seemed unable to look her in the eye. Farr thought it was because his macho sense of himself was too damaged by this salvo. He had lost face badly to a woman. Instead, his maddened gaze locked onto Farr, sitting comfortably and so far as anyone could tell, perfectly composed, externally at any rate.

Farr's apparent indifference made Martinez angrier than ever, his lips drawing back from his teeth like a hungry Dobermann on a short leash.

Farr didn't know how to respond. He lifted the glass and finished off his drink. His face felt scalding hot from the combination of alcohol and adrenalin. He could do with another, then he would be numb enough not to care for a while.

Alison Delaware glanced back at him.

'Don't say anything, Ricardo. Not a word!'

He wasn't planning to. The vodka had done its job well. His lips were numb and he couldn't feel the end of his own tongue.

'Can I have another?' Farr's eyes went to the minibar where the vodka and orange juice had come from.

'No. Not yet. We have things to do and don't have much time.'

We?

It must have shown on his face because she looked down at him and smiled. 'Wasn't that fun? I enjoyed it. Seeing Lieutenant Martinez's face!' She put her head back and laughed.

'God, I wish I had that on camera!' She looked at Farr and her face turned serious again. 'I'm sorry. It can't have been nearly as much fun for you – you're the one they want to arrest. It must have been really scary. What have you done?'

'I'm not sure. Miss Delaware—'

'Alison, Ricardo. Tell me how you got in.' She sat down on the side of the bed nearest to him. She had a narrow waist, he noted, and the broad shoulders of a swimmer with heavy, full breasts under the plain blouse. Delicate wrists, long fingers with plain, varnished nails cut short. The blonde hair was natural with a tendency to curl. Farr thought she was an intriguing mixture of the workmanlike and the feminine, the strong and the weak.

'I had a pass key,' he admitted. 'Or rather, a copy.'

'But why? Why not just call me?'

'I did. I asked at reception. I used the internal phones. I wanted to get hold of you quite badly.'

'It was the money, wasn't it?'

'Ohh—' He rubbed his face with his hand. Did he really have to tell her everything? God, he sounded like a fool. Like a cheap hustler. Well, Farr told himself, that's exactly what he was. But why he should feel shame, even self-doubt, in front of this young woman? He was attracted to her. He was attracted to lots of women, all the time. That didn't make him feel guilty, for heaven's sake. 'Well, yes,' he said. 'Partly that.'

'Partly?' Alison's blue eyes searched his face.

'I talked on the phone to James Plush and he said he'd given you the money and what he called the other thing—'

'It's over there. In the cupboard.' Alison didn't turn when

she spoke, but kept her eyes on him. 'In the big metal case. Everything you asked for, apparently.'

Farr felt very tired. It was as if he was very close to the end of a very long race lasting many weeks, and now he could see the end of it all in front of him.

At last.

'You didn't get my note, then.'

'What note?'

'I left a note for you at reception. They said you took it. That was – umm, yesterday.'

Farr put his hands over his face.

'Oh, shit.'

'What?'

'Nothing.' He shook his head.

'Tell me what happened just now. When you got in.'

He was relieved to have something else to talk about.

'I was looking for the money and the medical supplies. I shut the door behind me, drew the curtains, then put on the light. I searched the bathroom. You know, behind the cistern. Then all the drawers, under your bed.' Farr paused, but Alison nodded encouragingly.

'Go on, Ricardo.'

'Well, just as I was having a look at the case, there was this loud knock at the door.'

A smile crept across Alison's face.

'It happened again. By this time I managed to get the case back into the cupboard. I broke one of your hangers and knocked down a dress. I heard the key turn. Fortunately I had put on the chain. I went over to the door. I said, can't you see the sign? We're busy, I said. Come back later. I said this in Spanish, and I spoke roughly. I tried to sound impatient, angry.'

'Yes? What happened then?' Alison was looking excited, apparently enjoying the story.

'It was a woman. You know, one of the chambermaids. Poor girl. She wanted to turn back the bed. She said she was sorry, and went away. I debated the possibility of climbing out of the window. I looked out, but it was quite a drop and I don't like heights. I mean, I could have moved along the ledge to the next room.' At this point he remembered the noisy lovemaking next door. 'Or the one after that. Tried to get in through the window, then out of the door and down the stairs.'

'Why didn't you?' Alison seemed to be biting her bottom lip.

'Well, as I said, it looked risky. I don't have the head for it. I'm not hero material.'

'Aren't you?' She was grinning at him now, on the edge of laughter. Oddly, Farr thought, he didn't feel offended. He wanted to laugh too.

'So, what did you do?'

'Nothing. I turned the light off, drew the curtains back and sat down here and thought about it. I thought I'd give it ten minutes and try to slip out. I'm afraid in time of crisis I'm not very decisive. I like to think about things first—'

Farr paused.

'You know the rest. The girl – the chambermaid – reported me to the housekeeper, who told reception. A suspicious character in Miss Delaware's room. Reception called hotel security. Hotel security called the police. The police saw I was on the watch list, and they called state security. Sure enough . . .'

'Then I came in and found you.'

'Right.'

'Followed a minute later by Lieutenant Martinez.'

For some reason Alison found this terribly funny. She tried to say something, but couldn't. She was seized by a fit of giggles, then convulsed in mirth, rolling over onto her side of the bed. Again, she tried to speak.

'His face . . .' Alison cried in between gasps for air.

'Martinez . . .' was all Farr could say.

Farr found himself shaking with laughter too, then crying with it. He laughed so hard his sides and facial muscles hurt and the tears ran down his cheeks.

'I think we both need a drink,' Alison said, sitting up. She found tissues in the bathroom, offered one to Farr and blew her nose loudly.

'I suppose it's the tension,' she said. She bent down and opened up the minibar. 'Same again, Ricardo?'

chapter twenty-one

(Capricorn, November 1–2. Someone needs your
help. The weather has changed for the better and
so have your financial prospects.)

'I think you're terribly brave.'

'Me?'

'Yes, Ricardo. Doing this for your city – your country –
despite the best efforts of the authorities to stop you. They've
arrested you, questioned you, beaten you. You've done this all
on your own. That takes real guts.'

'There's nothing brave about it, Miss Delaware—'

'Alison.'

'Yes. Alison.' Farr was having difficulty with the 's' in
Alison's name. He felt the numbness spread from his lips
and tongue to the rest of his body. He could hardly feel his
legs at all. The chair was so comfortable. He never wanted to
get up again. He could sleep there quite happily, all night.

'Somehow you don't look like what I imagined a hero to
be.'

'I don't?'

'I thought you'd be the rough-hewn, unwashed intellectual
type with long straggly hair and a beard and fierce eyes and
wearing shabby clothes. A sort of perpetual student. A rebel,
quoting appropriate texts from famous Spanish authors and

you'd make me feel very small and stupid and unworthy.'
Alison smiled at him, her mouth turning up at the corners,
making little lines in her cheek that Farr wanted to lean over
and kiss.

'I'm sorry I don't live up to your expectations.'

Expectations came out as expectashums, but Alison either
didn't notice or didn't care.

'I prefer the way you are. You're much better-looking than
any dissident I ever met before – and I can assure you I've met
scores, well, dozens, anyway, from all over Central and South
America. Not that looks are important. You're so sweet. So' –
she searched for the word – 'helpless. Or maybe hopeless.'

Farr finished his second vodka of the evening. He liked
the idea of being admired for his courage. Admiration was
itself pretty rare, but the notion of bravery put a whole new
perspective on his character, and he thought he may as well
enjoy it while the illusion lasted. It was nice to be told he was
good-looking – well, in comparison with dissidents. Not that
he knew what dissidents were supposed to look like. Alison said
they were shabbily dressed intellectuals. No wonder he looked
better than they did. The only dissident he knew was a failed
dissident – Dr Garcia. He wasn't at all shabby. Alison clearly
knew nothing of Farr's affliction, and Farr had no intention of
enlightening her. She'd probably find out eventually, but what
did that matter? He wasn't quite sure he wanted to be thought
of as sweet, helpless or hopeless. In need of reform, certainly;
plenty of women had wanted to reform him before now, and
he had been quite happy to encourage them in their ill-placed
optimism – up to a point, the point usually ending in his bed.
The Cuban part of him found it hard to reconcile courage with
sweetness. The English side of him was confused (wasn't it
always?), and as usual had yet to catch up on his emotions,
mixed up both with the effects of the huge measures of vodka
and the physical proximity of Alison herself.

'They'll be waiting for you—'

'What?'

'They'll be downstairs. As soon as you leave this room they'll nab you. You know that, don't you?'

She was right, of course. Farr's mind threw up another series of images; the service stairs, the way out the back, through the kitchens, the iron fire escape that ended down at basement level where the garage opened up behind the hotel in a sweeping drive like an underpass. They would have that covered. What about disguises? A waiter's uniform, perhaps. In his mind's eye he saw the corridor, the lift doors opening, riding down to the lobby, the doors opening and himself striding brazenly through the foyer, the plate-glass front doors in front of him, the duty porter looking up at him, the fiery sunlight of the city in front of him. Beckoning him to the freedom of the streets. Then hands on him, grabbing him, the mocking voice of Lieutenant Martinez, his being half carried outside, feet pedalling furiously trying to find the ground, then pushed into the back seat of the drab radio car Martinez used, an old Skoda, and watched by scores of tourists and the hotel staff – Sanchez, Tomas. He saw Lydia, then, and Inez, both looking worried.

What now, Warren B., my old friend?

'We need a plan,' Alison was saying. 'Even if we could get the suitcase to your place or the hospital—'

Alison was right. They would be waiting wherever he went. They wanted him. They wanted the suitcase, too, apparently in the mistaken belief it contained plastic explosive. Or perhaps they knew perfectly well it didn't, but would plant some plastic in the case anyway. It wouldn't be the first time. There was no knowing the lengths to which Gomez would go for promotion. Right now he felt disarmed, powerless, incapable of speech. The carpet under his feet looked so soft and inviting, he wanted to slide off the chair onto it and go to sleep. Immediately.

'Ricardo, have you eaten anything today? I'm starving after

all that excitement.' Alison already had the room-service menu in her hands. 'Shall I order for us both? What do you like?' Farr's last thought was that Alison never really expected an answer to her questions. When she looked up again she saw that he was asleep, snoring gently, a half-smile on his face.

By the time Alison shook Farr awake, the waiter had come and gone with the food. No doubt he had reported Farr's presence when he got downstairs where Martinez and his men were waiting. He would have to if he wanted to keep his job – and working in dollar hotels was a rare privilege for most Cubans. Alison was saying the coffee would get cold if they waited any longer. He sat up slowly and asked if he could use the bathroom. Once in the privacy of the white-tiled room, he peered at himself in the big wall mirror and discovered to his relief that he didn't look quite as bad as he felt. After taking the inevitable leak, he tried to refresh himself by splashing cold water on his face. He still had puffy blue-grey bags under eyes that had a yellowish tinge to them. He told himself he didn't look all that terrible – just middle-aged and exhausted and rather scared. When he came out, Alison handed him a cup of coffee. She had pulled the two armchairs away from the wall and they sat opposite one another, the room-service trolley between them, Alison spreading a white napkin primly over a shapely knee.

Half a cheeseburger later, Farr was feeling revived, altogether different and above all, able to think.

'Better?'

'Much. Thank you.'

'I ordered a side salad. Have some. It's good for you.'

Obediently Farr stabbed a lettuce leaf with his fork.

'You slept for an hour and a half, you know.'

'I did?'

She smiled at him.

'I hope you don't mind my saying so, Ricardo, but this is quite romantic. It is to me, anyhow.'

She didn't wait for his response.

'Well, look at it from my point of view. I'm sitting opposite a wanted man, a leading dissident, it's after midnight and outside, down in the lobby, the secret police are waiting. You can't say this isn't – well, frankly, rather exciting!'

She put out her left hand and touched his fingers where they gripped his knife.

A leading dissident? God forbid!

Farr didn't think the situation romantic or exciting, in fact, but his mouth was full and he wasn't about to disagree with a new ally in his straitened circumstances. Would Alison have felt romantic if she had known she was alone with a man suffering from an acute and virulent dose of the clap impervious to all except the most modern antibiotics? It was highly unlikely. And it was all very well for these tourists who could come and go, protected by their passports and their embassies. For him there was no way out. Not really. He wanted the suitcase. He wanted what was in the suitcase, but as yet he had no idea how to get hold of it. It was right there, just across the hotel room, and far too heavy for him to carry on his own even if he could get out of the hotel undetected. He thought of asking Alison for the combination, taking what he wanted from the case and escaping, leaving it there. Trouble was, he didn't know what it was he needed. He couldn't pronounce or spell those funny names. He didn't know which to take and in what quantity. He might have to inject himself and he didn't know how. If this was another of Providence's cruel jokes, Farr didn't think much of it.

Farr attacked a slice of cheesecake while Alison poured him a third cup of coffee, emptying the pot.

'I have a plan,' she said. 'I sat there thinking about your situation while you were sleeping.'

He looked up at her.

'But first I really do need some information.'

'What kind of information?'

'I need to know more about you, Ricardo.'

'Me? What about me?' Farr didn't like the sound of this. The less she knew about him, surely the better it would be.

'You are Cuban, aren't you?'

'Certainly I'm Cuban.'

'You were born in Cuba.'

'Yes – Havana.'

It was hard going at first, but they covered the ground of Farr's parents, his childhood in Croydon, his running away and ending up in Santiago de Cuba.

'Do you mind me asking —'

What was the point of minding? Alison could ask whether he minded or not, but it was merely courtesy on her part. She might not look like a bulldozer (she looked anything but), yet she had that steady, irresistible pace of something massive rolling over and squashing any opposition, any doubt. He had never met anyone so self-assured, so single-minded —

—is it really true that you're a pimp?'

He nodded.

'I think that's awful. I'm sorry. But those poor women . . .'

'They'd do it anyway.'

'That's like an arms salesman saying wars happen anyway and if they don't get the weapons from me, they'll get them someplace else.'

'True, isn't it?'

'Hardly the point, Ricardo.'

'Isn't it? Is it better to be poor, to be hungry?'

'Maybe it is.'

'Okay, Alison. I'm a pimp. Though I don't quite see it that

way, however. I regard it as providing a service, a growth industry . . .' Farr told her about his vision for the future. He spoke quickly, earnestly. He forgot for a moment who he was and where he was. Alison watched him closely while he spoke. She didn't interrupt. He spoke about the growth of tourism, about Farr's Friendly Inns. He told Alison about Warren Buffett (it was quite a change, he found, to find someone who actually knew almost as much as he did about his guru), about his work as a tourist guide, ticket tout, driver and dabbler in just about anything that could earn him a few bucks, or even cents.

He described his working girls to her. He recalled the appalling thing that had happened to his precious Lada. In short, he discovered it was easy to talk to Alison. She listened. She was patient. She seemed to understand him in a way no one else he could think of ever had.

'Now your plan, Alison.'

'Yes. In a moment. First the money.'

Farr had almost forgotten.

They both pushed the trolley to one side and moved the chairs back to the wall. Alison put her hands behind her back and seemed to be fiddling with something under her blouse as if she was taking off her bra. Farr, who would have liked nothing better than to get into the big double bed with Alison but knew perfectly well – despite his rising excitement at the thought of it – that in his condition nothing like that was conceivable, was almost relieved when she produced a large and flat money belt instead, in effect a blue cloth strap with pockets and Velcro tapes to fasten it at the back.

'Now I think you gave Plush, what was it, two thousand dollars?'

'Right.'

'You want it all?'

'Well, would you—'

'I think it might be best if you took only what you think you'll need. If you're arrested . . .'

'If I'm arrested I won't see any of it again.'

'So how much do you want?'

'A couple of hundred.' If he could put a down payment on the tyres before he was locked up he would feel a lot better. 'Can you look after the rest for me?'

'Course I can. If you trust me.' She was grinning at him.

She pulled out two hundred-dollar bills and put the rest back.

But what if she left?

'You are staying in Cuba?'

She didn't answer at first. She asked Farr to help her do up the money belt, turning her back and hitching up the blouse again. He pressed the Velcro tapes together, looking at the curve of her neck and wanting very much to kiss it.

'How long depends on our plan and my news editor.'

'Your news editor?'

'I have to convince him it's worth my while staying on a few more days.'

She turned round again to face him.

'And the plan?'

Alison pushed the belt back under her blouse and tightened the strap so it didn't show. 'I think the best thing is to talk it through now. Then we'll sleep on it. You put these chairs together and there are spare blankets in the cupboard. We'll wake up really early and start work. If you agree, that is, Ricardo.'

Did he really have any choice?

chapter twenty-two

(Capricorn, November 2–3. People look forward to
your company. It's how you look at things. Don't
over-indulge or you'll spoil the party.)

Martinez couldn't see Gomez very well. The table lamp was
ineffectual, and all he could make out in the gloom was the
captain's outline, slumped in his favourite chair. Opposite
him was someone else, someone he couldn't identify at all,
except for the glint of buttons on his tunic and stars on his
epaulettes. Enough to tell Martinez that whoever it was he was
important.

'Well, get on with it,' Gomez said.

'He's spending the night with her.'

'In her hotel room?' Gomez sounded surprised.

'Right. I've got a dozen men posted outside, at the lifts,
on the stairs, in the lobby. We're watching his house, the
hospital and Dr Garcia's home. Two radio cars. Hotel phones
monitored.'

'And the suitcase?'

'In the hotel room cupboard.'

There was a pause, broken only by the sound of crickets.

'Why didn't you go in and pick him up along with the
suitcase?'

'You told me to be careful with the Canadian, Captain. You

also said you wanted to pick Farr up with the suitcase in his
possession.'

'What happened?'

'She physically prevented me from reaching Farr. She
accused me of attacking her—'

'Did you?'

'No, Captain.'

Gomez sighed. 'Go on, Martinez.'

'Seems he broke into the room, using a pass key. He was
searching it when he was disturbed by a maid wanting to make
up the bed. She reported it. By the time we got to the hotel,
the woman was already there. Farr was sitting in one of the
armchairs with a drink in his hand. She said he was her guest.
Asked us where our search and arrest warrants were. Started
shouting about the damage I was doing to Cuba's image, and
how she'd write news reports—'

In remembering, Martinez was becoming increasingly agi-
tated. The dim figure in the uniform coughed a wet, rattling
cough.

'I think we get the picture.'

'Sir . . . ?'

Gomez interrupted. 'You two haven't met. Allow me to
present Lieutenant Martinez, my deputy. Lieutenant, this is
General Reyes, of whom you've probably heard.'

Martinez came raggedly to attention.

Reyes made no attempt to rise. Instead he cleared his throat
again and said, 'Relax, Lieutenant. I'd like to know your views
on something. If you don't mind.'

'Of course, Comrade General.'

'Tell me. Is Farr a criminal in your opinion?'

'Undoubtedly.'

'Is that his fault, Lieutenant, or is Cuba to blame? Are we
all to blame for Farr's misdeeds?'

Martinez hesitated. He looked over to where Gomez sat,

but he realised he would get no reinforcements from that quarter.

'We are taught – the Revolution teaches us – that criminals are symptoms of the contradictions in capitalist society—'

'But we are not capitalist—'

'Of course. But the unexpected collapse of the Soviet Union, together with the tightening of the US blockade, has caused a setback . . . it has caused an upset no one could have predicted.' He added, quickly, 'A temporary setback.'

'Good, Martinez. But who is deserving of punishment?'

'There are rehabilitation programmes for people who are willing to learn from their mistakes – but as for the rest . . .'

The general muttered an aside to the effect that the very people one wanted most to enter the rehabilitation programme were those most likely to successfully resist it.

'You were saying, Lieutenant?'

'They have to be removed from society, sir.'

'You wouldn't shoot someone like Farr?'

Martinez was thrown by the question.

'Doesn't society have the right to defend itself?'

'Certainly.'

'A waste of a bullet, perhaps? Is that what you think? It's considerably cheaper than keeping these people alive, Lieutenant. Did you ever think about that? We are at war, you know. Not a war with tanks and planes, perhaps, but a war all the same, and no less bloody in the end.'

'We used to shoot subversives, saboteurs and the like, sir. Before my time. But I'm not sure Farr is in the category—'

'Aren't you? Are you sure?'

Gomez spoke up. 'General, there is no link between Farr and his friends and the pamphlets found in Manzanillo.'

'No? And the plane?'

'Missionaries. Amateurs. An entirely separate matter. Their Cessna ran out of fuel. They thought they could fly under our radar, but failed to take account of the extra fuel consumed at low altitude. They crash-landed off Cabo Corrientos—'

'Idiots,' Martinez said.

'Again, can you be sure?'

'General—'

Reyes held up a hand, the buttons on his uniform winking at Gomez and Martinez as he shifted in his seat.

'What's the charge going to be?'

'Murder, General. That way there will be no grounds for Farr's foreign friends to kick up a fuss. The prosecutor has already been briefed to demand the maximum sentence.'

'You'll make sure the trial is quick?'

'Oh, yes. He knows about that. So do the judges. And a long way from Santiago. A long way from anywhere.'

'You have witnesses?'

'We have a material witness who was at the scene and who will identify Farr at the line-up.'

'Excellent,' said General Reyes.

Farr didn't want to wake up. He tried to get back into the pleasant dream he was having, but Alison was shaking him and wouldn't stop. He pulled the blanket over his face, but she had put the lights on and he couldn't find the dream. Like stopping halfway through a book, he'd lost his place.

She led him to the bathroom and shut the door behind him.

'Have a shower,' she said. 'You'll feel better.'

Standing naked in the bath trying to work out how the power shower worked, Farr heard Alison calling room service. He wondered if state security would prevent them from getting anything to eat – or would perhaps put something in the food to knock them out and get them and the suitcase out of the room without Alison putting up another fight.

Farr was having a little local difficulty. First he managed to soak himself in what felt like freezing water, and he hopped about trying to get warm only to scald his backside with hot water when he turned the tap too far the other way.

'Pancakes,' she said when he emerged. 'Maple syrup, hash browns, eggs sunny side up, coffee, fresh orange juice, toast. Good, huh?'

He did feel better.

'It's still dark out there.'

'We've got work to do,' Alison said.

She sat cross-legged on the bed, already dressed in jeans and T-shirt, a plate balanced precariously on her knees.

'Do you know how to use a PC?'

'No. This is Cuba, remember?'

'No problem. You give me the facts, I'll shove them into shape. Okay?'

'Okay.'

'Sleep all right?'

'I could do with another ten hours.'

'When we're done then you can sleep as long as you want. You're going to need it.' She paused, looking at him. 'I'm really sorry,' she said. 'I wish it was me and not you. I don't want them to hurt you. I hate to think of you there and me here, with all this luxury and food whenever I want it. I'll worry about you all the time, you know.'

'You will?'

She nodded and bent over her ham and eggs, concentrating on eating.

'You're just saying that. Americans are so polite.'

Alison looked up at him, eyes narrowing.

'Is that what you think?'

He could see she was getting angry.

'Well—'

'Is that what you think, Ricardo?'

He remembered the way she had dealt with the secret police.

He didn't want to be on the receiving end of the same kind of treatment, not with a head that felt as delicate as his did.

'Let's get one thing straight, okay?' Alison shook her knife at him. 'What you see is what you get, Ricardo. I say what I mean. Especially with people I care about. I care about what happens to you. You got that, Ricardo? You listening to me?'

'Yes. Of course.'

Farr felt shivery. This American was having a peculiar effect on him, one he couldn't really pin down. He felt terribly thirsty. It must be the vodka, he thought. He emptied his glass of orange juice all in one go. Then he drank his coffee. He hadn't even started to eat yet. When he looked up he saw that Alison was watching him.

'What is it?'

'Nothing. I was thinking.'

'Thinking?'

'Thinking. Wondering what it'll be like for you.'

'Don't,' Farr said. 'It'll be bad enough without thinking about it.' He knew he couldn't do anything else but think about it. Prison. It terrified him.

'You trust me, don't you?' Alison leaned forward and put her empty plate back on the trolley.

'Of course I do.'

'The toast's all yours. But I wonder if you will still trust me when you wake up in whatever place they put you, and there's no water and no food and no news—'

'Stop it, Alison.'

'Okay. I'm sorry. I know I talk too much.'

'I don't mean that. Just let's pretend that nothing is going to happen. That we're having breakfast and then we'll take a walk and maybe stop for a coffee or ice cream. Like ordinary people.'

'Is that what you want, Ricardo, to be ordinary?'

'I suppose not. Only at times like this. When I'm scared.'

'You're scared?'

'Of course I'm scared.'

'I am too. It takes courage to admit to being frightened, especially for a macho Latin male.'

'You do talk an awful lot of rubbish sometimes, Alison.'

She laughed, delighted for some reason. 'Is that so?' She got up off the bed and walked over to him. Her legs were showing because the front of the towelling gown was partly open. Alison made no effort to tighten the cord around her waist.

'You don't mind if I sit here in your lap, do you? Just for a moment? Before we start work? I need to be hugged.'

Farr didn't have to think about it.

'No, of course I don't mind.'

'Hold me tight.'

Farr put his arms round her.

chapter twenty-three

(Capricorn, November 3–4. You owe it to yourself
to have fun. Others may be hurt if you don't say
how you feel. They can't be expected to guess.)

Gomez sounded indignant and incredulous. 'You ask what
will happen to you? You will get what you deserve, that's
what'll happen! You'll be placed in the custody of the prison
department. You'll be processed – like any other common
criminal.'

'What do you mean – processed?'

Farr knew perfectly well, but he was playing Gomez along,
playing dumb.

'There's a procedure for suspects, just as there's a procedure
for everything else in our socialist state. You will be photographed and have your prints taken. You will be stripped of
your clothes and personal belongings. You will receive prison
work clothes. You will be placed in a holding cell. On the day
of your appearance you will be able to wear your own clothes
one last time.'

'Just one day?'

In response Gomez puffed out his cheeks and touched his
moustache, the gestures of a man of importance whose patience
is unreasonably tried.

'I am confident that your trial will last less than that. I have seen the papers. With luck it'll be over in an hour or two. That will save the state time and money.'

'What a comfort it will be to know that.'

This was a cradle-to-grave welfare system, and the state knew what was good for its prisoners even if they failed to appreciate it.

'I won't be questioned?'

'You may be examined in court.'

'You mean——'

'There's nothing I want from you, Farr. We've finished with you. State Security has no further need of you — understand? You are to be formally charged with murder. You will not be granted bail.'

'Murder!'

'What did you expect, Farr? Did you really think you could get away with it? The boy you attacked in the park. You killed him. You were seen attacking him.'

Farr remembered the game of canasta and Varga mocking him about the pickpocket, saying then that the killer was wanted for murder. Making a joke of it, teasing Farr with it.

'Sure there was a pickpocket. He attacked my colleague. The punk had a knife. I stepped in to protect Plush . . .'

'Please.' Gomez held up a hand. 'Your colleague, as you describe him, is a long, long way away and his lies won't help you. The best thing you can do is make a full confession and ask for the court's mercy. The police will take your statement. They will read you your rights. You will have legal counsel. All the proprieties will be observed, believe me.'

He's washing his hands of me, Farr thought.

'My rights, Captain?'

'And please. Farr. No more Captain. As of the beginning of this month, I am Major Gomez.'

No, indeed. No longer a mere Captain in State Security.

Major from now on. Major Gomez told Farr, not entirely without a note of self-satisfaction in his voice, that he had been promoted to a new command. The entire Santiago de Cuba province was now his bailiwick, and all who inhabited the area, some one million souls, were in his solicitous care. Martinez – did Farr remember Martinez? (How could Farr forget?) Martinez was promoted to Captain and the city itself was now his responsibility.

Gomez said that he and Martinez had been elevated for completing their tasks during the trade exposition. Everything had gone smoothly. There were no unusual incidents, or at least if there were, they had escaped the attention of the foreign media. Law and order had been maintained. Foreign terrorist conspiracies were snuffed out.

'You deserve it, Major,' Farr said, his face deadpan.

'Thank you – I'll be pushing papers behind a desk. It's administration and management from now on, Farr. I personally won't be dealing with—'

'Counter-revolutionary and antisocial elements. No more dirt like us under your nails.'

'You put it succinctly.'

Farr said, 'You lied to me, Gomez. You said we were friends. You asked for my help. It's an odd friendship that I'm sitting here waiting to be fitted up with a fake murder conviction and you're standing there preening yourself in your new major's uniform.'

Gomez went pink. 'How dare you—'

'You said you'd try to help.'

'I did. But you went too far. You involved foreigners in a plot to undermine the state. You had materials smuggled into the country—'

'Have you found these materials?'

Gomez looked away.

'That gives me immense satisfaction, Felipe.' Farr used the

first name to provoke, not to appease. 'At least something hasn't worked entirely to plan!'

Gomez got up from his desk and nodded to the two uniformed policemen waiting behind Farr's chair.

They stepped forward and took Farr by the arms, one on each side, one hand gripping the upper arm just below the shoulder, and with the other hand Farr's forearm.

'It's because you couldn't find any so-called evidence——'

Farr was being moved backwards. Gomez wouldn't look at him.

They lifted him up and turned him so that he had his back to Gomez. To finish his sentence Farr twisted his head round to get what he thought could well be his last glimpse of the secret policeman. Instead of being pulled, he was being propelled forward.

'——it's because you couldn't pin anything on me you've invented this murder charge. Right, Major?' They were doing something with his hands, twisting them around behind his back. He felt, but couldn't see, the handcuffs snapped tight onto his wrists. Almost immediately he felt his fingertips tingle and then his hands go numb as the blood supply was cut off.

Farr tried to slow down by dragging his feet. He made one last effort to turn, but the policemen just held him tighter and started to pull him from the office, lifting him slightly off the floor. They seemed indifferent. They knew their business. To them it was just a job . . . routine.

Farr raised his voice as he was pushed through the door.

'How's your sister, Major Gomez? How's Amelia doing now, huh? Did she tell you what she got up to in my room at Las Americas on Tuesdays and Fridays? Did she tell you, Major? Or did you know? Did she call you from the States and give you all the lurid details? Hey, did she? Did she tell you what she liked most? Did you put that in your reports to Havana?'

Gomez didn't move at all until the prisoner had been carried out of his office and he could no longer hear Farr's maniacal laugh ringing down the corridor, mocking him.

Farr was taken straight to a line-up. He was told nothing that could have prepared him for what happened next. Under bright lights and facing what appeared to be a wall mirror, Farr was lined up with six other Cubans. All male, all adult – but otherwise they had nothing in common with one another. They ranged in age from their twenties to their sixties. They were tall, short, fat and thin; it was as if the police had run outside and collared the first seven men they saw. Which was probably pretty close to the truth of it. A cop hung a giant figure seven around Farr's neck. They were prodded into the room in single file, Farr leading, and told to sit down on a bench, toes on the numbers painted on the floor and matching the numbers around their necks. After a few minutes they were told to stand, take a step forward, turn to the right, face front, then the left. A slow and dignified pavane of fake justice, Farr thought. Going through the motions for form's sake.

'Number seven! Remain where you are! The rest of you – move out!'

That was it. He had been identified. Whoever it was had pointed the finger. That one, over there. The foreign-looking man in the dirty clothes with three days' growth of beard. The only foreign-looking man in the line-up, after all. How convenient! Farr didn't need to be told. He felt a great sadness, a resignation settle around him like the noose around the condemned man's neck. He went numbly through the processing Gomez had spoken of, his thoughts and feelings shut off as if a tap had been turned tight closed, silently shuffling like an old man in his ridiculous prison slippers from the handprints to the photographer, standing against a wall with Prisoner Number 769825 held up in front of him. Front, right profile, left profile. His face was expressionless. Another

loser. Another example of street pond life vacuumed up by the
organs of state to protect society from its own worst instincts
and appetites. Farr didn't speak, and the warders said nothing
to him that wasn't absolutely necessary. They did this all the
time, every day, to dozens of people, people who stared back
at their uniformed, armed captors with the same numb, blind,
inevitable hopelessness. 'Step forward.' 'Sign here.' 'Wait.'
'Move forward.' At every stage, hands would guide him, pull
him or push him or hold him still. Steel gates, windows, bars
and chains clanged shut or rattled open. The world was a series
of barred barriers opening and closing. The guards thought
nothing of it, but despite his best efforts Farr winced at each
physical contact, each and every dehumanising touch. He felt
like a post office parcel being stamped and sorted, passed from
one postman to the next. A piece of baggage. Pass the parcel.
This was the famous conveyor.

Farr told himself he wasn't there. He wasn't home. He
was someplace else, left behind. He was stalking the carpeted,
air-conditioned corridors of the Casaverde. He was sitting
outside on the balcony enjoying a *mojito* with Maria in her
midnight-blue lurex or leaning on the bar near the pool with
Lydia, laughing at her innocent stories over an improbable ice
cream. He was taking a stroll at sunset along the seafront,
Inez holding his arm. He was sitting in a bar, hunched over
a Jack Daniel's and gazing into the quizzical blue eyes of Alison
Delaware. Or sitting alone on a hard chair among the family
groups, pensioners and teens at 208 Heredia Street, absorbed in
the rhythms of Afro-Cuban music. It was always free admission
at Casa de la Trova.

How he missed it all!

No, Ricardo Farr was not present. Not today, thank you,
comrades of the prison service. He was somewhere else
entirely.

There were, of course, a few other things Gomez had not

told Farr. The succession of roasting days and chilly nights in a succession of cells, the long road journey out into the sticks, the way the manacles on his ankles chafed the skin raw, the pain making it difficult to maintain the illusion of not-here-in-being. The cup of water for breakfast and, rarely, a teaspoon of sugar to go with it as a special treat, created a terrible, gnawing hunger that quickly made food and the desire for it the overwhelming obsession of every fibre in Farr's otherwise well-fed frame. Stomach cramps were constant, and quickly followed by diarrhoea, and with nowhere to shit he fouled himself and wept like a child because he couldn't help it and above all because he knew they wanted him to feel the sting of humiliation. In the evening, the indigestible corn mash had no impact whatsoever except to bring the hunger pangs to new, exquisite heights of torment. Gomez didn't tell him either of the way the prison truck heated up like an oven on the move from one place to another and often back again, baking him alive as he tried to figure out where they were headed.

East, most certainly.

East. Inland. La Maya, a one-horse town. Mayari Arriba. Not even a horse. Then Seboruco. Matahambre. Nothing on the road to nowhere, and Farr beginning to hallucinate from the heat, thirst and the sudden drop in protein intake.

He could only glimpse the countryside through the barred slit in the side of the truck, twisting himself up, ankles screaming with pain, to see out, guess the angle of the sun, the time of day, the direction. Always east or north-east, Farr thought. It was a land of immense distances surprising for an island: hilly, rolling countryside, lakes and forests and dusty pastures went by, hour after hour. Few cars and even fewer people. No one to see him, hear him. Dirt-poor *campesinos* would have no interest in the fate of a well-fed pimp. Not in someone who preyed on their womenfolk, sold their virtue to satiate the casual lust of foreigners for a handful of dollars and callously murdered a youngster who had only tried to fill his belly by cutting loose a foreigner's wallet. Was this the eternal hell Christians believed in? Had he already died? Only there was no one to answer. No one to hear. They drove on into the night, Farr watched by a lone prison guard clutching a primitive-looking sub-machine gun and nodding off into a fitful sleep and vivid dreams of a smiling Alison, of swimming pools and seascapes, waterfalls, rivers and fountains, of mountains of slow-roast pork and huge ripe mangoes – unable to lie down or stand, Farr moaned to himself, the sound blotted out by the prison truck's engine, his tongue huge and swollen in his aching mouth with its soft, bleeding gums.

chapter twenty-four

(Capricorn, November 27–28. Your sign does
not bless you with an easy disposition. Get out
more. Fresh fruit and vegetables will restore your
humour.)

Farr's awareness of his own trial was fragmentary. He remembered washing in cold water, and attempting to comb his
tangled hair and full beard with trembling fingers. His hair
came down over his ears and collar, filthy and knotted. He
remembered jumping back, startled, at the stranger's gaunt face
with cracked lips and frazzled, maddened eyes that glared back
at him from the dirty mirror. That's me? He stepped up to the
image, wrinkled up his nose and stuck out his tongue to make
sure. He remembered too putting on clothes that were vaguely
familiar as his own but no longer fitted him. He looked down at
himself and was surprised that his trousers were so baggy, the
collar of his shirt so big. He recalled a surge of sudden panic;
how would he cope in the courtroom? Someone, possibly a
sympathetic guard, lent him a length of twine to use as a belt.
He could have it as he was taken out of his cell to the court,
but he had to hand it over on his return for fear he would hang
himself with it; in any event, Farr contented himself with the
thought that as he would be sitting down most of the time, no
one in court would notice his pants anyway. The authorities

had forgotten his shoes, or perhaps they had been stolen; on the other hand it might have been intentional — maybe he wasn't supposed to feel too normal, too equal. Shoes gave a human being a sense of being equal to all the other people who wore them. The community of shoe-wearers was privileged.

As for the rest of it, Farr was conscious of very little that happened in the whitewashed courtroom itself when the time came. Did he perhaps nod off in the dock, wedged between the two prison warders? It wasn't really a dock; it was a scarred schoolroom desk with three chairs, Farr slouched on the centre one, sometimes putting his head down on his folded arms. Was it a form of partial amnesia? He wasn't sure. He saw his lawyer's face for the first time, in court, the lawyer turning, giving him an imperceptible nod. Yes, I'm your defence. That was it. They didn't say anything to one another, not then or later. He heard his own plea of 'not guilty' from his own mouth, a croak that had to be repeated twice for the benefit of the three old men on the judge's bench — again, it wasn't a proper judge's bench but a school bench. The judges, all with faces as wizened as old crab apples, wore jackets but no ties. A rumpled pink sash that crossed each judge's chest was the only badge of office. Farr had to be helped to stand up, and the warders put their hands under his arms so he wouldn't fall over once up and swaying on his feet. Was that the first hearing or the second? Were the two events held in the same place? Farr didn't know. Were they separated by an hour or a week? Farr couldn't tell. He felt no fear, no sense of apprehension at the prospect of a heavy sentence. It wasn't him they were trying, was his main thought. They had his body already, but not him.

Time shrank to instant cravings and the relief of sleep — the terrible wait for food and water, the chill of night and the furnace of day; a cycle of survival was all that mattered now. The world and everything in it was a tight loop of pain. Every sensation, thought and impulse was reduced to the shortest

possible focal length: water and food, then sleep, only thirdly
the issue of being warm or cold. Cleanliness, nice clothes, the
scent and touch of a woman – they simply didn't figure at
all in Farr's shrinking universe. There simply wasn't anything
else. He no longer felt any arousal when he tried to summon
up Amelia, not even longing for Alison whose sweet features
had retreated and finally become irrevocably blurred, the way
television sometimes tries to blot out a face or car registration
during one of those American 'real life' police procedurals.
It wasn't until some time later – to Farr it might have been
years – when he was established in his communal cell in a
municipal jail that his fellow prisoners told him their third-hand
and contradictory versions of what had happened to him.

What they heard had happened to him was not, he had
the presence of mind to realise, synonymous with what had
happened to him. It was an approximation. What he did
not know, even then, was that he had a reputation that
went further than the twelve-by-ten-metre cement-and-breeze-
block cell and its nine occupants, the burning corrugated-
iron roof over their heads, the lime-green lizards with eyes
like marbles that skittered across the walls, the bars, the
pail out in the little courtyard that was in almost constant
demand.

'What's this?

Joaquim Yara bent forward, taking a closer look at the older
man's body.

Farr was pointing at himself, or trying to.

'What's what?'

He was lying on the floor of the cell, flat on his back. He
held his filthy prison shirt up to his neck with one hand. With
the other he tried to direct Yara's gaze to purplish blotches on
his skin that seemed to be linked together and went around his
sternum and up over his shoulders.

'What are these marks on my chest? They go right round like a necklace—'

'Pellagra, man. We've all got it.'

'What is it, though? This pellagra . . .'

'You're an ignorant mother, Farr, you know that?'

'Yes.'

'How long have you been here?'

'I don't know.'

'Look at my legs.'

'They're all swollen.'

'Right. So are yours. So's Enrique's over there. And Hector's. Ariel's ankles are splitting . . . If you press your thigh – right, like that – the dent stays there until the fluid seeps back. You're dying, that's what it is. You're suffering an acute form of immiment death.' Joaquim giggled, a tinkle of hysteria at the back of his throat. 'There are more fancy ways of describing it, of course – it's sometimes called protein and vitamin deficiency, and it's getting so bad you will die. We all will. Of state-administered starvation!'

'Why don't they feed us?'

'Have you looked at our hosts?'

'What do you mean?'

'Our guards. They're starving too. They used to enjoy beating us, but they don't have the strength for it any more: rag-and-bone men. Not as badly off as us, certainly, but they haven't been paid for months. They've got families to feed. The village people won't help them – they stay well away. No one wants to have anything to do with the prison. Too much pain and blood. Bad vibes. People round here are superstitious, and anyhow they fear authority.'

'You're just going to lie there, Joaquim, let it happen, watch us die one at a time until it's your turn?'

'Who do you think I am, Farr? I'm a composer, a musician. I got locked up because they don't like my songs. Charge?

Enemy propaganda. Full term – thirteen years. Just like you, Farr. I'm not Spartacus, you know. They've had me for a year and I'm lucky to be alive. I'm no rebel leader intent on freeing the slaves and marching on Havana. I hardly have the strength to sit up.'

'Why don't we grow our own food? Keep our own chickens and pigs?'

'They used to take the prisoners out every day to work on the prison garden. There was food then, yes, but the prisoners ate little better. It all went into the guards' pockets.'

'And now?'

'Where've you been, Farr? There's a drought, haven't you heard? No rain. The so-called rainy season didn't happen, not in the east. They say it's the El Niño effect.'

Joaquim turned his back on Farr, spindly knees up to his chin.

He started humming to himself, lost in his own world.

Farr pulled himself up.

'Enemy propaganda?'

Joaquim made no reply.

Farr scratched vigorously at his own stomach through his filthy prison uniform. He could feel the lice moving about in the waistband of his blue prison trousers. If only lice were big enough to eat, Farr thought, he'd mash them up into a protein-rich paste with the teaspoon he had managed to hide and was gradually sharpening and straightening to make a crude blade. Why not? It would be like eating himself, after all.

Joaquim was still humming.

Farr had no chance with the cockroaches. There was too much competition. He was one of the oldest and weakest captives, and the roaches all went to the youngest and fittest. Natural selection, and it was probably as it should be. The young deserved to live more than the old. What did roach taste like? A little crunchy, but who the hell cared about taste?

That brief conversation was Farr's first inkling that his murder trial had collapsed, that he had been promoted, as it were, from the rank of dangerous felon to saboteur of the Revolution. The bad news was that a political prisoner (there was no official distinction between the two) was in practice treated infinitely worse than a convicted murderer.

The pellagra was a good example of his superior status.

'Joaquim – when did you last smell onions and peppers frying with garlic on a hot skillet? When did you last taste beans and braised steak?'

Joaquim added percussion to his humming, rat-a-tat-tatum, drowning out Farr's voice.

Death was no vague date with the future. It was no theoretical inevitability. The realisation that it was imminent, that he bore the marks of its steady advance, drove Farr frantic. He told himself they were killing him as surely as if they had put him up against a wall. Only they didn't have to do anything so dramatic or decisive. All it took was a barred cell and a lock and a failure to give him and the other prisoners enough to eat, and he was a dead man. He was dying on his feet, though very quickly he found it hard – and painful – to stand at all. He needed to rest after the slightest physical exertion. He could pull himself upright by clawing his way up the wall, but it was easier to sit. Even sitting was becoming awkward. His buttocks had disappeared, his body having consumed all the stored fatty tissue that would have provided the padding most people took for granted in sitting on a hard surface. It was easier to lie supine, inert, and let the mind drift. Sleep was the painless way to go. It provided the only comfortable escape. Joaquim was there already, floating away from the rest of them inside his own head. No! Farr knew it and he fought it; he told himself he must think and then act, but the longer it took to come up with a solution, the less able he would be to act at all.

Time was running out fast. It was one thing to face a gradual
death over weeks or months through disease, another entirely
to watch himself turn into a skeletal shadow, creeping across
a filthy cell floor, murmuring to himself dreamily, feeling his
own physical being slowly alter its nature, almost preparing
itself for the shallow pauper's grave that awaited him behind
the prison. Life was ebbing away, a rip tide of tissue.

What did he have left? A week? Two?

I must think while I can.

He stared at the bars, ran his fingers over the lock, watched
the guards, memorised the prison routine, listened to everything they said.

What would Warren Buffett have done?

Think, for Chrissakes!

Think!

'Beny—'

The guard turned slowly.

'What's the date, Beny?'

Farr had his arm through the bars. He hung there. It helped
because he could stay upright without putting all his weight on
his painfully swollen feet.

'What the fuck do you care? You won't make Christmas
anyhow, shitface. None of you will.'

Farr brushed the remark aside. All the guards cursed and
used abusive language. It was like the army. It meant nothing.
It wasn't personal.

'I'm not thinking about Christmas, Beny,' he said patiently.
'I'm figuring out a way to get us all some fresh food.'

Beny, a tall man with a thick moustache that drooped down
on both sides of his mouth, giving him a hangdog expression
of infinite pessimism, grunted in contemptuous disbelief.

'Beny!'

Beny turned away from the two-tier gallery of cells.

'Beny, damn you!' Farr slammed his cup into the bars. He did it again and again. He found he enjoyed doing it. It made a terrific din, and then Joaquim and Enrique joined in, not knowing why Farr was doing it or what he wanted – but just for the hell of it. Beny came back with two of his comrades.

'What's your problem?'

'The date, Beny. Tell us the date. Please.'

'November the twenty-seventh.'

'Thank you.'

'Anything else you gentlemen would like, now we're here? Perhaps some *sofrito*, followed by some *fru-fru* or perhaps *picadillo*? Washed down with a few *cuba libres*, huh?'

The three guards laughed.

'Yes,' Farr said. 'Now you mention it, there is something.'

Joaquim and Enrique crawled away, fearing that Farr was inviting trouble unnecessarily. For their part, Beny and his companions stepped closer to the bars. Beny's sweaty face was menacing.

'Oh, yeah?'

'I want to see the boss.'

'He's at home, and he doesn't speak to treasonous scum.'

'He might, though, if the treasonous scum explained how he could get hold of some fresh meat and vegetables – enough to feed everyone here and without any work or payment on his part.'

'You're full of shit.'

Beny shuffled away with his companions.

Farr raised his voice.

'What have you got to lose? Ask him, damn you.'

Silence.

Farr's voice rose to a scream.

'Ask him!'

chapter twenty-five

(Capricorn, December 11–12. Think things through. Don't lose your temper; it's never a pretty sight. Friends send greetings.)

Commandant Luis, as he was known, was slumped across his desk, sound asleep, his mouth open, saliva sliding down onto the rough wooden surface. He didn't stir when Beny and Farr entered, but quivered and twitched and made strange throaty noises. Beny came to an approximation of attention, scraping his feet together and coughing ostentatiously to get his superior's attention.

'Ahem! Commandant! Prisoner Farr . . .'

Commandant Luis opened his eyes, blinked and after a moment's reflection, shut them again. Then he lifted up his head, but he kept his eyes shut. He groaned. He slid back in his chair, raised his chin, putting his head back, and then opened his eyes once more and squinted at the prisoner under eyelids that looked swollen and bruised. For his part, Farr had to hold onto the side of the desk nearest him. He looked back at the prison governor, a man time and the Revolution had left far, far behind. His skeletal form was draped in a uniform shirt both sweat-stained and threadbare, the batting protruding from the collar, the cotton trousers ending several inches above his ankles and so worn there was no colour left in them. The commandant's feet were bare. The brown belt and holster slung across the back of the commandant's chair were cracked and worn with age. The leather had entirely lost its shine.

A strong smell of stale rum filled the room when Commandant Luis spoke.

'Okay, Farr.' Commandant Luis kept one hand over his eyes, shading them as if the light hurt, peering at Farr like a man looking out to sea, the sun in his face. The commandant sighed deeply, a sigh of someone who had heard it all before – the appeals for clemency, assertions of innocence, offers to turn informer, the squeals and yelps of dementia, the blubbering of fear and tearful, pathetic pleas for mercy. Commandant Luis was well over sixty, and well acquainted with the peculiarities of human nature, and he had seen it all, knew it all and no doubt done much of it himself. Very little could surprise Commandant Luis.

'Say your piece, prisoner, and then get the fuck out.'

He turned his head and spat something green and nasty onto the floor.

Farr spoke for a minute – almost to the second. He had rehearsed what he was going to say, using his fellow prisoners as his critics, honing it down and keeping it simple and to the point. Above all it had to be practicable and brief, covering all possible objections and difficulties that the commandant could throw at him.

When he finished, Commandant Luis shut his eyes again for several seconds.

'So you're a celebrity, Farr.'

'I wouldn't say that, Commandant.'

Luis's black eyes burned with something Farr couldn't identify, something that made him feel acutely uncomfortable.

Hate? Anger? Scorn?

'If you're lying to me, Farr, if this is some kind of trick or stunt you're trying to pull, you're a dead man. Hear me?'

There was a sticky white froth in the corners of the commandant's lips. Commandant Luis turned, tugged the pistol out of the holster, checked to see there was a round in the chamber, and, satisfied that there was, gently placed the weapon in front of him, next to his right hand.

Farr said nothing. The gun was a worn antique of dull metal, all the blue gone from the steel. They were going to die anyway, weren't they? A bullet might be preferable to the indignity and pain of a slow death by starvation. Farr counted the seconds. There wouldn't be another chance. Would this impoverished revolutionary swallow advice from a self-styled capitalist and stooge of the imperialist media? Farr looked at Commandant Luis and Commandant Luis stared back at him, his eyes mere slits as if at any moment he might go back to sleep again. The commandant had skin like ebony, tight and shiny where it stretched against bone, sunken cheeks and a full, contemptuous mouth that suggested he had witnessed most of what the world had to offer, and was impressed by none of it. His hair was curled tight and completely white all over, as if someone had rubbed ash into his scalp.

'Take off his cuffs.'

Beny hesitated, then complied and Farr felt pain as the blood rushed back into his fingers. It was all he could do not to cry out.

Commandant Luis put a hand out and touched the telephone.

God Almighty, Farr thought, he's going to do it!

'The number?'

Farr gave it to him, one digit at a time as Commandant Luis dialled, ever so slowly. Farr's heart thumped so hard he thought he was going to faint right there. He had to force himself to breathe evenly, deeply. He watched the commandant's long, bony forefinger do the dialling. He must have swayed a little because Beny held him firmly by the upper arm, keeping him upright. Farr was not a praying man. He wasn't even superstitious, but if ever he felt like praying to the God in which he couldn't bring himself to believe, he knew it was this moment.

Farr learned that there had been two so-called trials, both hastily organised in village schoolrooms and a long, long way from Santiago, the media and the reach of foreign diplomats. The first collapsed when the state's star witness staged a protest of her own, during which she had pointed out that Farr had been the only foreign-looking suspect in the line-up and that that was why she had picked him out. She had seen two foreigners in the park, one of them immensely tall and wearing a broad-brimmed cowboy hat, but it was his companion who had struck the youth, then kicked him – but it was too dark to make him out clearly. Yes, it could be the man in the dock, but the witness had her own protest to make against the system she detested, and had to be dragged, kicking and screaming, from the courtroom. Farr didn't even know her name. No one else in his cell did, either. He remembered the black leather festooned with zips and chains, the punk hair style and make-up, the ring through her lip (was it her tongue, too?), her Parthian shot of abuse – 'cocksucker' – as she and her companions scattered through the trees of Cespedes Park. She was a member of what Farr knew to be an outlandish underground group known as *roqueros* – rockers – heavy-metal addicts and alienated teenage nihilists who took the Cuban slogan Death or Socialism to heart, preferring an early death to the official version of socialism and state welfare. Farr had heard it said that members of the roqueros' extremist fringe had even injected themselves with HIV-infected blood – and spent their final days locked up in the sanatoria established by the authorities to isolate the island's AIDS sufferers.

Farr's second trial, hastily arranged three days after the first and involving more erratic journeys by prison van from one town to another, had reverted to the political crime of enemy propaganda. Farr knew it must have been a far from perfect solution for the authorities, but neither the prisoners nor the guards could enlighten him as to why that particular charge had been brought. The prosecutor demanded the maximum sentence of thirteen years, and after two hours it was all over. Farr hoped it was because Alison had carried out their plan, and that this was what lay behind the 'propaganda' – but he had no real way of knowing. Alison, Plush and the rest of them – Garcia and Amelia, Maria, Lydia and Inez – seemed to belong to another universe now, a dream as faded as ancient parchment. He had not seen a newspaper or heard a radio news bulletin since his arrest. That was presumably why Gomez had had him shipped out east, and had these trials improvised on the hoof, as it were, well out of range of anyone who might have taken an interest in his fate.

Commandant Luis put a hand over the mouthpiece.

'The name. Give me the name.'

'Carlos Rodriguez.'

'Mr Rodriguez, please.'

Farr looked at Beny. He had to sit down. Beny let go of him and Farr sat carefully down on the commandant's office floor, holding onto the wall and sliding down slowly. From there, staring at the commandant's horny feet, he heard half of the conversation.

'He's here, Mr Rodriguez, but he can't come to the phone just now. Yes, of course he's alive. He's right here. He will supply a month's contributions at a time and can start work on them immediately. From January the first. Yes. No problem. But the payment – that is something that has to be changed. No, not money, Mr Rodriguez. Mr Farr wants his wages in kind – in food. Well, let's say chickens cost— Yes, that's fine. Every week would be best. By weight? Yes. Let me explain where it should be sent. Can you start at once? Luis Vilero, Commandant, Palenque Jail, Palenque. Sure. That would be good. Thank you. How much? I understand. We appreciate it. I will pass on your good wishes. Who am I? I am Vilero, the prison commandant. I will tell him. Yes, I will pass on your good wishes . . . Yes, yes.'

For four days nothing happened. For four days and four nights Farr lay in the cell, listening to the world around him. He slept very little. He watched the grey first light creep in between the bars and listened to the pail of water being brought in the early morning by the duty prisoner, the rattle of the bars as 'breakfast' was announced, the ritual tramp and shouted obscenities of the guards at morning roll-call. No one talked to him. They left him alone. At night he heard the whispers. Farr had lost his marbles. Farr had big *cojones* going to Commandant Luis, no question, but the old man would surely kill him for making a fool of him. Silly fucker – his con tricks wouldn't work with old Luis, no sir!

In the old days the two galleries of cells had housed three hundred prisoners, crammed so tight they could barely sit and had to take turns sleeping. Luis was there then, too. There was a confrontation over prison dress. The politicals demanded to be treated differently, and there had been brutal fights. A guard had died, and the firing squad had worked all night to exact vengeance. Then came the releases in the 1980s, and again after the Pope's visit. Now they were down to nine prisoners and six guards – all that was left – and Luis, a local man who had risen through the ranks, was given command of the old shell of a prison. Most of the cells were empty, save for the odd village drunk or petty thief.

Sometime before dawn on the fifth day, Joaquim died, all hope drained out of him. He didn't make a sound. He didn't say anything. He just didn't wake up with everyone else, and when his body was discovered at roll-call, two prisoners were 'volunteered' to haul his corpse out. Farr wept. He turned his face to the wall. For the first time in his life he felt a failure. He felt it was his fault the boy had died. He should have kept his big trap shut. Joaquim and the others had believed him. Not at first, of course. But when he came back, alive and in one piece, from the commandant's office, he could see the hope seep back into their eyes. Trouble was, he yearned for the respect of other people; he couldn't resist talking more than he should, offering more than he had to give.

Farr told himself he wasn't guilty the way the State said he was. He didn't do anything wrong as far as the charge brought against him was concerned. The law was crooked, its enforcers more crooked still. But Farr told himself he was guilty as hell, guilty of all the other things he had done in his life, guilty of promising what he couldn't deliver, guilty of pride and guilty of greed. He cried for Joaquim, he cried for the youth he had inadvertently killed and finally he cried for himself. He cried like a child, helplessly. He had hated Garcia for his goodness and simplicity, and not content with that, had taken his wife. He had hated Garcia because he had offended him when it was Garcia who should have done the hating. Now his boasting had taken the life of a virtual stranger, and someone a lot more principled than himself, to teach him that lesson.

I deserve to die, Farr thought.

It's justice that I do.

He lay soaked in self-pity on the cement, in the midst of other men yet terribly alone, keeping away from the bars, knees drawn up to his chest, ears pricked for Commandant Luis approaching quietly on bare feet, his old revolver in hand, Beny sliding open the barred door so Luis could slip in and finish him off.

None of the prisoners would try to stop him, Farr knew.

Hell, they'd be doing him a favour, a kindness.

chapter twenty-six

(Capricorn, December 12–13. Mars spells trouble,
Pluto confusion. Stick to your plan and you will
have nothing to worry about. Enjoy the good
weather.)

Farr was having the most wonderful dream. He was feeling
happy. He was smiling, enjoying himself. Alison was offering
him something, a bowl, and it was full to the brim with the
most delicious food. He could smell the garlic, the cumin,
the parsley and the meat. Onions, too. Chicken, was it? She
was saying, 'Take it, Ricardo. Go on, there's plenty, eat.' He
couldn't see her face, not really; he could see her long pale
arm holding out the plate, hear her voice. The food was very
close to his face, but the sun was in his eyes, the sea – he could
hear the sea and the cry of gulls – and he was trying to sit up,
smiling back at her, nodding and putting out his hand to take
the plate. He felt relaxed, pleased. Somehow he couldn't get
hold of the plate now, and in the end it was his own voice that
he heard, and it woke him up.

'I can't—'

'Yes, you can. Here, let me help you.' It wasn't Alison's
voice. It was Hector's, and someone else was propping him
up.

'Give him room.' Farr didn't want to wake up. He wanted to

go back to the dream. It was so nice. But Enrique was towering above him and using his hands to push the other prisoners back. 'Let him get some air.'

'They took it all. I don't have the money—' Farr said, not knowing why he said it. Something that had happened earlier.

'He's talking to himself.'

'He was dreaming.'

'Don't let him overdo it.'

'You've already paid for it, friend.'

The voices of his fellow prisoners seemed a distant chorus, nothing to do with him. Something hot and metallic touched his teeth, then pushed between his lips. Instinctively he pulled away and started to fight them off, but they were holding his head. A spoon . . . then hot liquid, with a taste so vivid, so fierce it burst like a firework display in his brain, a frenzy of heat and flavours, a sunburst of colours, trickled hotly over his tongue and headed down his throat.

Instinctively, like a calf nuzzling furiously for its mother's teat, Farr grabbed the plate with both hands . . .

'Hey, watch it!'

He put his mouth to it, stretching out his lips, ignoring the spoon, the hands that held him, the voices urging restraint and caution, grunting in his effort to lean forward. Never mind if it scalded him.

Farr lapped up the broth. He made a loud sucking, grunting noise. He found sucking more effective than lapping, so he stuck to that method. He pulled the plate in to his chest with both hands, wildly, furiously, ducking his head lest anyone try to get it and the food away from him. He held it there, elbows in to his ribs, chin and nose in the gravy. The slivers of meat, the little bits of onion and tomato, the rice and beans floating in the greasy mixture, they were all sucked up, chewed and swallowed. His jaws worked frantically to process as much of the soup as he could as fast he could so he could suck in more.

clap

The heat of the food and its effect on his rotting gums and chafed lips made his eyes and nose run, but Farr didn't care. While this was going on, his eyes darted back and forth like an animal guarding its prey from competing predators, anxious lest it be taken from him by force.

'Slowly does it, friend.'

'*Puneta*! He'll make himself ill.'

Farr took no notice. His mind wasn't in charge. His body was. His need for food was supreme, the instinctive demand pushing everything else aside as he frantically vacuumed up everything on the plate. When there was nothing else he tipped it up, and when the last drops had fallen onto his swollen tongue, he licked the plate. No matter that some of it had dribbled down his chin and leaked into his matted beard. Farr licked the bowl the way a cat licks, in long, studied strokes.

'Good, huh?'

Yes. It was good.

The voice was Beny's.

'No more now, or you'll get the shits all over again.'

Farr looked up. He looked up because of the applause rippling around him. It started with a few slow handclaps, and now everyone was doing it. Standing – and in the case of the weak, sitting – in a circle around him, bringing their hands together, guards and prisoners. Banging their tin mugs and bowls on the bars in unison, making a fearsome racket. They were all smiling at Farr. Applauding him. They had given him the first helping. Now it was their turn.

'Close the door – Beny, outside, please.' When they were alone, Commandant Luis nodded at Farr. 'Sit.'

Farr pulled the only other chair back from the desk and sat down. He folded his arms and waited.

'How's it going, Farr?'

'We've formed a committee. Hector does the writing.

Enrique, Jose and I divide up the zodiac into three stars each, and we revise each other's work. Hector puts down the first draft. We try it out on our colleagues before we produce the final version . . .'

'You'll finish the first month in time?'

'It's nearly four hundred entries, and we're about halfway through.'

'Anything you need?'

'More paper and pencils would be good. If you can let us use this office of yours for an extra hour it would help. When you don't need it, that is.'

Luis nodded. 'It's done. However, there are one or two other matters we need to discuss.' He leaned forward, elbows on the table, fingers to his lips, frowning. 'There was a matter of backpay. I didn't tell you before. You were too sick. Two hundred pesos in all. We used it to buy fruit and vegetables.'

'Good. I've no problem with that.'

'No – but there are complications.'

'Such as?'

'Local people quickly noticed that we had money. My mistake. And of course not all the guards are so discreet. Within a week or so we all began to put on a little weight and looked healthier, and I think some of the warders' wives found their husbands were taking more interest – if you take my meaning – and that prompted talk. News spreads fast in a place like this. So now everyone in the damn village knows we have a famous astrologer among our guests of the state—'

'Damnation.'

'That's not all.' The commandant paused, as if trying to find the right words to express it. 'Your friends at *Diario* back in Santiago have run a story about the astrologer who is feeding an entire prison, guards and inmates alike, with the income from his predictions. On the front page.'

Farr was secretly delighted, but he tried to look suitably

appalled. He looked down at his feet and shook his head, trying to hold down the excitement bubbling up in his chest.

'The only consolation is that they had the decency not to say where it was. The prison, I mean.'

'That's good.'

'What I'm trying to say is that I don't know how long this will last. Before the authorities put a stop to it.'

'What do you propose?'

'Ask for a raise when you send off the first month's contributions. In cash. Not much – but something we can put aside for lean days. A sort of emergency reserve.'

'That's a good idea, Commandant.'

'You're a different man, Farr. A week ago we thought you were going to die. We thought—'

'I know.'

Farr didn't want to remember. How he Farr and four of the other prisoners who couldn't walk had taken a cup of broth each day. As their strength returned, the ration was increased, with half an orange in the mornings and a slice of tamplain at night. Now everyone ate together at noon in the courtyard outside the cells, guards and prisoners sitting in a circle. A large plate of chicken or pork and vegetables, a chunk of bread and a portion of fruit. Jose, a prisoner with a penchant for cooking, had been elected by the prison to add variety to the diet. That very day they had eaten *sofrito*, a paste of finely chopped onion, garlic and green pepper cooked in olive oil along with *picadillo*, or meat hash.

'Farr—'

'Yes?'

'When prisoners are starving, they make no trouble. They are too weak . . . When I was young it was used deliberately to keep them docile, you understand.'

'And when they are properly fed they start to make demands, become difficult and then there's trouble —'

'Yes. That's exactly it. You know. It would be a pity —'

'But you know too, Commandant, that you can stop this food any time you want. And while you can do that, we are not going to give you any trouble. You have my personal guarantee. If you like, I will talk to the others about this. There are only eight of us and six of you. You have the keys to the cells and the guns and cudgels. If we are stronger, so are your men. I have the stars and between us we can keep matters calm.'

Luis looked relieved.

'But there's one thing I must ask of you,' Farr said quickly, knowing he had to capitalise on every opportunity that presented itself. 'In confidence, Commandant. A personal favour. It's how all this business started with me. A matter of antibiotics . . .'

The very next day, and exactly two weeks after the first consignment of food had arrived at the jail, the commandant appeared in person outside the cells and asked Beny to let Farr out. He had something to say to him.

'Feel like a walk?'

'Certainly, Commandant.' Farr had become the unofficial, unelected spokesman for the eight prisoners, but he always made a point of calling Vilero by his rank. It put a little distance between them and, Farr thought, reassured the old prison officer that his authority was still intact.

'Have you ever seen what our garden looked like?'

'No, Commandant.'

Commandant Luis used the key on his belt to let them out of the big double doors into the street. Farr stared at everything around him. He felt light-headed at all the space and colour, especially the dusty road rising and falling into the distance, the blue hills, the warm breeze in his face. They walked together around the prison building.

There was nothing left of it, just a rectangle of dry red

earth, overgrown with weeds. Farr leaned against the wall. He felt dizzy.

'I thought,' Commandant Luis said, 'that after a while, we could perhaps bring all this back to life. We could irrigate it, perhaps, trap water from the drainpipes when the rains come . . .'

'We need tools and seeds.'

'I was thinking in the long term. When the rains do finally arrive . . .'

'You didn't really bring me out here to talk about your agricultural ambitions, Commandant.'

'I had a call yesterday.'

He picked his words with care, not sure of the best way to proceed.

'Yes?'

'I shouldn't tell you any of this, you understand, but I felt I should prepare you. Prepare all of us, in fact. The call concerned you. It was from Havana. You're leaving us.'

'When?'

'They're sending transport. Tomorrow morning sometime. Have you heard of the Villa Marista?'

'Everyone's heard of the Villa Marista, Commandant. It's State Security headquarters.'

'That's where the call came from.'

'Why me? Why now?'

'They didn't say. Those people—'

He left it hanging in the air. The way he said it. Those people. *Que hombres . . .*

They turned and started to walk back. Farr thought, I could knock him down easily. He's old and frail. I could take his gun and be off. A few days on the run would be better than a bucket of water and electrodes clipped to lips and balls . . .

'Don't even think it,' Commandant Luis said, glancing at

Farr and smiling at him. 'I've seen that look on a hundred prisoners' faces. Their graves are round the back.'

At the double doors, Commandant Luis hesitated.

He looked down at the ground and poked at something with his foot, suddenly embarrassed.

'We're grateful to you, Farr,' he mumbled. 'I'm sorry it's ending like this. I thought—'

'Nothing's ended, Commandant.'

Commandant Luis looked up.

'"Farr's Stars" will go on. The committee will carry on perfectly without me. Hector knows my style, the others know the basic characteristics of each sign. We've plotted what planet goes where for the next twelve months. They have all my notes. Just make sure they keep to the deadline.'

'And the newspaper?'

'Who's going to tell them?'

'But if they find out somehow?'

'It's in their interest to keep it to themselves, don't you think? Their readers want the astrology column. Apart from the sports section, it's the most widely read part of the paper. They carried the story that their astrologer was keeping an entire prison alive. Are they going to tell their readers that's all finished? That "Farr's Stars" was made up? That it's written by a committee? Of course not. It's cheap at the price.'

'Cheap? What is?'

'Maintaining circulation for what? Three chickens and a few yams? The odd leg of pork? Isn't that a small price to pay to give the citizens of Santiago a little bit of hope, Commandant?'

'Only it's nonsense. We both know that.'

'Yes, Commandant. We all say we prefer the truth even if it hurts – only it's not true for most of us. I'd rather be told a sweet lie that makes me feel better about the future. I think that goes for most people who buy the *Diario*, don't you think?'

chapter twenty-seven

(Capricorn, December 13–14. A change of career seems likely. You may well make a sudden journey. You can't put off others' demands on your time.)

An ominous silence settled over the prison, a sense of siege, an air of threat like the electricity in the air at the approach of the first summer rainstorms, the tension affecting both prisoners and guards alike, making them tetchy and irritable with one another over trifling matters. Enrique kept dropping things, Hector was late on latrine duty, Alfonso nearly got into a punch-up with a guard over the next week's menu and the committee of astrologers argued fretfully over the nature of Aquarians. Orders were given for the following day's meal to be prepared in advance, so that the strangers would detect no smell of cooking. It would also ensure that the next day's distribution and consumption of rations would be swift. The visitors could not be permitted to see the extent of prison cuisine.

The food store was broken up and items distributed to the guards' own homes, the cell and courtyard were washed down, the little luxuries men accumulate during years of captivity carefully hidden (for Farr that meant inserting his home-made knife in a crack in the wall). Who knew what these people would be like, how many there would be, and what they would want – apart from Farr? The two words Villa Marista were enough to spur everyone into a frenzy of activity. Finally, shortly before midnight, Commandant Luis left instructions that he was to be woken at first light and made his way home, while Farr and his fellow committee members worked into the early hours preparing as many of the January forecasts as they could under the paternal eye of Beny, the commandant's deputy. Farr was now a supervisor who checked the final phrasing, the planetary references and made sure that each prediction was 'true to character' for the sign concerned. All the real work was left to the men who would stay behind.

In the morning, prisoners and guards shook Farr's hand.
'Good luck.'
'Hey, I'll buy you a drink when I'm next in Santiago!'
'Keep one of your girls for me!'
'Bring us some rum when you get back . . . or else!'
'Can you deliver this letter to my family?'
'You're checking out of this hotel? What is it with you, Ricardo? You prefer the comforts of the Villa Marista, huh?'

Farr didn't know what to say. Neither did anyone else, not really. The flippancy of the farewell remarks, the effort to make a joke of it, slaps on the back and finger-crunching handshakes, the hugs and kisses on the cheek were all well meant – intended to cheer him, show him how much they would miss him. But he thought they looked at him as if he were already dead. Not there. Already scratched off the list – another ration to be shared out, another space to be taken over in the cell, after all! Farr told himself that would have been exactly his own reaction. A New Business Opportunity. Wasn't that what he used to call somebody else's misfortune and his opportunity to exploit it? How odd, how extraordinarily out of place that phrase seemed . . . He knew that they knew few men and women who had ever been granted the hospitality of Villa Marista were allowed to walk out whole and free again. Whole and free. Whole and free. What a wonderful, beautiful and improbable dream . . .

I'll settle for home, Farr thought, and maybe one of those ordinary, day-to-day jobs I used so much to despise.

When they did finally come for him, it wasn't until the next evening and everyone, including Farr, was so thoroughly tired of waiting, the event itself seemed an anticlimax.

The first man in the black leather jacket asked, 'Where's the *extranjero*?'

His companion said, puzzled: 'Foreigner? He's foreign?'

'Isn't he a foreigner?' The first man was asking anyone but no one in particular, as if he didn't really expect an answer.

'He looks like a foreigner.'

The first man looked at the papers in his hand. 'His name is foreign-sounding.'

'This way, gentlemen.' Commandant Luis, respectful but insistent, led the two agents to his office. There was no need for them to see things they didn't need to see.

'Are his things ready?' The man in the leather jacket held out his State Security ID, a little card behind scratched plastic. He had a fleshy face and protuberant eyes. He was clean-shaven. He smelled of soap, and there was the bulge of what appeared to be a pistol under his arm.

'He's wearing his own clothes,' Commandant Luis said. 'There's nothing else. He has nothing else.'

'We have the release order transferring him into our custody,' said the second man. 'We both sign. In triplicate. You keep a copy. I sign for the Interior Ministry.'

They signed, taking turns to bend down over the table, take up the pen, the first agent pointing to the right place. Commandant Luis was last. He straightened up and carefully folded one of the copies.

'That's it?' he asked.

'Sure,' said the first agent.

'What happens to him?' It was Beny, unable to resist the

temptation to ask, to take something back for the guards and prisoners. The other three men turned their heads and looked at Beny as if they hadn't seen him there, by the door.

'We take him to Havana,' said the second agent. He had on a very rumpled blue tropical suit. The sleeves almost covered his hands and the collar was too big for him, so much so that there was a gap of a couple of inches between the back of his neck and the jacket. His belly hung out over his belt.

'Where's the prisoner?' The first agent glared at the second hard as he said it. His eyes said: shut the fuck up in front of these civilians.

Commandant Luis shot a glance at Beny.

'He'll get him for you,' Commandant Luis said.

'Has the prisoner been searched?'

'Searched?'

'Strip-searched. He must be strip-searched.'

Commandant Luis went to the door and called Beny.

'Beny—'

'Yes, boss?' Beny turned round.

'Make sure Farr is strip-searched. Now.'

Commandant Luis gave Beny an exaggerated wink.

'Are you Ricardo Farr?'

'Yes.'

'You don't look at all like your picture,' said the second agent. He said it doubtfully, as if Farr might be an imposter.

Farr looked at their feet. Mr Long – his own name for the taller, first agent – was well-shod in shiny black leather shoes with tassles to match his black leather jacket. The shoes might not be Italian, but they looked it. That meant he was *nomenklatura*. Not just Party, but one of the gilded elite with access to dollar shops. His companion, Mr Short, the second agent from the Interior Ministry, was nowhere near in the pecking order. His shoes were leather but old and torn, the heels worn away to the uppers. Mr

Short was meaner than Mr Long, less sure of himself and that meant more aggressive. Farr resolved to keep well away from Mr Short if he could, and to try to get on the right side of Mr Long. Beny opened the door of the commandant's office and stood aside. As a reflex Farr put his hands out, wrists together, for the cuffs.

Mr Long shook his head. It was a look that was neither friendly nor hostile.

'We'll have to get his beard and hair cut,' Mr Short said to Mr Long. 'And do something about – those.' Mr Short contrived to look at Farr's clothes without looking at Farr himself.

Commandant Luis and Farr said goodbye. They didn't speak. Their eyes met across the desk. Commandant Luis did not want to show these men from Havana that Farr was more friend than captive because he might suffer for it, while Farr did not want to get the old man into difficulties over the food and other privileges. Left alone, they would have embraced, clasped hands, wished each other well. This was all they could do: a look of complicity. Farr said to himself, goodbye old friend.

Farr turned. Mr Short went first, Farr in the middle, then Mr Long. When they reached the front doors, the sound of the prisoners could be heard quite clearly. 'Ric-ar-do! Ric-ar-do! Ric-ar-do!' They were chanting his name and banging their tin mugs against the bars in unison, the way Cubans did it in the old days for the President. Fi-del! Fi-del! Mr Long and Mr Short did not react. They had decided not to hear it.

Mr Short got behind the wheel of two Ladas welded together, a Creole Limo in local parlance, its paintwork so faded in places it seemed somewhere between pink and beige. Mr Long held a rear door open for Farr, who slid along the back seat to make room. Mr Long got in after him. Farr turned round just in time to see Commandant Luis raise a hand before the dust from the street kicked up by the tyres obliterated his last view of the prison.

'We'll find a barber in Bayamo,' Mr Long said.

'Right,' said Mr Short.

'And a new shirt and pants,' Mr Long added, looking sideways at Farr. 'He'd better have socks as well.'

'Right,' Mr Short said again.

'His shoes are okay,' said Mr Long.

'Uh-huh,' said Mr Short.

The two agents said nothing at all directly to Farr until they reached the airfield at Bayamo. If they spoke at all it was across him, about him, but never to him. Farr didn't mind. He was busy getting used to the huge distances, the sky, the sense of movement. Again, he had the sensation of being light-headed, and he had a slight pain from behind the eyes. Perhaps they weren't used to focusing on things so far off. On the way Mr Short stayed in the car and Mr Long read a paperback book in a chair behind Farr, while the barber cut Farr's hair short and shaved off his beard. Farr could make out the title in the mirror: *Como Ganar Amigos e Influir Sobre Las Personas*. How to Win Friends and Influence People. It was Mr Long who bought a short-sleeved blue shirt, a pair of Manila trousers and socks for Farr. It was Mr Long who waited while Farr changed into them and it was Mr Long who paid for the items in cash.

When they finally reached the airfield it was quite dark. Mr Long shepherded Farr on board the Cubana Antonov-24 and they sat next to one another. Mr Long still had his gun, a Russian Tokarev. As far as Farr could tell, they were the only passengers. Mr Short, meanwhile, waited until the steps were taken away and the cabin door shut before climbing back into the Creole Limo and driving away into the gathering darkness.

As the aircraft rumbled along in the dark past the control tower towards a line of palm trees illuminated by the runway lights at the far end, Mr Long went straight to sleep, hands folded across his stomach, leaving Farr in charge of himself and his fears and staring out at a night sky filled with stars.

chapter twenty-eight

(Capricorn, December 14—15. One of your rare endearing qualities is your failure to notice what other people are really up to. Have a nice day.)

It was still dark, and a long, winding drive led uphill to what appeared to be a Spanish-style farmhouse with a steeply pitched roof of tile, low eaves and a broad veranda running along the front of it. Mr Long hit the horn twice and almost immediately the front door opened, illuminating a profusion of potted ferns and miniature palms. A figure trotted out hurriedly, his legs moving with almost comical speed in small steps, wrestling with a jacket and trying to push his arms into the sleeves. He ran down the steps to the car. Mr Long leaned across the front seat and opened the car door.

Gomez was fatter than ever, and it wasn't just the effect of the grey double-breasted suit. He bulged out of his clothes, his neck spilled over his shirt collar. He seemed swollen, as if someone had been blowing him up, Farr thought, like an inner tyre and using a foot pump. Gomez got into the car by sitting on the seat first, then pulling his legs in after him like a woman in a tight dress. Gomez didn't say anything. He was wheezing from his exertions. He gave no sign of having noticed Farr at all.

'Let's go,' Gomez said to Mr Long, who turned the car out into the road, backed up and headed back the way they had come, the headlights picking out high fences and railings of Vedaro's extensive properties. Mr Long seemed to know exactly where they were going. He was a *habanero*. He needed no instructions.

The sky was pale in the east.

'Felipe,' Farr said. Gomez didn't respond.

'FELIPE!'

Farr was tired of being treated like a non-person. First the road journey with Mr Long and Mr Short, the barber and men's outfitters; then the flight, finally the official Skoda at Havana. Mr Long had hardly said a word all the way.

Gomez was putting a hand in his jacket pocket now and Farr half expected him to pull a gun on him. Instead Gomez was holding something out over the back of the front seat, but he still didn't look at Farr.

'Take it.'

'What is it? I can't see in this light.'

Farr was holding it up, trying to get the grey light outside the car to illuminate the stiff pages. It must be a sick joke, some new trick to play on his nerves, to soften him up before whatever it was they were planning happened.

'Felipe, would you tell me what the hell is going on?'

Gomez said nothing for what seemed like a long time.

'Major Gomez, would you please—'

'All right.' Gomez turned round in the front seat and glared at him. 'You're trying to make out you don't know. All right. You can have your little joke. I don't mind. After all, you're a big name now, aren't you? A celebrity.'

'For God's sake—'

'We had a deal, remember? You helped me with the trade show and I promised to help you . . .'

'By sending me to prison for thirteen years?'

'By getting you deported. By getting you out of here.'

Gomez turned round again, facing the front, the anger in his voice matched by the stiff way he held his head.

'Why, Felipe? Why are you doing this?'

Gomez didn't say another word until they reached Marti International Airport. Then they all got out of the car.

'Got the passport?'

'Yes.'

Was this really happening? Was he dreaming?

'Come along.'

Gomez led the way.

Farr could see a crowd of people at the bottom of the steps leading up to the aircraft. In his right hand he carried the new Cuban passport with his picture and exit visa stamped in it, along with his ticket.

He was walking alone towards them, his legs a little unsteady because of the acres of open space around him, breathing in fumes of high-octane aviation fuel, the air so humid it felt like being wrapped in hot, wet towels. It felt . . . it felt very strange. He was used to walls and bars, gates and guards. He knew Gomez was back at the terminal, watching him through a pair of binoculars with the silent Mr Long for company. The Revolution was spitting him out like some indigestible lump of gristle, and its servants wanted to make sure he got out and didn't reappear again with tourist baggage from an incoming flight. Looking ahead, Farr could see James T. Plush, hat in place. He stood out like a lighthouse, an obelisk at least a foot taller than anyone else. The diplomat Delaware was standing next to him, frantically trying to keep the hair down on his bald patch with both hands. There were photographers and what looked like two television crews. He scanned the little crowd again, but he couldn't see Alison.

It didn't occur to him that they were waiting for him, that the plane had been held up for him.

'Ricky, old son! How ya doin'?'

Farr said something back but he didn't know what it was.

J. W. Diaz

His right hand was being pumped up and down and squeezed. He pulled his cheek muscles to form a smile, but he somehow managed to freeze his face in a look of terrified constipation, and a tick quickly developed in the corner of his mouth. It was all too much for him after the quiet of his cell and the company of the other prisoners. That was . . . only the previous evening. He just hoped his bemusement and rising panic wouldn't look as idiotic on video as he felt. Someone had shoved a camera in his face and a reporter was shouting questions at him over the high-pitched whine of the plane's engines. He couldn't make sense of any of it. He nodded and smiled his ghastly smile and mouthed 'excuse me' and 'no comment', and while one side of his face seemed to do things quite independently, Farr pushed to get through like a drowning man scrabbling to get ashore, to get away.

Farr found himself stumbling up metal steps behind the huge rear end of Plush (who was talking loudly to no one in particular), Delaware right behind him.

Someone in a blue uniform took his boarding card and showed him to his seat by the window. The next seat to his was empty. He was alone at last. He kicked off his shoes, stretched his legs. He took a glass of sparkling wine from a smiling stewardess who came back a moment later to show him how to use his seat belt. He was given a blanket, headphones and a menu that promised fresh fruit and mushroom omelette, croissants and coffee. Farr started to salivate.

Just as the aircraft began to roll, Farr noticed a familiar scent. He was trying to see something out of the little porthole. He breathed in, tasting the smell. It was so different from prison smells. It was strong, sweet and feminine. Something reminded him—

'Hi, Ricardo.'

She had slipped into the next seat.

'Alison—'

242

She bent forward across the armrest. They kissed clumsily. He didn't want to let go of her.

'Our campaign worked so well, Ricardo. I must admit I had my doubts at the time . . .' She leaned towards him and kissed him again. 'You've lost so much weight! You poor darling!'

'I have?'

'Did you really feed all those people on your astrology column . . . ?'

'There were only fourteen of us.'

He thought of Alfonso, Enrique, Hector, Jose and poor Joaquim, God rest him. Of Beny and the old man Luis. His chest felt tight, and there was an odd pressure at the back of his throat. He realised he wanted to cry.

'Did you see the cuttings?'

'Cuttings?'

'The stories.'

The plane lifted its front wheel off the ground. Farr felt it lift, then the other wheels came off and they were rising steeply. Farr gripped the armrests. He stared out of the porthole, not wanting Alison to see how scared he was. He had never flown in a big jet before. He shut his eyes.

'Here you are.'

He saw the headlines. The photocopies seemed to be in reverse order. Dissident To Be Freed, Cuba Says. Writer Leaves Prison. Cuba Dissident Feeds Jail With Astrology. The bylines were Alison's, mostly. Plush was there too.

'There's more. Remember our little plan?'

'Sure.'

Vaguely he did.

Dissident Reveals Epidemic. Dissident Fights For Hospital. Cuban Jailed For Smuggling Drugs. English Writer Held Over Epidemic Campaign. Havana Denies Dissident's Epidemic Claim.

'What happened to the suitcase?'

Farr found he was holding Alison's hand, but he didn't know how it got there. They had levelled off, and the cabin crew was preparing to distribute hot food.

'Oh, you mean the antibiotics? My father took them to Dr Garcia at the hospital. The Canadian government made a big stink about the whole thing . . . Then the European Union offered to help on condition—'

'On condition?

'On condition they freed you, of course!'

'My God.' Farr couldn't see anything but sky. 'Your father thought I was a spy. He thought I sent coded messages in my *Diario* column.'

'Daddy thinks everyone's a spy. He thought you were CIA because you talked all about Warren Buffett and were such a keen capitalist. Did you see James?'

'James Plush? Yes.'

'His newspaper is offering you a job. Did you know?'

'I'm no hero, Alison. I'm no celebrity.' He leaned closer to her and said in a whisper, 'I'm a pimp – remember?'

She shook her head. 'No, Ricardo. No. You can be whatever you want to be. That's behind you now.'

'But I can't write.'

'Yes, you can. I know you can. You just need to learn to type. How many journalists can really write? You'd make a superb reporter.'

'So where are we going?'

Alison had an envelope in her hand with Farr's name on it.

'I promised Dr Garcia I would give you this the moment we left Cuba. He seemed to think it very important . . .'

Farr turned it over.

'It won't bite. Nothing's going to hurt you now, Ricardo. And I won't look over your shoulder, either.'

Dear Ricardo,

I hope you don't object to the familiar form of address; I feel I know you so well by now. I knew you when you came that first time to hospital and I examined you. I pretended not to know. I couldn't really tell if you were convinced by this deception or not. That is why I'm writing to you. I want to apologise. Not only did I deceive you, but I was guilty of professional misconduct. I could argue that the means justified the ends, but I know you well enough to know you wouldn't be fooled by that. I did what I did because I felt I had to, and I must also admit I did so because I wanted to hurt you.

Of course I knew about Amelia. So did my brother-in-law. In fact I went to see Felipe about my little problem. I don't mean Amelia. I'm referring to the epidemic. We talked about you. My marriage had broken down some years ago. Amelia and I stayed together for all the wrong reasons, of course; for the children, out of habit and because, as you know, I'm a cautious man. There was also the matter of Felipe's career.

You were not Amelia's first adventure. I think you must have suspected as much. At any rate, when you came to the hospital I couldn't believe my good fortune. Felipe and I needed to find a way to get hold of the antibiotics we needed. The state wasn't going to do anything until the trade show was over. Felipe did what he could by using his special powers – arrests, curfews and so on. What we needed was a *marisca*, a smuggler of cunning and innovation we could control but who would be sufficiently determined to do the job. You were that man. I misdiagnosed gonorrhoea – deliberately. You were, understandably, anxious to obtain the new antibiotics available only in the United States and Europe and you did so. I encouraged you in the belief that you would die if you failed. Trouble was, you had the drive, but you were far from 'tame'. You slipped through Felipe's grasp and we couldn't find the drugs. Your 'mules' arrived and were arrested – but they had nothing on them and Felipe could not use his usual methods to extract information. We tried pressure. Felipe invented a foreign conspiracy and a story about plastic explosive. Incidentally, my arrest and the stone-throwing incident outside my home were all Felipe's creative work. Eventually, it was a Canadian diplomat, Delaware, who brought the drugs to me. They had been distributed among the cases of the various television crews who came to Cuba for the trade show and gathered together by Delaware's daughter, Alison, but we weren't to know. Felipe tidied the loose ends, keeping you out of the way (or so we thought) and ensuring, at least during the trade show, that there would be no adverse publicity. I got what I wanted. So did Felipe. You will be glad to know the epidemic has been brought under control, and the rate of infection is declining rapidly.

Anyway, I apologise. I lied. I admit I was happy when Felipe told me you had been imprisoned. It was that American journalist, James Plush, who really got you off the murder rap. Felipe told me Plush sent a deposition to the court, through the Swedish Embassy. It was all hushed up, but I expect you know all about that by now. It may be some consolation to know that many Cubans would have preferred to use a machete or a shotgun to deal with a man such as you, but that was never my way.

Amelia has settled in northern California. I believe she has sent the money she owes you to Señor Plush.

I will miss the children, but I was never much of a father to them. I tell myself Amelia can give them a much better life than I ever could in Cuba, but I'm not sure it's true.

Oh, I almost forgot! The fact is that you have something known as a 'non-specific urinary infection'. It's nothing, little more than an irritation. The pains you complained of were not as bad as you imagined they were. If you take the six tablets in the envelope with this letter – one after every meal – you will be rid of it in a couple of days.

My best wishes for your new life . . .

Yours sincerely,
Ernesto Garcia

'Ricardo?'

Farr took one of the tablets, reached for the coffee cup on the tray and swallowed it.

'You okay?'

He crumpled up the note and shoved it in a trouser pocket 'Oh, yes. I'm fine. Never felt better in fact.'

Plush was in the aisle, holding a plastic bag.

'Ricky, we wanted to give you something. I mean the foreign press. We all chipped in – we wanted to thank you for all the stories you gave us. And for putting up such a great fight.'

Alison said, 'Open it.'

Inside the bag was a box and wrapped in tissue was a pair of shoes. None like Farr had ever seen. Loafers. Bright yellow. Little rubber studs at the back. He put his nose to them, breathed in the new leather smell and pressed his cheek against the soft suede.

Plush spoke. 'They're car shoes, Rick. Fashionable in Hollywood, and a helluva long way up the food chain from sneakers. But we couldn't decide on the colour so we took a vote. Oh, and you don't need a car to wear 'em, either.'

'It came down to crocodile yellow or titanium,' said Alison. 'I had the casting vote and I decided the crocodile yellow was more you.'

Plush moved aside for a member of the cabin crew. 'Alison always has the casting vote, but I guess you know that.'

'They're just beautiful,' Farr said, stroking the suede with his fingers and suddenly feeling emotional. He bent down and took off his shoes and slid his bare feet into the loafers. When he sat up and looked out he couldn't see anything but pale blue sky. He kept looking out because he didn't want anyone to see his face.

'Where will you go, Ricardo?'

'I reckon I'll try the newspaper.'

'It's in Miami.'

Florida. He'd heard so much about Florida. It wasn't Cuba. It wasn't home, but it was a place where he wouldn't have to be a criminal to make money and wear a pair of J. P. Tod's worth not a cent less than three hundred bucks. Just like the film stars. Maybe he'd start with the newspaper and then branch out — start his own business.

'Ricardo, my people say there's an opening in our Miami bureau if I want to take it. I've applied, and it's not a hundred per cent certain I'd get it, and of course it would be a few weeks before I will know for sure . . .'

Alison paused, having run out of words.

'Are you . . . are you pleased, Ricardo?'

'Pleased that you're going to Florida, too?'

'Am I being terribly presumptuous?'

She looked anxious that he would say 'no' or, worse, show utter indifference.

Farr watched her face, the way her smile made little dimples in her cheeks.

'Of course I'm pleased, Alison,' he said. He smiled reassuringly at her, wanting so much to take the worry out of her eyes. 'I'm very pleased. To tell the truth, it's really the best news I've had all day.'

If you enjoyed this book here is a selection of other bestselling titles from Review

MY FIRST SONY	Benny Barbash	£6.99	☐
THE CATASTROPHIST	Ronan Bennett	£6.99	☐
WRACK	James Bradley	£6.99	☐
IT COULD HAPPEN TO YOU	Isla Dewar	£6.99	☐
ITCHYCOOBLUE	Des Dillon	£6.99	☐
MAN OR MANGO	Lucy Ellmann	£6.99	☐
THE JOURNAL OF MRS PEPYS	Sara George	£6.99	☐
THE MANY LIVES & SECRET SORROWS OF JOSÉPHINE B.	Sandra Gulland	£6.99	☐
TWO MOONS	Jennifer Johnston	£6.99	☐
NOISE	Jonathan Myerson	£6.99	☐
UNDERTOW	Emlyn Rees	£6.99	☐
THE SILVER RIVER	Ben Richards	£6.99	☐
BREAKUP	Catherine Texier	£6.99	☐

Headline books are available at your local bookshop or newsagent. Alternatively, books can be ordered direct from the publisher. Just tick the titles you want and fill in the form below. Prices and availability subject to change without notice.

Buy four books from the selection above and get free postage and packaging and delivery within 48 hours. Just send a cheque or postal order made payable to Bookpoint Ltd to the value of the total cover price of the four books. Alternatively, if you wish to buy fewer than four books the following postage and packaging applies:

UK and BFPO £4.30 for one book; £6.30 for two books; £8.30 for three books.

Overseas and Eire: £4.80 for one book; £7.10 for 2 or 3 books (surface mail).

Please enclose a cheque or postal order made payable to *Bookpoint Limited*, and send to: Headline Publishing Ltd, 39 Milton Park, Abingdon, OXON OX14 4TD, UK.
Email Address: orders@bookpoint.co.uk

If you would prefer to pay by credit card, our call team would be delighted to take your order by telephone. Our direct line is 01235 400 414 (lines open 9.00 am–6.00 pm Monday to Saturday 24 hour message answering service). Alternatively you can send a fax on 01235 400 454.

Name ....

Address ....

....

....

If you would prefer to pay by credit card, please complete:
Please debit my Visa/Access/Diner's Card/American Express (delete as applicable) card number:

Signature .... Expiry Date...............